AW... 1975

S0-AWZ-917

Seagulls Under Glass
and
Other Stories

Books by Peter Tate

SEAGULLS UNDER GLASS AND OTHER STORIES
MOON ON AN IRON MEADOW
COUNTRY LOVE AND POISON RAIN
GARDENS ONE TO FIVE
THE THINKING SEAT

Seagulls Under Glass and Other Stories

PETER TATE

DOUBLEDAY & COMPANY, INC.

GARDEN CITY, NEW YORK

1975

ACKNOWLEDGEMENTS

"Mainchance." Originally published in *Alchemy and Academe* (Doubleday & Company, Inc.), copyright © 1970 by Anne McCaffrey. Reprinted with permission.

"Mars Pastorale." Originally published in *New Worlds*, 1967.

"The Gloom Pattern." Originally published in *New Worlds*, 1966.

"The Post-mortem People." Originally published in *New Worlds*, 1966.

"The Day the Wind Died." Copyright © 1969 by Mercury Press, Inc. From *The Magazine of Fantasy and Science Fiction*. Reprinted with permission.

"Same Autumn in a Different Park." Copyright © 1967 by Ultimate Publishing Company, Inc. From *Fantastic*. Reprinted with permission.

"Crumbling Hollywood Mansion, Crumbling Hollywood Man." Originally published as "Protest" in *Galaxy Magazine*. Copyright © 1974 by Universal Publishing and Distribution Corp.

All of the characters in this book are fictitious, and any resemblance to actual persons, living or dead, is purely coincidental.

ISBN: 0-385-01827-4
Library of Congress Catalog Card Number: 74-12717
Copyright © 1975 by Peter Tate
All Rights Reserved
Printed in the United States of America
First Edition

For MARK AVERY TATE
who, every day, brings his
father a present of joy.

Contents

Seagulls Under Glass
and
Other Stories

MAINCHANCE

Introduction

"Mainchance" is the story that must be told and I tell it as well as I can. At the outset, it was a challenge; at its first publication in Anne McCaffrey's admirable and under-estimated *Alchemy and Academe* (Doubleday), it gyrated between Baconian research and metaphysical statement. In 1975, for me, it has the added urgency of a firm conviction which will never be more timely. Present Babels are manifold and the tale is for (and against) those who believe them impregnable.

Lest this sober note should act as a deterrent, let me hasten to add that laughter and fancies, outlandish people and breath-taking schemes lie further within.

We're just getting the heavy stuff out of the way first. And I never said it wasn't *enjoyable*. . . .

"... For by a machine three fingers high and wide and of less, a man could free himself and his friends of all danger of prison and rise and descend. Also a machine can easily be made by which one man can draw a thousand to him by violence against their wills, and attract other things in like manner. ..."

ROGER BACON, Alchemist (?1214–1292)

Hubert Dreyfus compares cybernetics with alchemy:
"... Because a few people have climbed some very high trees, they think they can solve the problem of getting to the Moon."

He drove the monoprop across the blue shale courts of heaven; a big man who deliberately kept the controls on manual because he liked to feel the craft fight a little before it answered his prods and pronouncements.

A big man with the most important human job in the world—guardian to a machine which, in more primitive days, might have ranked for deification.

There was nothing clumsy about him. The body moved perfectly to inner direction, and inner direction came from the elements that mediaeval men had called humours. Fire, water, air . . . a life-force that seemed to move like a torrent in the veins; that was Adams.

Young. A wealth of curly black hair—and underneath it, a chameleon brain that attacked knowledge and took it into captivity.

Adams, then, exercising his wrists on the manipulae of the monoprop, saw the blue sea turn brown with the rising stratum. I'll come upon it from above, he thought. This is as it should be.

The monoprop rode over land. He turned it to follow the grey-ribbon road into the foothills. And there, ahead of him, glinting in the sun—

The Tower.

So it had come to this. There was no other kind of heritage available to him. Priorities, pressure, a strength of conviction had robbed him of flesh-and-blood mathematics, a multiplication out of a division, a product of his cylindrical root.

To see it dazzle—to have it greet you with a tax on your eyes—that was a sad thing, the sadness autumnal rather than bitter.

And while he analysed the vague nausea, a downdraught found the plane and tried for destruction.

When he brought the monoprop out of the current, his mind was clear, his brow moist, his co-ordination uncluttered with regrets and hang-nail thoughts.

The Tower was closer (of course) and he began his grounding manoeuvre. He cut back speed, lost height, yellowed his window to negate the glare.

Able now to regard the structure in detail, he found it sharp and clinical. If he had anticipated any more spectacular an impression he would have been disappointed, but he had kept himself carefully detached. Out of expectation came disappointment and disappointment, like everything else, disturbed his chemistry . . . made him a slightly different man.

The road ran headlong into the mountain seventeen thousand feet below.

The monoprop threaded itself into the eye of the needle.

It had been a time of undeclared interests, individually and in the dealings of great nations. And since such a condition quickly bred mistrust it soon became well-nigh impossible for one power to enjoy—or even to contemplate—any amicable relationship with another.

The result was a resurgence of nationalism which showed itself in a welter of small local wars. They were dirty wars where starvation was used as a weapon and no distinction was drawn between the halt and the healthy, the young and the old, the combatants and the innocently involved.

As they grew in number, so the United Nations—never much more than a myth, since it was founded on a premise of mutual honesty that just didn't exist—declined in influence.

Those who watched the world scene began to suspect that civilisation could not continue for much longer without a major conflagration. Even the cynics were wont to cite the Millennium, though without any real understanding of the word.

What few Christians were left in a world that had gone sour on religion (even as religion had gone sour on Christianity) were under persecution. In a way they were blamed for conditions—and ridiculed when they pointed out that the Scriptures had prophesied (Matthew, chapter 24, verse 14, and on) what would occur.

Since the world feared the Millennium—in whatever form it might come, speaking whatever language—steps were taken by those who retained enough influence to implement a kind of solution.

If man could not be trusted, then some substitute had to be found . . . something that could make use of all knowledge that the world provided without being corrupted by the power that that intelligence could give.

A computer. Without doubt the largest computer that had ever been visualised. A machine that worked not with the formalised language of mathematics but with the broader linguistics of humanity. No one source could be used to stock its memory banks or to prepare its programmes. This function must be conducted by the best cybernetic brains world-wide.

Out of this common task grew the first friendship of an international nature that had been evident for quite a while. It was like a revelation. People, finding that they could communicate, began to do so. But they were wary of divisions. The whole business of living was geared to a broad-plane togetherness.

When organisation introduced itself, it was tiered or pyramidic and involving all nationalities. The tariffs came off; the barriers came down. There was free mobility of labour, of living materials.

It was an ideal existence which could not have been imagined even ten years before. It came about with the haste of desperation. It was welcomed as a salvation.

And behind it all, balanced between one side of the world and the other (on the narrow umbilicus of land between what had been North and South America) and remaining wonderfully noncommittal was . . . Multiple Algorithm Random Deduction Unicentre.

MARDUC symbolised the self-sufficiency of man in the face of destiny; the perfectness of the present. There was no need to consider the future.

There was, however, a need to consider a human attendant for the machine. He would act in liaison, over and above any technician strength. His qualifications would be unique. Apart from an excellent working knowledge of the machine, he must be a product of the system, must believe in its infallibility and must possess an extensive general intelligence. There were not too many such people around.

Just enough, it would seem, and so scattered to be representative of the world as a whole. A short list was drawn up and agreed. Then came the democratic thing—a contest that could favour no particular candidate. A receptacle was produced, the names plunged therein, a piece of paper withdrawn.

The name on the paper was "Adams."

The walking man came west out of the sunrise, following the coast road until the hampering presence of dust in his open sandals persuaded him onto the beach.

There he followed the line of the sea, dangling his sandals by the fingers of his right hand. As yet, the strand was still cool from the night, and the water, creaming about his toes, comforted and caressed. The sea that had been called Mediterranean, untouched by fishery development and artificial stimulants of tide and temperature, retained its morning breezes and the man feasted on them.

Even its salty status quo was intentional. Along the sides of the hills which ran olive fingers down to the sea, the terraces of orange and vine needed such daily changes. But the man was not aware of this or at least not concerned by it. His own inner peace found a parallel in the crumbling white citadel villages that nestled inland between soft green feminine swellings. Occasionally he stopped, one man alone on the meandering shore, and turned his eyes outwards and then upwards across the paling dome of the sky.

Once he looked down at his feet and seemed to be searching among the surf for a word. "Michelangelo," he said suddenly.

When he reached a rocky promontory, he dried and dusted his feet carefully on a handkerchief he drew from a pocket of his tidy but worn suit and replaced his sandals. Then he began to climb.

Thus he entered Midi Settlement as it started to stir. He sorted out the control buildings and found himself a seat near them.

He took a polythene wrapper from another pocket of his suit and extracted a piece of bread and some cheese from it. He ate sparingly, running his eyes along the uniform rows of dwellings. When doors began opening, he folded away the food and stood up as though it were important.

As the men filed past him, he smiled. "Hello, brothers." They regarded him suspiciously. They wondered at his smile.

All morning, he wandered unhindered up and down aisles of tomatoes and olives. He even took his shoes off again to paddle along rows of green rice. He spoke to the bent workers. "A pleasant day. Perhaps a little warm. Make sure your necks are covered."

Not once did he stop and not once did the workers answer. But they straightened and watched him on his way in curiosity. As the sun rose higher, he took the handkerchief from his pocket, knotted it at the corners, and laid it over his perspiring scalp.

Soon, the men left their labours and sat in silent groups, huddled into scant patches of shade. The wanderer selected one such group and sat down a few yards distant. He took out his bundle of food and ate more bread and a substantial part of the cheese. He paid the men no particular attention but he knew their eyes were on him. He looked up, smiled, and went back to his meal.

"You," said one man eventually. "Are you looking for work? Because . . ."

"Because nobody need be jobless?" The stranger laughed. "No, I don't need a job."

The men fell back into a sullen silence.

"And I'm not a spy."

"You must be something," said the first man defensively. "What's your classification?"

"I don't have one. Or rather—no classification applies to me."

"Listen, if you're a human being, you're classified. All of us . . ."

"Not all." The wanderer interrupted gently.

"Well, who . . . ?"

"Free men are not in subjection to some distant tin god."

"Wait a minute. If you're here to start trouble for us . . . I'm going to call the supervisor." The man stood up.

"Please—let me explain. I am here to talk, no more. I am not an agent for a revolutionary movement. I'm not trying to trap you into any kind of indiscretion against the system. I just want to begin a conversation between us. I want to hear *you* talk. Tell me—have you ever thought what is at the end of this?"

The spokesman lowered himself to the ground and leaned his weight against the shadowed wall of a shed. "At the end there is nothing," he said. "Now we are allowed to live and work and make the best of life as it is. It is a pretty thankless business, but it is the best the world offers."

"So they tell you."

"Who?"

"Why, the man in the Tower and his infernal machine. That's where it comes from, doesn't it?"

"It's common sense, no matter who tells it. Nobody's hungry, there are no wars, we don't waste time and energy believing in things that will come to nothing. All in all, things are pretty near perfection."

"But you don't smile."

"We . . ." The spokesman bit back a hasty denial. He tried to think of the last time he had consciously felt happiness. "Life is a serious business," he said.

"Particularly with nothing to look forward to."

"We've been through all that . . . more times than most of us care to remember. I told you, we don't waste our energy."

"Don't you ever have any inclination to—ask a question?"

"Our instructions in all matters are explicit."

"And there is nowhere in you a desire to challenge any ruling or to apply your own sense of reasoning to any circumstance?"

"If we felt a thing was not just, we would challenge it."

"But you consider the system incapable of being unjust."

"I didn't say that. Our powers of judgment are still such that we can perceive an anomaly. You seem to think that because we accept this regimentation, we have become some kind of vegetable. In fact, a lot of us have come to the conclusion that if the world is to avoid committing genocide, then this is the only way to do it."

"And you think a—preacher—like myself is misusing his time."

"I think you are redundant."

"Yet if I could persuade you that I had something to offer—if I could prove to you that the power of the Tower is treating us as anything but redundant, what then?"

"We would—have to think about it."

"If having thought about it, you might decide the power should be asked a certain question . . . ?"

"Then we'd do it. Wouldn't we?" The spokesman glanced at his colleagues. They nodded.

"Thank you," said the wanderer.

> Sol gold is, and Luna silver we declare;
> Mars yron, Mercurie is quyksilver;
> Saturnus leed, and Jubitur is tyn,
> And Venus coper, by my fathers kyn.
>
> GEOFFREY CHAUCER: Canon's Yeoman's Tale

First Beginning of my beginning; First Principle of my principle; Breath of breath, First Breath of the breath within me; Fire which, among the compounds which form me, was given by God for my own compound, First Fire of the fire within me; Water of water, First Water of the water within me; Earthy Substance, model of the earthy substance which is within me; O my Perfect Body, fashioned by a glorious arm and an immortal hand in the world of darkness and light; lifeless and living—if it please Thee to transmit and communicate a rebirth to immortality to me, who am still constrained by my natural condition, O that I may, after the violent constraint of my impending Fate, contemplate the immortal Principle thanks to the undying breath . . .

> Four roots of Empedocles (fundamental matter)
> invoked in Prayer to Mithras (*c.* 200 A.D.)

MARDUC came in sections. The central processing unit sat in the uppermost chamber of the Tower while the myriad peripheral units were situated on same-level or lower-level floors. The high-speed data channels were joined, where visually practicable, by laser beams and where not by underfloor wiring.

Further down the Tower were the software quarters where compilers prepared programmes in the special language built into the computer. Disc storage, drum storage, closed storage had all been incorporated to grasp the extraordinary intelligence.

Ten years of modification had been devoted almost entirely to improvement of programming techniques. Users in the late sixties had found increasingly that they were better able than the manufacturers to provide software for their machines. Thus concentration had been on coherence and machine-time salvage.

By the mid-seventies most of the problems that faced humanity had fought themselves to a solution. To say that the possibility of error no longer existed would be over-simplification of mammoth proportions. But the programmers safeguarded against this with parameters that emphasised cause and effect, so that judgments formed on impulse were out and a comprehensive and honest consideration of all factors was in. That, they reckoned, was about as close as they could be expected to get.

And there was the urgency. At some stage, it was bound to become necessary to suspend their attempts at prediction and to place their trust in the progress they had made.

The face of MARDUC, then, was undistinguished, the voice deadpan and not always faithful to inflection. The boast of perfection lay in the process validity of the machine rather than any fine finish.

Adams, confronting MARDUC for the first time, found himself with a sense of anticlimax. Perhaps it was inevitable after the build-up. He looked for reasons and thought, The thing lacks glamour. He brushed the thought aside quickly.

You are disappointed in me.

He sat down too fast in the contoured chair adjacent to the input speaker. Surely the thing couldn't read thoughts too.

"No." His first defence was denial.

It was predictable. I have no supernatural powers but I am aware of factors that are formula. It is natural that you had a somewhat—rosy—impression of marduc.

Holy cow, a computer with an inferiority complex. "I am not bothered by how you look, marduc," said Adams. "You're here for the same reason I am—to do a job. I don't suppose I look all that keen to you."

Now *that* was a stupid comment to make.

Keen meaning sharp. I do not form opinions, sir, but it is logical that unless you were entirely capable of carrying out the work we are to do, you would not be here. therefore, welcome.

"Thank you, marduc. As you say, it is logical and our relationship is founded on logic. I appreciate your welcome and for the record I would like to say that I look forward to working with such a fine example of man's ingenuity. That said, I think we might perhaps move on to the more formal business of our meeting. Can you give me a regional briefing?"

Adams settled back in the chair. He closed his eyes to concentrate, kneading his lower lip between forefinger and middle finger of right hand. Marduc went briskly but comprehensively through his report and Adams let him flow without interruption.

At "Midi," the machine paused.

"What's the matter?" said Adams absently. He acknowledged his slip with a wry grin. But marduc had been made familiar with vernacular.

I am collecting latest information from midi. It appears that there is a suspension of labour. I am endeavouring to ascertain the cause.

Adams waited, not yet curious.

Work has stopped, said marduc after a while. my information is that the men are demanding a dialogue with you.

"For what purpose?"

They will not tell the supervisors. they say they will talk only to you.

"Yes, well so much for direct channels. What does Supplementary Intelligence yield?"

There have been reports of the presence of newcomers in the

AREA. ONE WAS SEEN ON THE SETTLEMENT A FEW HOURS PRIOR TO THE STOPPAGE. HE WAS OBSERVED TALKING TO CERTAIN OF THE MEN ALTHOUGH IT IS NOT KNOWN WHAT WAS SAID.

"So it is possible that his visit had nothing to do with the cessation of labour."

POSSIBLE, BUT . . .

"Appreciate that I am reluctant to pay too much attention to these—preachers. All the same, give me what you've got on the Newcomers."

NEWCOMERS BELIEVE THEMSELVES TO BE WHAT THE CATHOLIC CHURCH USED TO CALL "OF THE APOSTOLIC SUCCESSION," THOUGH THAT IS NOT TO SAY THAT THEY HAD THEIR BASIS IN CATHOLICISM. IN FACT, THE OPPOSITE IS TRUE, SINCE EARLY NEWCOMERS DREW A PARALLEL BETWEEN THE ROMAN CHURCH AND ITS INVOLVEMENT IN TRADE AND POLITICS AND THE "GREAT HARLOT" OF THE BIBLICAL BOOK OF REVELATIONS. IN FAIRNESS TO THEIR TENACITY, THEY HAVE SURVIVED THE GENERAL DISINTEREST OF THE WORLD IN METAPHYSICS AND THEIR DOCTRINES ARE SUBSTANTIALLY UNCHANGED.

. . . IF ANYTHING, THEY HAVE THRIVED ON THIS DISINTEREST, STATING THAT SUCH A "FALLING AWAY" WAS PROPHESIED IN THEIR BOOK. BY NATURE THEY ARE PERSISTENT BUT POLITE. ANY INTERFERENCE IN ANYTHING AS SECULAR AS A LABOUR DISPUTE WOULD SEEM TO BE FOREIGN TO THEM. NEVERTHELESS, IN THE ABSENCE OF ANY ALTERNATIVE, THE PROPOSITION SHOULD BE CONSIDERED.

"My feelings exactly. Now, I think, I shall go to Midi."

WITH RESPECT . . . EVEN A COMPUTER NEEDS RATHER LONGER THAN YOU HAVE TAKEN TO CONSIDER ALL THE ASPECTS OF THIS MATTER. ARE YOU HAPPY THAT THIS WOULD BE THE WISE THING TO DO AT THIS TIME?

Momentarily, Adams felt anger. It was one thing to question the machine's capacity, but to have it questioning his . . .

"Quite happy. This is as good a time as any to show that the administration is approachable. Above all, we must keep the confidence of our workers—and show them, too, that we have confidence in them."

POINT TAKEN. I SHALL MAKE FLIGHT ARRANGEMENTS. HOW MANY WILL TRAVEL?

"I go alone."

BUT THERE IS DANGER. A HUMAN LIFE—NO MATTER WHOSE LIFE— BECOMES PUNY BEFORE AN UNBALANCED HAND ON A TRIGGER.

"I go alone. I shouldn't have to repeat things for you, MARDUC. If I took a crowd of security men with me, how approachable would I be? It would defy the whole point of my going. Perhaps I should put it in terms you would be more likely to understand. In the international war games of the past, computers were briefed in two types of rationality. One was 'minimax,' which meant selecting the move that would do maximum damage to your adversary while achieving minimum cost to yourself. The other was 'mainchance,' the all-or-nothing calculation that was impulsive and obviously much more of a gamble. This, I would say, is a 'mainchance' situation. I don't think the people of Midi will fail to appreciate that I am taking a risk. That fact alone could do some good. Do you follow my line of reasoning?"

I ACCEPT WHAT YOU SAY. MEANWHILE I HAVE FOUND A SPOKESMAN FOR THE WORKERS. HIS NAME IS JONES. HE HAS SUGGESTED A MEETING AT NOON THEIR TIME TOMORROW AND I HAVE ACCEPTED THAT SUGGESTION. MIGHT I SUGGEST SOME SLEEP IN THE INTERIM?

"Granted," said Adams. And let's hope it's always that easy, he thought. He felt an unaccountable nausea in his stomach.

. . . Next succeeds the reign of Mars, which shows a little yellow, mixed with luteous brownness; these are the chief colours, but transitory ones of the rain-bow and peacocks-tail, it shows most gloriously. . . . Now the mother being sealed in her infant's belly, swirls and is purified, but because of the present great purity of the compound, no putridness can have place in this regimen, but some obscure colours play their part as the chief actors in this stone and some middle colours do pass and come, pleasant to behold. Now know that this is the last tillage of our virgin earth, that in it the fruit of the sun might be set and maturated; therefore continue a good heat and thou shalt see for certain, about thirty days off, this regimen, a citrine colour shall appear which shall in two weeks after its first appearing, tinge all with a true citrine colour.

> Typical mediaeval account "of the appearances in the matras [retort] during the nine months' digestion."

The walls were talking again. The old man moved restlessly on the straw palliasse. No matter which way he twisted, the words were still there, pounding like water droplets into an empty bucket.

WHY . . . WHY . . . WHY . . . WHY . . . WHY . . . WHY . . . WHY . . .

"Why what?" he said finally.

WHY DO YOU FUNCTION THUS?

"Who asks?"

MULTIPLE ALGORITHM RANDOM DEDUCTION UNICENTRE. FOR BREVITY
I AM CALLED MARDUC.

"I know all that. I mean who behind you? Who really wants to
know? Who tells you to ask?"

NOBODY. EVERYBODY. I AM THE SERVANT OF THE COMMUNITY. THE
INFORMATION I SEEK IS FOR THE BENEFIT OF THE SYSTEM.

"Even I cannot be fooled by such a proposition. You know—I am
sorry—you are *aware* in your intelligence that your status is not
that of a menial. Even your name . . ."

MARDUC. THAT HAS SOME SPECIAL KIND OF SIGNIFICANCE FOR YOU.

"I would put it higher than a significance."

THERE WAS A MARDUK OR MARODECH WHO SLEW THE SERPENT DRAGON
TI'AMAT TO BECOME KING OF THE BABYLONIAN GODS. YOU SEEK TO ES-
TABLISH A LINK. I AM NOT A DEITY. I AM A HIGHLY SOPHISTICATED
PIECE OF MACHINERY.

"You are what people make of you. Your measure is the emphasis
they place upon you."

A DISCUSSION ON SEMANTICS IS NOT IN LINE WITH MY PROGRAMMING.
I HAVE ASKED YOU A QUESTION. IN CASE YOU DO NOT UNDERSTAND I WILL
REPEAT IT. WHY DO YOU FUNCTION THUS?

"If you mean why do I talk to people about a future, I would say
it is because I hold the conviction that they should concern themselves beyond today. More than that, it is in their best interests to
consider tomorrow."

YOU USE TODAY AND TOMORROW IN THE REAL-TIME SENSE.

"I use the words as temporal co-ordinates."

This was how it went, back and forth, up and around the cell,
words upon words—why this? who that? what who? who what? The
old man trying to tie the machine in knots; the machine clinically
precise, pedantic—unflappable.

How long had it been now? It seemed like a week, but it could
not be that long since the Tower guards had come to his home at the
foot of Popocatepetl and told him that his presence was required.

How long in this terrible dark room with the walls moving and
muttering about him as he tried to sleep? He had been warned of
persecution—should really have glorified in it, since it signalled the
imminence of the reward—but he was frightened. He knew that,
despite his efforts, MARDUC had probably absorbed his fear. Sometimes he thought he heard the machine sniffing about his prison like
a dog.

Still, he played his side of the game and tried to read a meaning into the logistics, tried to keep a stalemate between them.

I AM FAMILIAR WITH THE TENOR OF THE CONVERSATION. I CANNOT PROCEED UNTIL YOU HAVE ANSWERED EACH QUESTION SATISFACTORILY.

"Then ask a different question," he said. "A different question would yield a different answer. That I guarantee."

WHAT IS YOUR OBJECTION TO THE SYSTEM?

"It is ungodly."

WHATEVER YOU MAY MEAN BY THAT, IT IS INHERENT IN ME TO POINT OUT THAT THIS SYSTEM, IN COMPARISON WITH ITS FORERUNNERS, IS FAR MORE—WHAT YOU WOULD CALL—"GODLY." THERE IS NO WAR, NO CRIME, NO HUNGER . . .

"No faith."

EXPLAIN FAITH. THE VAST MAJORITY OF OUR CITIZENS HAVE FAITH— IN US.

"That is not what I mean by faith. Faith is an example of obedi- ence; a belief that will accept promises; a desire to maintain integ- rity. Faith is a hope that does not require visibility."

IN WHAT WAY WILL THE FUTURE DIFFER FROM THE PRESENT, BY YOUR INTERPRETATION?

"You know my interpretation. Consult your memory. You know even as I know that to restate it would be a waste of your time and mine."

YOU MEAN THAT MY PROGRAMMING ECHOES THE WORLD'S INCREDU- LITY.

"The world's incredulity does not make it any less the truth. Such an attitude was prophesied. . . ."

PROPHESY. BRIEFING STATES: PREDICTIONS FROM CULT MYTH, RELI- GION, EARLY HISTORIC DOCUMENTS WERE FOUND TO CONTAIN MANY COMMON THEMES. SINCE IT IS NOT DENIED THAT CULTURE GREW FROM CIVILISATIONS IN MESOPOTAMIA AND THE INDUS VALLEY AREA IT IS NOT STRANGE TO FIND THESE PARALLELS. THEIR RELEVANCE IS IN THE TRACE- ABLE SPREAD OF SOCIAL SYSTEMS AND NOT IN ANY HOPE OF REALISATION. THEREFORE, FOR ALL OTHER PURPOSES THEY MAY BE DISCARDED.

"That is an opinion."

IT IS A CONSIDERED STATEMENT.

"I maintain it is an opinion."

WISHING DOES NOT MAKE IT SO.

"What is the object of these questions? You must surely require more of me than data which are already established within you."

THE NEWCOMERS ARE MAKING A NUISANCE OF THEMSELVES. THEY ARE HOLDING UP ENDEAVOUR.

"You must be mistaken, tin man. My brothers are passive people. They do not prevent any man from doing what he wants to do. They merely suggest what else he might be doing."

THE ACTUAL DEGREE OF PERSUASION IS BUT A SMALL MATTER. THE FACT IS THAT A CERTAIN SMALL PORTION OF OUR FIELD-LABOURERS HAVE STOPPED WORK AND YOUR PEOPLE—ACTIVE OR PASSIVE—ARE RESPONSIBLE.

"That is your information."

THAT IS UNQUESTIONABLY THE POSITION.

"And what do you want me to do about it?"

THE MEN HAVE BECOME IDLE BECAUSE THEY CONSIDER WE ARE PAYING TOO MUCH ATTENTION TO YOU. ON BALANCE, MY INSTRUCTIONS ARE TO AGREE WITH THE MEN. I AM PREPARED TO RELEASE YOU. BUT THERE IS A CONDITION.

"I would have been surprised if there had not been."

YOU MUST CONVINCE YOUR PREACHERS THAT THEIR WORK IS FUTILE.

"But how do I do that when the signs they see all around them are of fertility, not futility?"

The old man sat down on the edge of his bed . . . somehow in his contest with the voices, he had moved to the centre of the room, and his legs, he suddenly found, were weary. . . . He smiled. For some reason he had a feeling close to contentment. "Besides, I have no control over them."

HOW DO YOU SAY THAT? YOU ARE THEIR LEADER.

"Computers shouldn't listen to rumours. But then, I suppose they have no choice. . . . No, I am not their leader. I may be held in some regard but that is only because I am aged in the truth. They have but one leader—and you will never lock him in a cell. . . ."

IT FOLLOWS THAT IF THEIR LEADER IS UNSEEN, INVISIBLE, INTANGIBLE, THEN HE CANNOT BE CONTAINED IN A CELL. IT IS ALSO LOGICAL THAT IF HE IS ANY OF THESE THINGS HE CAN DO LITTLE TO INTERFERE WITH EVENTS ONE WAY OR THE OTHER. WE HAVE A—REPRESENTATIVE—OF THAT BODY IN OUR CARE AND WE SHALL SEE HOW THEY REACT TO OUR TREATMENT OF HIM. CONSIDER THAT.

The voices went away. The old man lay down on his thankless bed with his stomach churning.

If Our Lord could stand nails through his hands, he thought, surely I have the strength to . . .

Then sleep came like an answer.

After he had issued all his decrees,
Allotting to the Anunnaki of Heaven and Earth all their portions,
The Anunnaki opened their mouths
And cried to Marduk, their lord:
"Now, O Lord, who has brought about our deliverance from toil,
What shall we do to show you our gratitude?
We will build a shrine whose name shall be called
The Resting-Place for Night—come, let us rest in it.
We will create a shrine . . . ;
On the day of our arrival we will rest in it."
When Marduk heard this,
His face shone brightly as the day, and he said:
"So let Babylon be, which Ye have desired to construct;
Let a city be built and a well-girt shrine be erected."
Then the Anunnaki worked with their spades
And shaped bricks for a whole year;
And when the second year came,
They raised the top of Esagila on high, above the Apsu.

Enuma Elisha, Babylonian poem

Then the sons of the true God began to notice the daughters of men, that they were good-looking; and they went taking wives for themselves, namely, all of whom they chose. . . . The Nephilim proved to be in the earth in those days and also after that, when the sons of the true God continued to have relations with the daughters of men and they bore sons to them, they were the mighty ones who were of old, the men of fame . . .

Genesis, chapter 6, verses 2, 4

And they kept on bringing forth to the sons of Israel a bad report of the land that they had spied out, saying, "The land which we passed through to spy it out is a land that eats up its inhabitants; and all the people whom we saw in the midst of it are men of extraordinary size. And there we saw the Nephilim, the sons of Anak, who are from the Nephilim; so that we became in our own eyes like grasshoppers, and the same way we became in their eyes."

Numbers, chapter 13, verses 32–33

Adams set the monoprop down in the exact centre of the communal plateau.

He moved out of the shadow of the craft and rotated slowly, taking in the tidy streets of tidy houses, radiating like wheel spokes away from the plateau. Each pastel house was shuttered against the sun. Nothing moved on the baking streets. At their extremes, the dwellings rippled and took on crazy dimensions in the heat haze.

Noon exactly. The sun at its peak. It pierced his light fibre suit and sucked perspiration from his back. Moisture moved on his legs and his legs moved in retaliation, seeking to make their own breeze. Moving together towards the rim of the plateau.

Noon was a bad time to call on anyone round the Mediterranean. Adams was uncomfortably aware of this and more than sorry that the fact had not occurred to him when he agreed to the time for the meeting.

Where was everybody, anyhow? And hard on the tail of that question came another, to answer it—Wasn't it obvious? Perhaps that was the idea—let him arrive in the mid-day sun and keep him hanging around until the day cooled, even if he didn't.

The tiers of benches which could rise from the plateau at the touch of a button were harnessed below floor-level. Nevertheless, Adams kept carefully to the permanent way that ran between them.

He descended the steps to the promenade that ran the circumference of the plateau, its inner edge shadowed meagrely by the plateau overhang. Somewhere, a fly muttered, a generator throbbed. Only the sky moved; clouds meandering like lazy sheep across a lush pasture.

Behind him, a child moaned in fevered sleep.

He turned.

The men stood or squatted in the thread of shade against the wall. The women sat hunched on canvas frames, stools, benches, left-out-in-the-weather chairs, no-good-for-anything-else chairs. Children were cradled in their arms, some sleeping. The others, like their parents, were looking at him. They all watched him as though dumb.

Adams braced his legs against a sudden gastric weakness.

"I am sorry for bringing you all out in this heat," he said eventually. "The time was fixed with one of your members. A man called Jones."

The group near the steps shifted. A man emerged. A knotted handkerchief covered his sparse hair. His face was furnace-red and running with sweat. "I am Jones," he said. "As for arranging your visit, I was told when you would be here. That was all. If I had been asked I could have made the point. I was not."

Adams chewed his lower lip. "There seems to have been some kind of misunderstanding," he told the people. "You men will be paid for today. Now go to your homes and return when it is cooler.

Can we say six o'clock? I cannot afford too long away from the Tower."

That's for sure, he thought. Somehow, he was more inclined to accept Jones's version of the arrangement than MARDUC's and that didn't make a lot of sense. A human being, after all, was much better qualified for deception. We humans have to stick together. . . . The phrase popped out uninvited. It was so much of a cliché it was funny.

"Jones," he said. "I'd like a few words with you."

He motioned the man up the steps. A child—perhaps the same child—grumbled and was hushed as they walked away from the edge of the plateau.

"It appears that you and MARDUC are in dispute," he said.

Jones gave him a quick glance. "I've told you what transpired," he said. "If you don't believe me, there's nothing I can do about it. I suppose the computer's got the conversation on tape. Check it if you feel the need."

"Don't assume automatically that I'm going to call you a liar, Jones. My powers of magister aren't so tied to MARDUC yet that I accept him as gospel. But I have to say this—if computers tell lies, that must be some kind of a breakthrough."

"And you wonder why I take the onus for granted." Jones laughed shortly, mirthlessly.

They were at the craft. Adams started up the steps, but Jones stayed on the plateau.

"Come on up," invited Adams.

"Unless that's an order, I don't see the point."

"For crying out loud, don't be so—obstructionist. Can't two men have a straightforward conversation anymore?"

"Two men, yes . . ."

"Meaning?"

"Look . . ." Jones took his time as though explaining to a wearisome child. "I think you are asking rather a lot of my belief in democracy if you suggest that there would be anything straightforward about our conversation."

Adams found his lower lip between his teeth again. "I expected to find some kind of—gulf—between us. But if I'm trying to bridge it, why can't you? If it makes it easier for you to accept, I have a purpose for talking to you. I *want* something. I am *using* you to get it. Is that more in line with your idea of our relationship?"

"Much more in line. No, I don't think I'll come up. I'll say what I've got to say when everybody can hear it."

Then he turned. Adams watched him back across the plateau. He did not retreat into the craft until he saw the beginnings of movement on the rippling streets. And he went quickly, as though the sight offended him.

At the UHF he dialled MARDUC's restricted frequency. When the computer responded, he said, "Tell me again of the arrangements for the meeting here."

THE SPOKESMAN, JONES, SUGGESTED NOON LOCAL TIME AND I AC-CEPTED THAT SUGGESTION.

"He says you made the suggestion. More than that, you made it a definite instruction."

IF THERE IS SOME COMPLICATION RESULTING FROM THE ARRANGEMENT IT IS LOGICAL THAT HE WOULD ENDEAVOUR TO COVER HIS BACK. IS THERE SUCH A COMPLICATION?

"There is. The timing was all wrong. Noon here is blazing hot. I cannot imagine anybody volunteering to hold a meeting at that time."

UNLESS THERE WAS AN UNDERLYING MOTIVE.

"You mean unless he wanted to make things look bad for me."

SUCH PEOPLE MUST EXIST.

"That was my first thought. . . ." Adams cut himself short. At times, he was coming dangerously close to confiding in the machine and he cursed the naturalness of their exchanges.

MARDUC hummed and waited. "What is it?" said Adams uneasily.

IS THERE SOMETHING ELSE YOU WISH TO PUT ON RECORD?

"Nothing."

WHAT ARE YOUR ARRANGEMENTS NOW?

"I shall be here until this evening and then I will be meeting the people in more amiable conditions. In case there is another attempt at verbal juxtaposition, is there anything else I should know?"

NOTHING.

"Good. Then conserve your circuitry. I shall want a briefing when I get back to the Tower. I shall also want to file a report."

The afternoon smouldered into early evening. Adams, enclosed in the cool green pod of the monoprop, dozed intermittently, holding himself back from deeper slumber in case he overslept his appointment.

The sun fell behind the range of hills bordering the settlement and a breeze sprang up. Again there was movement on the static streets.

As he banished the blinds, Adams saw the seats come up out of the plateau like . . . words evaded him . . . like . . . rising giraffes.

The people came down the streets and creamed up over the plateau, moving in a flickering current across the tiered rows.

Jones was waiting in front of the seats with two microphones. He handed one to Adams and kept one. Adams blew on it and it responded with gentle thunder.

"Once again, I would like to say that I am sorry you were caused to wait for me in the mid-day heat," he said. "I hope no-one has suffered any ill-effects. I hope, too, that now we are in the cool of the evening, we may arrive at a solution that is mutually satisfactory in our problem here. . . ."

He licked his dry lips and tested his throat. He did not want his voice to carry any hint of indecision.

"You men have withdrawn your labour," he said. "I am here to find out why. I am here, too, to evidence the Tower's belief that all matters of contention can be resolved in an environment of peace and reason. I am going to ask your spokesman, Jones, to tell me why this action has been taken. You will hear his questions; you will hear my replies."

He swung back from the crowd and nodded at Jones. "Now . . ."

"It's about your prisoner," said Jones.

[Angels cast down from Heaven] betrayed the secrets of worldly pleasures—gold, silver and their products; instructed men in the art of dyeing fleeces . . . laid bare the secrets of metals, the virtues of plants, the force of incantations and all the knowledge coveted by men, including even the art of reading the stars. . . .

TERTULLIAN (150–230 A.D.)

The third daye again to life he shall uprise,
And devour byrds and beastes of the wildernesse,
Crowes, popingayes, pyes, pecoks and mevies;
The phenix, the eagle whyte, the gryffon of fearfulnesse,
The greene lyon and the red dragon he shall distress;
The whyte dragon also, the antelope, unicorne, panthere,
With other byrds, and beastes, both more and lesse,
The basiliske also, which almost each one doth feare.

Alchemical Effusion (fifteenth century)

Even in the time it took Adams to regain the Tower, his temper was not abated. He took the el to the upper chamber, fuming at its apparent lack of haste. He went through the door, slammed it, stood regarding the machine with his hands on his hips.

Only then, when mere flickering dials met his angry stare, did he wonder whether wasting such emotion was not supreme folly.

"You didn't *tell* me we had a prisoner," he said eventually.

WE HAVE A PRISONER, said MARDUC.

"The information comes too *late*. I asked you if there was anything I should know before meeting those people and you replied in the negative."

I WAS NOT AWARE THAT THERE WAS A LINK BETWEEN THE ONE CIRCUMSTANCE AND THE OTHER. I WAS GOING TO MENTION THE PRISONER TO YOU IN OUR BRIEFING TONIGHT. MY INTENTION WAS TO BE ABLE TO PRESENT YOU WITH A COMPREHENSIVE REPORT WHICH WOULD HAVE INCLUDED SOME PROGRESS ON THE MATTER OF HIS INTERROGATION.

"His interrogation. By whose order do you hold him for interrogation?"

THERE WAS NO ORDER. BY THE POWER VESTED IN ME, I AM PERMITTED TO SAFEGUARD THE SYSTEM FROM LIKELY CAUSES OF HARM.

"You should have sought my guidance before you acted."

I WAS ABOUT TO TELL YOU.

"I don't believe that." Adams was surprised at his own choice of phrase. "I believe that if I had not found out from another source, you would not have informed me until your intended line of action with the man had been completed."

IT IS NOT POSSIBLE FOR A COMPUTER TO CONSCIOUSLY KEEP THINGS BACK FROM ITS ATTENDANT.

"I don't believe that, either. It may not be possible for a computer to be dishonest, but it is certainly possible for you to delay utterance on any matter until your programming tells you that best advantage may be served by its revelation. And if that isn't deception, it's the next best damned thing. . . ."

I ACCEPT THAT OUR INTERPRETATIONS OF REAL-TIME MAY DIFFER INASMUCH AS YOU ARE A MAN AND I AM A MACHINE. IF SOME INCONSISTENCY SHOULD ARISE AS A RESULT OF THAT, IT IS SOMETHING THAT CANNOT BE RESOLVED AS LONG AS WE ARE WORKING TOGETHER.

Adams sat down in the feeder seat. He tugged at his lower lip. He felt exhausted, though very little of the last few hours had been spent in actual physical exertion.

"You'd better tell me from the beginning. Where is he?"

DOWN IN THE BASEMENT LEVEL.

"And why is he being held?"

WHAT DID JONES TELL YOU?

"I know what Jones told me. I want to hear from you."

HE IS AN OLD MAN AND HE TALKS A LOT OF RUBBISH. HE TAKES UP WORKERS' TIME.

"Surely one old man can't make that much difference."

HE IS A REPRESENTATIVE. THERE ARE OTHERS OF A SIMILAR PERSUASION WHO MAKE THE SAME KIND OF TROUBLE THROUGHOUT THE SYSTEM AREA.

"By talking?"

I DETECT THAT YOU ARE STILL ANNOYED WITH ME. I CONCEDE THAT YOU MAY HAVE REASON TO BE FROM YOUR HUMAN VIEWPOINT. AT THE SAME TIME I WOULD COUNSEL AGAINST LETTING THAT CONDITION LEAD YOU INTO A FALSE ASSESSMENT OF THE SITUATION HERE. TOO MANY OF THESE PEOPLE: TOO MUCH TIME WASTED ON LISTENING AND OUR SYSTEM COULD SUFFER IRREPARABLY. WHILE ACKNOWLEDGING THAT THEY HAVE A RIGHT TO THEIR OPINION I WOULD ADD THAT I AM PROGRAMMED TO CONSIDER THAT NO OPINION IS WORTH THAT MUCH.

"I guess you can't avoid being dogmatic—that's how you're fed—but it's a pity. There is a lot to be gained from flexibility. You miss something by not having the capacity for personal experience. . . ."

I WOULD DISPUTE THAT. RATHER, EMOTIONAL INVOLVEMENT CLOUDS THE ISSUE IN THESE MATTERS. I CITE THE INDUCTIVE SCIENCE OF THE BACONIANS AND THE CONSCIENTIOUS PRODDINGS OF DESCARTES. . . . NOTHING WORTHWHILE EVER EMERGED SIMPLY BECAUSE THESE PEOPLE CONTAINED THEMSELVES WITHIN RIGID DISCIPLINES. THERE WAS FAR MORE PROGRESS MADE BY MEN WHO READ MYSTICISM INTO THE SCIENCE ITSELF. CONSIDER HOW ALCHEMY FATHERED CHEMISTRY . . .

"I'm not starting a major debate, MARDUC. I take it you say you made this—arrest—because you are sure the hazard exists."

OTHERWISE I WOULD NOT HAVE TAKEN THE STEP.

"Fine. Now do you mind if I prove it to myself?"

THAT IS YOUR RIGHT.

"Get him up here."

Adams stood up and pushed the contour chair into a position which afforded easy vantage to himself and the computer. He balanced himself on a technician's stool. By the time he had done that, the old man was at the door.

He looked tired—Adams made a mental note to inspect his quarters. He came with an air of quiet dignity and looked vaguely surprised to see Adams. He took the chair as directed, sinking into it as though his muscles had betrayed him. Adams shifted on the stool.

"There is no need to be nervous," he said. "Take as long as you like to answer my questions. Feel free to ask questions of your own. First of all, I want you to tell me your objections to this system."

The old man folded his hands carefully into his lap. "You said I could ask questions. I wonder if I could give you a warning."

Adams looked at the computer, but there was nothing to see. Another human would have been returning his glance. For no good reason, he missed such an intercourse.

"Yes," he said.

The old man licked his lips. "There is a precedent for this structure, both physical and spiritual. History shows that circumstances conspired to overthrow that structure . . ."

"You speak of the Tower of Babel," Adams interrupted. "Or Birs Nimrud, as it might more rightly be called. The symbol of the Babylonian Empire. Overthrown by the Abyssinians, revived, then laid waste by the Medes and Persians . . . and yet out of that up-and-down empire came the Code of Hammurabi, which had a profound effect on law covenants right up to contemporary times. Out of the Plain of Shinar came cuneiform writing and a remarkable basis for medicine, botany, geology, astronomy, alchemy . . ."

"All of which," cut in the old man, "formed a sound platform of academy for a world bent on severing itself from any suggestion that it might not be self-responsible, self-helpful, and self-sufficient. I see you know something of Babylon."

"I know more," said Adams. "In all probability, the machine knows more again. You find a parallel in this edifice in which we sit. Perhaps you are going to suggest that we shall shortly be reduced to talking nonsense. . . ."

"I suggest nothing. What is to be will be."

"That's for sure," said Adams—and before he could take it further, MARDUC started up.

ARGUE WITH THIS, OLD MAN. THE HEBREWS, A NOMADIC TRIBE, CAME INTO THE FERTILE PLAINS OF THE DELTA AND BEHELD, WITH WONDER AND DREAD, THE SOARING ZIGGURATS OF THE BABYLONIAN CITIES. THEY DESPISED THE MULTITUDES, SPEAKING ALL THE TONGUES OF THE NEAR EAST: THEY DESPISED THEIR ADVANCED METHODS AND TECHNIQUES AND WERE HOSTILE TO THEIR MYTHS—BUT WERE NOT ABOVE BORROWING FROM THEM AS THEY HAD IN THE PAST FOR THEIR VERSIONS OF THE CREATION AND THE FLOOD . . .

There the old man cut him short, leaning forward in the chair.

From apparent exhaustion he had moved into a kind of dynamism. Adams wondered at it—even more as he listened.

"It is a pity you have no means by which to question the information fed to you. Had you so, you might ask why the process might not have been reversed, with the pagans parodising the Old Testament and revising doctrines to suit themselves. You might ask if the common ground in the various myths of the period might not work as much in favour of the truth as you say they do in favour of the other. You might also ask why the name of yhwh has been, throughout history, more prominent . . . more *permanent* . . . than the names of Marduk or Anu-Enlil-Ea. You might ask and find no answer. You might then know the meaning of blasphemy."

"Hold on, old man," said Adams. "Who says we cannot ask and answer? Between us, we have *all* information. We can solve any problem merely by dissemination . . ."

"My pardon, sir, but you have all the information you were *given*. That is my point. Was that intelligence pure? Was it unadulterated, untampered with? Were there no—programmer opinions . . . involved? No knowledge is valid without a proper appreciation of the *un*known. . . ."

Adams stood up—he had to do something, he thought. If he stayed seated, he might never rise. "Such an appreciation of nothing in particular is a luxury the business of running the system will not allow.

"We deal in data. We utilise discovery, experience, the products of great minds. What went wrong with previous governmental forms might well be that they spent too much time dwelling on things they did not know. Such preoccupation is impractical. Our philosophy is simple. It is the whole object of this machine that stands behind me. If you don't know something, find it out. If you can't find it out, it isn't worth knowing. All knowledge is in the public domain. There are no secrets, no oracles, no revelations granted solely to saintly men. We know this is so because we make it so. . . ."

The old man pushed himself up from the chair. "That is admirable in its simplicity. I am surprised, though, that with your vast resources of knowledge and behaviour you should not have arrived at a proper attitude of humility. I maintain that you cannot assess how much you know with taking into account how much you don't know. Now, if there's nothing else . . ."

Adams waved his hand in a gesture that was meant to imply indifference. "Not at the moment. Hold yourself in readiness."

He kept his eye on the door long after the old man had gone.

MARDUC cut in on his careening thoughts. So I HAD HIM ARRESTED. "You did—right," said Adams slowly. But he still had a picture of the old man leaning forward in his chair, possessed of energy, battling for his beliefs. He was wondering why *his* commitment allowed him to be so weary.

Whenever men are so presumptuous as to attempt a physical explanation of theological truths; whenever they allow themselves to interpret sacred texts by views purely human; whenever they reason concerning the will of the Deity and the execution of his decrees; they must necessarily involve themselves in obscurity and tumble into a chaos of confusion.

GEORGE LOUIS LECLERC, Comte de Buffon, 1749

Plac'd in this isthmus of a middle state,
A being darkly wise and rudely great,
With too much knowledge for the sceptic side,
With too much weakness for the stoic pride,
He hangs between; in doubt to act or rest;
In doubt to deem himself a god or beast;
In doubt his mind or body to prefer;
Born but to die, and reas'ning but to err;
Chaos of Thought and Passion all confus'd,
Still by himself abus'd or disabus'd;
Created half to rise and half to fall,
Great lord of all things, yet a prey to all;
Sole judge of Truth, in endless error hurl'd;
The glory, jest and riddle of the world.

ALEXANDER POPE, *Essay on Man*

Jones found the wanderer on the beach, watching the moon lay a silver trail across the quiet night sea. The man must have heard his approach—he moved awkwardly in his shoes on the fine sand and had not seen the need to remove them—but he made no movement.

For a while, Jones thought he might be praying and stood back away, not out of any particular appreciation of the fact but as a simple courtesy. Then the wanderer turned. In the moonlight, something glistened on his exposed cheek. "It's all right," he said. "Did you—ask?"

"Yes. But there wasn't much of an answer. He said he didn't know anything about any prisoner." Jones was pondering the moistness on the man's face.

"Believe me, what I tell you is . . ."

"I believe you. You could both be right. It—kind of—threw him for a moment. A man like that would hardly condemn himself with a deliberate untruth."

"You sound as though you quite like him. Yet you weren't too sure yesterday."

"Well, I . . ." Jones turned the suggestion over in his mind. The tide came and went about his feet. "I was quite prepared to believe that he has some good qualities. He was—human. I guess that was what I wasn't expecting."

"He didn't know anything about it. And yet it is a fact. Then the computer must have been responsible. MARDUC . . . with a name like that, it is hardly surprising."

Jones shivered a little as the breeze penetrated his shirt. "What's the name got to do with it?"

"It's all very complicated. Maybe one day . . ." The wandering man left the sentence unfinished and turned his eyes once more to the sea.

Jones changed his weight from one foot to the other. "Look—I don't pretend to know how the minds of you people work. But if there's anything you want to—well—talk about . . ."

The man turned suddenly and started to walk briskly along the water-line, his bare feet kicking up the surf like splinters of glass. Jones had to run to catch up. When he spoke again, he was becoming impatient. "We stopped work for you, didn't we?"

The wanderer slowed. "I'm sorry. Forgive me. I have a lot on my mind. Sometimes it is not all that easy to accept your calling. Under it all, you're still . . ."

"A human being," said Jones. "You're worried about your friend. Who wouldn't be? But the way Adams was moving when he left here, I reckon he was going to have something to say to that computer. Your friend will be all right."

"He won't. As soon as MARDUC knows it's been challenged, it'll just go ahead with whatever it intended to do. And that is to rid the system of us. It'll *kill* . . . Adams won't even know."

"Then we have to tell him. That's easily done."

"We were warned of a great tribulation. Maybe this is the beginning of it. Maybe we should not interfere with the course of events."

"That's ridiculous. A friend of yours is in danger for his life and all you can say is, 'Maybe we should let it happen.' What kind of religion is that, anyhow?"

"This is all so. . . . This is advanced thinking. If I tell you now, it'll mean nothing. All I can say is that we believe that losing this life isn't important as long as you don't lose your integrity."

"And how does that affect you at this time? It means, I suppose, that you can't beg a member of this system for mercy. Well, I don't have to believe in that. You stay here with your mysteries. I'm going to *do* something."

"I said you wouldn't understand," the wanderer called weakly. But Jones didn't hear. He was already racing back up the beach.

Even the Earth, which is innocent in itself and committed no sin, is nevertheless compelled to bear sin's curse. . . . All creatures, yea, even the Sun and Moon, have as it were put on sackcloth. They were all originally "good," but by sin and the curse they have become defiled and noxious.

MARTIN LUTHER

Surely to alchemy this right is due, that it may be compared to the husbandman whereof Aesop makes the fable; that when he died, told his sons that he had left unto them gold buried underground in his vineyard; and they digged all over the ground, and gold they found none; but by reason of their stirring and digging the mould about the roots of their vines, they had a great vintage the year following: so assuredly the search and stir to make gold hath brought to light a great number of good and fruitful inventions and experiments. . . .

FRANCIS BACON, *The Advancement of Learning*

MARDUC got Adams out of bed with the message that Midi station demanded immediate personal contact with him. Adams was in the screen room before he had properly collected his thoughts. But he pulled himself together when he saw Jones's anxious face on the visual link.

Jones was breathless. At the same time, he was not too sure of himself or of Adams. The result, when Adams appeared before him, was a brake on the tongue. "The . . . the prisoner," was all he could manage to say.

"I've gone into it," said Adams. "I've spoken to the man. He is in good health and staying with us for a while for further discussions."

Then that was that. Adams was up with the situation; had taken his own steps. Might even have confirmed the computer's course of action.

"You . . ." Jones swallowed, gave himself voice. "You bloody murderer. You're no better than . . ."

"Wait a minute. Wait a minute," said Adams. "What is all this?"

And the Midi link circuitry blew.

I AM SORRY. I AM DOING MY BEST TO RECTIFY THE FAULT.

"I'm giving you fair warning." Adams swung angrily on the processing unit. "If you've done anything to that old man, MARDUC, it'll be the last damned thing you'll ever do."

He went from the screen room at a run, dived for the emergency slow-grav shaft and found himself chewing on empty words as he slid down the pole to the base of the Tower. Now, more than at any time in his life, like a knife twisting in his stomach, was the pang, the hunger to talk to somebody. Not just someone who would listen; someone who could offer him a crumb of comfort.

He hit the platform heavily at basement level, picked himself up, raced along the corridor; and flung aside the security man who stood at the door of the isolation room. With the key taken from the prostrate guard, with his heart hammering in some limbo between his ears, he got the door open.

The old man sat on the edge of his bunk.

Adams stayed in the doorway, swaying slightly on his heels. The sight of the Newcomer, apparently unharmed, had wound him down quickly. Again he found himself wondering whether he had not been foolish. After all, he had only Jones's emotional outburst to go on, and . . .

And what? MARDUC's blown circuit just as Jones might have said something important—could that have been deliberate?

The Newcomer was watching him. The guard had picked himself up. Adams stood half in and half out of the cell, accountable to both of them. The guard came to the doorway and looked in.

"He's all right, then."

Adams moistened his lips. "Did you think he might not be?"

"Mr. Adams, when a man arrives on the scene like you did, there's only one reason. Somebody's in trouble."

Adams was off the hook. "Seems I was wrong."

"Not wrong, Mr. Adams. It's never wrong to care that much about anybody." The old man had risen from the bunk. "Now that you're here, could we—perhaps—talk?"

Adams moved into the room. "Leave the door open," he told the guard. "Even listen."

He turned a straight-back chair to face the bunk. He sat down. He motioned the Newcomer to the bunk.

"I was under the impression that you were in danger," he said.

The old man smiled wryly. "From whom if not from you? I'm sorry. That was ungracious. The truth is, I never suspected anything else."

"But nobody . . ."

"No *body*, no. You see, we—you and I—are at the mercy of logic. If MARDUC has any qualms at all about anything, it consults precedents. Depending on what those precedents are, it takes action . . . and if the precedents provided for it as experience are of a certain conviction, then one has little difficulty in anticipating what the thing will do. You know what it—thinks—of my religious beliefs. It has been so briefed as to conclude that I have no value at all to the system it represents. Therefore, why should it have any compunction about getting rid of me?"

"But if you were in fear of this, why didn't you say?" Adams didn't wait for the answer. He had another question. "And why didn't your—Friend—take some action to protect you?"

The old man's lips were set in a gentle smile. "Forgive me if I appear to find that a little naive—I have been too long in the company of people who take such matters for granted. If my Friend were to intervene whenever anybody got into trouble, life would be carefree and faith would be cheap. First of all, you have to understand that a man has no fear of death when he knows that something better awaits him. You look tired. Perhaps you would like a long sleep. Perhaps you would like to wake up and find that all your problems have been solved. That's a fairly common wish, wouldn't you say? Well, if your Friend—your very close, very real friend—had promised that that was what would happen when He implemented His will on earth, would you not go gladly to the grave?"

AND THERE YOU HAVE IT, said the walls. THE DEATH-WISH CATEGORICALLY STATED. THE MADNESS THAT SENT MARTYRS INTO THE HANDS OF THE MANSLAYER.

Adams shifted uneasily on the hard chair. He had forgotten that there was always another occupant in the cell, taking record of every word. He felt guilty and that was wrong, too. He should not have to feel guilty.

IF YOU BELIEVE THAT, YOU ARE LOST. STEP ASIDE AND LET ME KILL HIM.

But Adams stayed where he was. He knew with a certainty that lay like a blizzard in the pit of his stomach that the point had been reached—the point that had actually been inevitable since the mono-prop had threaded him into the Tower. The point where he had to divide his psyche from his function; to decide whether he was a man for his own sake or the unprotesting agent of a purpose.

And even as he put the predicament into words, he realised that there was no time—machine time, real-time, any time—to arrive at an answer. So he argued.

"Then you'll do what he wants. Is that in your programming, to give an enemy what he wants?"

THAT IS ONE OPTION. WHETHER HE WANTS IT OR NOT CANNOT ALTER THE FACT THAT IT MAY BE THE BEST FOR ALL CONCERNED.

"For all . . . Have you considered what you mean by 'all'? How do we explain away his death to the people who consider him so worthwhile that they have stopped work pending his fate?"

THEY WILL ACCEPT OUR RULING WHEN WE EXPLAIN. THEY HAVE HAD THEIR FILL OF THESE EMPTY PROMISES OF THE MILLENNIUM. WE ARE THE MILLENNIUM.

"You are on your own. I have ordered that he shall not be harmed. I will not support your action. You will be a maverick, a machine that must be destroyed."

THEN YOU DIE, TOO.

So it had come to this. Adams beckoned the guard, indicated the old man. The guard came and went, leading the Newcomer quietly from the cell.

Well, at least he didn't have to decide now where his loyalty lay. The machine had made it clear he was held in no higher respect than the old man he had just dismissed.

Out of that prospect came—almost—an exhilaration. The humours moved within him; body chemistry built a compound and began a reaction.

He was on his feet before the machine, his right hand clasping and unclasping as though it sought to feel some weapon within its compass.

"Fine," he said. "Kill me."

The walls fussed and mumbled. He watched the ventilator grid. As far as he could work out, that was the only form of armament MARDUC had immediately to hand, some chemical pumped into the shaft and piped to the cell.

Still the walls whirled within themselves; tape turned on tape; sensor sought algorithm.

"What's keeping you?" said Adams. "Come on, you're all words. Let's see what else they put inside you. Let's see some discipline."

He found his lips curled back against his teeth, half smile, half snarl. He was ready to laugh.

MARDUC spoke.

MY DATA ARE INSUFFICIENT. I MUST KNOW THE COUNTEREFFECT HAZARD BEFORE I CAN CONSIDER AND APPOINT THE OPTIONS AVAILABLE TO ME. THAT IS MINIMAX. WHAT WILL YOU DO TO ME?

And now Adams *was* laughing—so hard that he choked and his eyes streamed. Endgame. End of endgame.

"Nothing," he said. "I will do *nothing*."

After that, the computer got a little incoherent.

Later, Adams saw the old man out at ground level. He walked with him to his simple but clean dwelling in the foothills where the shadow of the Tower fell at this time of day.

He watched the Newcomer move into the house and saw him go first to his bookshelves, running his hands over the spines in a caress.

"I'll come and see you when I get a moment," he said. "There's a lot I don't understand and I can't promise that I ever will."

"At this stage, you don't have to make any promises," said the old man. "It's enough that you are prepared to listen. If it's easier, I can come to you."

"But . . ." Adams gestured at the shadow that lay, beanstalk-twisted, across the rocks.

"It's only a tall building," said the Newcomer. "Isn't it?"

DAYLENGTH TALKING BLUES

Introduction

If it is spring when you read this, Peter St. John Martineau, Blind David, The Man With The Bicycle, and The Girl With The Unfinished Face bid you welcome. Come to Cardiff and I will point them out—just four of the shabby immortals who seem to have nothing and are therefore credited with nothing.

But think about it. Think about *your* local never-dies. The tramp who was old when you were young and is now no older, though you are counting grey hairs. The busker, the girl dwarf, the Peter Pan eccentric, his jacket heavy with a thousand badges.

If I were a writer of science fantasy, I would say it was their regular contact with flying-saucer personnel that was keeping them so robust.

Instead, I have been putting two and two together in a neglected branch of research where the layman might still come up with the answer of four quite by accident. Take what you know of gerontology and lay it alongside your store of data on leaf-fall and its reasons. The parallels are undeniable, the unknowns are impressive and—don't laugh—this could even be a breakthrough.

Peter St. John Martineau, the beggar with the prep-school name, reads it on the label of his Cyprus wine bottle. Blind David, forever underground inside his mining valley head, finds it figured out in Braille upon the autumn leaves which settle on his accordion in sympathy with the one sad tune of his repertoire. The Man With The Bicycle mouths it over and over as he wheels his velocipede up arcade, down lane, round and round cul-de-sac. The Girl With The Unfinished Face shouts it from her news-stand along with cries of the latest crises.

They know the score. That is their secret and their privilege. It is safe with them.

Peter St. John Martineau lives in a corner that is not even a porch near the entrance to the telephone exchange. He may be sprawling asleep in daytime and standing poker-straight at night. The hours make no claim on him.

Occasionally he will walk, but only to the nearby river-bank, there to relieve himself.

People are good to him. I have seen bags of food change hands. They offered him a home one time but he refused it. He is after the vacant shop-lot next door to Her Majesty's Stationery Office—he being stationary, you understand. He is very attached to the civil service.

People are good to Blind David also. He was found one night hopelessly drunk, rolling on the pavement near his usual venue. In his possession and intact was a hundred and ten pounds.

The morning judge told him he was lucky. The woman who served him faggots and peas in the market and was careful not to spoon up any black ones said the same thing.

Shortly after the news of his good fortune was flashed to the thousand corners of South Wales, he disappeared.

The Bicycle Man used to have a name when he kept a tobacconist shop in City Road and his son had a bicycle. Now his son has the shop and the father has the—

Every day, the same shopping bag seemingly bulging with vegetables. No matter how the hands of the clock stand, you will see him pass and he will see you but there will be no recognition.

Hill, the name was. Rugby, the conversation was. Buying Dad's Old Tavern, the occasion was.

Strange, that bag of legumes smells of Old Tavern.

The Unfinished Girl is elegant, a *Vogue* showpiece below blurred features. She has made herself worth looking upon and yet defies anyone to catch her eye. How do you say: "I wasn't seeing your face"?

The prospect is distressing. Newspaper-selling is the vocation of the halt and the lame in this town and these are her colleagues.

Her special friend is a man whose gait is so awkward that he cannot keep his arm around her, no matter how hard he tries. Instead, he scripts the air with lurid details of sensations not contained in the papers he carries.

Any prosecutor citing the Trade Descriptions Act would find the defendant unfit to plead.

The consolation is that they make money hand over fist. And the Unfinished Girl's profit goes on a wardrobe to impress her hunch-backed, club-footed, faithful beaux.

How is it that when you have put twenty years between yourself and childhood, those memory figures persist, as solid as a clamour at your ear, a keyboard melody, a tyre-mark across your foot?

They know the score. That is their secret and their privilege. It is safe with them.

Peter St. John Martineau has a new thick overcoat and a stocking cap. It makes him stand out lightly against the soot-black stain on the wall where he lives. Hitherto, stain and derelict have been second-dimension synonymous, like something that might look better with the sun on it.

Why does Peter choose the telephone exchange? Is he waiting for a trunk call?

Blind David—we had a typing error once: "blind Rhondda miner" instead of "Blaenrhondda miner" and it was funny until you thought about it—could be seen upon the lane that divides St. John's Churchyard down the middle. He shared the location with men who sell fell-off-lorry transistor radios, junk jewellery, and Christmas wrappings but did not/could not run with them when the law showed up.

Under his feet, brass numbers marked graves that had become a common thoroughfare. Why did he stand on death? Was he waiting to put down roots?

The Bicycle Man has been seen actually treating his wheels as they should be treated, i.e. propelling them by means of pedals. He is the slowest cyclist the world has ever seen and how he does not fall off is a vandalism of Newtonian physics.

Riding or walking, he is never lacking his cloth cap with poke (which is South Welsh for "peak"), foul meerschaum, and grey-brown-indeterminate jacket. When the weather is inclement, the outfit is supplemented by fly-away gaberdine mackintosh, threatening to catch in spokes and therefore providing an element of excitement for the observer.

One false move, one breeze out of place and he could be unseated, down on the road, under a bus with pipe-smoke drifting in epitaph, but the years proceed and this does not happen.

Why does he take the risk? Are there letters in the smoke?

The Unfinished Girl has a Little Black Riding Hood cape for gloomy days when the High Street draughts drive her and her news-box into the nearest arcade and a succession of petal-lace blouses for balmy summer days which call her back to her site near a bus-stop.

The bus which calls at this stop plunges down to dockland that used to be called Tiger Bay before they exorcised the shanty-town wraiths with concrete plazas and high-rise flats. The people endure and are conquering their fear of heights. Now they all ride at the top of the mast.

Invariably, there will be some person in the bus-stop queue who will engage the Unfinished Girl in animated conversation. When the girl tries to smile, it would bring a tear to your eye, which is stupid. It is, after all, a smile. Why does she smile? Has she found some good news in her pile of pulp?

This is what Blind David traced with his fingers upon the crisping foliage:

A typical leaf loses chlorophyll, anthocyanin, nitrogen, phosphorus, sodium, iron, magnesium, and water and changes carbohydrate constituents before it is discarded by abscission.

The leaf detects the shortening of days and the hormones are liberated within it. These auxins trigger the chemical resurgence and subsequent cell-wall dissolution.

The falling of a leaf is voluntary euthanasia more than suicide. It is certainly not murder by the trunk of the tree.

He could not understand a word of it while he was sober.

This is what Peter St. John Martineau found on a raisin-wine label:

Human urine and saliva are the richest natural sources of the auxin indole-3-acetic acid (IAA) which regulates plant growth and life and may even prove to be the main deterrent to the resurgence process.

He read, considered, and moved to the river-bank. There he relieved himself upon grass and shrub, knowing the feeling of creation. For the final polish, he hawked and spat.

This is what the Unfinished Girl read hand-stamped in the late-news column of her city-final papers:

Daylength is more critical even than sunshine. There can be no sunshine and yet plants will grow, photosynthesising with light no stronger than one foot-candle (that is the intensity of light one foot away from an ordinary kitchen candle). But if there should be no daylight at all . . .

The item was not murder, price rise, or local strike, but she shouted it nevertheless. Kitchen candles were her illumination when her money was gone to freer-spending friends. Daylight she knew like no other.

This is what the Bicycle Man learned from the habitual contents of his pipe:

W. W. Garner and H. A. Allard of the U. S. Department of Agriculture first linked daylength with flowering in 1920. They concluded that growth regulators of the auxin nature were especially active in their experimental subject, the Maryland Mammoth tobacco plant.

The Bicycle Man was not at all surprised. With a shopful of varieties, he had stuck to Maryland Mammoth for years.

A blind man cannot see when he has had enough to drink. Blind

David only knew when he began understanding the message of the leaves. Then he ran ahead of the rest before the law.

Now Peter St. John Martineau knows he has something to offer and something to possess, he has gone from the telephone exchange corner, leaving a body-shaped smudge.

A rough male voice shouting at the mouth of the arcade, selling lies as latest sensations. Ask about the Unfinished Girl and he accuses you of taking her away.

Lunchtime. A week of lunchtimes taken at various hours, trodden over familiar ground and no tyre-tracks on road or boot. No scent of Old Tavern or Maryland Mammoth.

Daylength talking blues: Given that plants and animals share the definition of heterotrophe, the enzymes of glycolysis, the citric-acid cycle, and the pentose phosphate shunt, the common auxin bond lacks only documentation.

Ergo: Death equals leaf-fall.

Ergo: In the balance of nature that defies A. I. Oparin and his carbon-cycle hypotheses, those who miss the luxuries of circumstance instead enjoy the riches of cute hormones.

Ergo: It is December. My ghosts will be back to see every spring. That is their secret and their privilege. It is safe with them. And out of my reach.

SKYHAMMER

Introduction

Joe Gaskell has had an undistinguished secret-service career. He was called in to probe the "Moonface Scenario" caper where astronauts, for no apparent good reason, began reciting some ripe Cyrano de Bergerac during their walkabout on one of the last Apollo shots. His inquiries called for a great deal of legwork and some pretty dull interviews with space experts around the world before he found that the astronauts were only doing it to keep their ground buddies at Cape Kennedy employed (like, with another Apollo mission?). It was heavy going for Joe and pretty heavy going for editors also, to judge from the response.

Then he starred in "Skyhammer," written for British Milford 1, taken along to Milford-on-Sea—and crowded out for reasons of time.

His next assignment was a little better—he had a bit part as a security man in my last novel, *Moon on an Iron Meadow*. But it was so small a role that it was doubtless overlooked.

So here, because he is a nice guy and losers have as much right to protagonism as heroes, is "Skyhammer." It is livelier than "Moonface" because Joe learned his lesson. It is a chronicle of forced lightning—and though Bob Silverberg informs me he has seen more snow than lightning since he has known San Francisco, the quarries of Joe Gaskell are about to change all that.

You may enjoy the trip to Venice, as well. Joe did—but typically, he got wet in several ways.

Rain falls on the Piazza San Marco, an insubstantial drizzle which would have had the Venetians of five years ago studying their cellars and the measuring rods along the Grand Canal.

Now there is no persistence of flood. The pumping stations around the lagoon have lengthened the history and driven back the water. If anybody can build a pumping machine, it is an Italian, but Russian money has gone into these devices. Since the excommunication backlash of '75 slew the Christian Democrats and tipped the Vatican into the Tiber with the rest of the sewage, the Soviets have been anxious to place their funds here.

The Italian Communist Party, having managed for long enough without much help from the Kremlin, was first cool in response but now is glad because the local economy is still meagre. The public-ownership plan which took the Communisti to power was built on silt. Art treasures were to be sold and the profits shared. But there were too many treasures and too few buyers.

Rain falls on the Piazza San Marco and on the man who sits under a tattering Martini sunshade drinking Trebbiano as thin and dry as the music of the string quartet at his back. Standing out of place among the basket chairs for the only customer. While their black umbrellas hover above them like crows.

Joe Gaskell. An American and an agent of intelligence, though he is not here to prepare a report of the new regime. He is here because of his migraine.

Damn and hammer, the lightning strokes were falling on San Francisco when Martin Slade called Joe Gaskell across the Bay City sealink complex for a conference about the weather.

He noticed the way Joe's forehead was puckered despite the dark lenses that both of them had begun to wear.

"Never known a summer like it," he said.

"Makes me sick," said Gaskell.

"Same here."

"No, Chief. Really physically sick to my stomach. Migraine sufferers can't stand strong light."

"And you have migraine?"

"It's on my record. Along with my beauty spots and my passion for Italian wines. Idiosyncrasies—that's the heading. My migraine is an idiosyncrasy." This latter comment delivered in a rising pitch.

"How do they define your temper, Joe?"

"I'm sorry. I guess the conditions are getting to me."

"You could do with a holiday."

"I could do with a workable blindfold."

Slade sat forward. If his eyes could have been seen, they would have been seen to be peering intently. "You're no good to us that way. You'll take a break."

"Can I pick my own spot? I have friends one mile down a Welsh coal-mine."

"No doubt they'll come in useful sometime, but not this time. We thought you might like a few weeks in Venice."

"Venice! But that corner of the Adriatic's even worse off for electric storms than this place—"

"Not this year."

"What?"

"Not this year. Plenty of rain—you can't help that, so close to water—but no lightning."

"Unusual."

"Exactly."

"Then I'm on an assignment."

"No, Joe." Slade removed the shades from his elongated, equine face to promote sincerity. "You're there because it's away from the fireballs. In your own interests. Understood?"

Gaskell returned the gaze from his polaroid haven. "So I'm looking a gift-horse in the mouth," he said archly.

"I didn't put it that way but I guess it was what I meant. Give us a little credit. You've done a lot of good work. We look after you. Come back fresh and you'll be looking after us."

What a fine liar I am, thought Slade. What a statesman.

"So I get to go where I want to go?"

"Surely, Joe. A mere suggestion on my part." What a statesman. "Where would you like to go?"

Gaskell thought about it while voltage lacerated the sky above Frisco. A right setting for a passion which lingered in settings and maybe a day or two at the Verona vineyards. Little ol' wine-drinker, me.

He said: "Venice."

There are so many amoebic sections of so many imaginations at a Miami Science Fiction Convention that you would read in a little simple intrigue without even thinking about it.

That's a place where you can mention Roger Zelazny with impunity. That's a place where you can hand over a copy of *Nine Princes In Amber* without arousing the slightest suspicion. The piece of paper appended is a Doubleday review slip seven years old but science-fiction people have this hoarding fetish. The lemon-juice lettering which appears before the match is of more recent vintage.

The first cypher entry says 2/28/1. The page is 2, 28 the line, 1 the place of the word in that line. Complete cypher reads: 2/28/1, 50/32/1, 81/1/1, 96/23/8, 110/16/5, 129/18/1, 11/2/8, 31/29/6.

The message from Moscow via Miami is: JUST PUT HIM WHERE WE CAN FIND HIM.

A look inside Martin Slade's head. No search for motives, this, but a little physiology as he beats his way about the office scarred by natural neon in the night made day by flickering devilglow.

See the brain, fitful in oscillation. Its electrical activity on a normal day with the sky silent and just a fibreglass sheen of dioxides coming off the dipping streets would be mostly slow, around five cycles a second. At the subliminal end of the spectrum, the activity would be up to around ten cycles a second (the alpha rhythm).

Tonight, three hours after his conversation with Joe Gaskell, three days before Joe Gaskell will sit in the Piazza San Marco rain sipping Trebbiano and still knowing nothing, Martin Slade's brain is oscillating evenly at twelve cycles per second. He has tried to shut out the current from his National Security Agency office eyeball to eyeball with the sky at the top of the L'Enfant Plaza. He could have gone home but that removed him from the problem.

Instead, he stayed to fight it out and now could not go home if he tried. He made one last good move and we shall see what that is.

Now Martin Slade is no longer sane.

Joe Gaskell was less than happy with the Trebbiano. It made him reach too hastily for the cheese. It was a bad wine that set him thinking of something else or perhaps the wine did not exist that could seduce him from the burden he had to bear.

He had quit. Not the NSA, not even his commitment. But quit San Francisco while the sky fell and the panic climbed to meet it. The drive to the airport had been a nightmare, with the street lighting short-circuited and at least a dozen diversions around twisted metal too hot to handle and broken people too dead to be raised.

He was nauseous yet at the recollection. The lightning was a new phenomenon and though it had brought back a familiar kind of pain to Gaskell, its effects on the rest of the population had only begun to be made manifest.

He had not known before his conversation with Slade, even during the conversation, that the flickering was taking its toll on others who were less than freaks. He could not be sure that even Slade realised, though he would concede that Slade was not ignorant of a matter merely because he did not mention it or pretended surprise when his attention was drawn to it. The instance of the migraine . . .

Venice was an assignment. Slade had denied that, too, but only because he wanted Gaskell in the right condition to make up his own mind.

So the agent had acted in harmony and left Slade thinking that his fabrication had succeeded like a charm.

Venice had to be an assignment. That was the only way in which Gaskell could tolerate his presence here while his home cracked wide and millennial chaos ensued. Somewhere in Venice was the means to order that chaos. How Slade knew was his own business. Why he had chosen Gaskell was less of a riddle. Gaskell had contacts . . . and migraine.

When would the contacts be made? That was the tear-jerker. Gaskell had been sitting here going through his vino vocabulary for two days.

And right on cue, a bulky shape blotted out the poor light, shook itself like a dog, and dropped into a seat beside him.

Oskar Samov. A cold-war confrontation in six cubic feet of space beneath a frail Martini parasol.

"Excuse me, sir," said Samov, "but would you mind if I shared your shelter?"

A waiter swam out from the cafe, cursing discreetly because the string quartet forced him into a roundabout route.

Samov regarded Gaskell's bottle critically. "Merely a coffee with milk," he said.

"Are you well, Oskar?" asked Gaskell without enthusiasm.

"Neither of us is here because he is well," said Samov. "One monopoly the capitalists do not have is on headaches."

And that reaction was unexpected. Gaskell had known Samov

from his CIA days, when the bluff Caucasian was an agricultural adviser to a succession of Latin American nations. When he had recognised him now, he had considered that the man was working closer to home. That Venice was his patch. That he was here, maybe, to explain the intricacies of these irrigational wonders which bordered the lagoon.

The pain was starting now behind his right eye. The vapourous glare was bothering him. Shortly, the one side of his head would be separated from the other as surely as with a meat cleaver. Wine and cheese, chocolate and nuts, travel and television, all triggers. Travel and anxiety, his particular beasts. He must have nodded.

"You are not surprised to see me?"

"Never surprised to see you, Oskar. Maybe surprised that you expect me to be."

"Then you know about Moscow."

"Nothing. Not—lightning?"

"Like San Francisco. Only worse."

"It can't be worse," argued Gaskell. Blood and debris and madness.

The waiter came with Samov's coffee. The rain fell insubstantially.

"All right. Just as bad."

"Why are you here, Oskar?"

"Because you are here."

"How did you know I would be here?"

"You were sent."

"I—find that hard to believe." But he didn't. Only moments ago, he had credited Slade with the initiative.

"Then why are you here, Gaskell?"

"I was sent," conceded the American.

"Yes, but why?"

"I was expecting you to tell me. At least, I was expecting somebody to tell me. If Moscow's in the same way, I guess you and I just sit here and wait for that third party to come and name the ransom."

"I think not. That is not why we sent for you."

"If you sent for me, how the hell do you ask why I am here?"

"San Francisco is expendable. Why didn't you try the trick on Washington or New York? That would have been comparable with our Moscow."

"You're talking yourself straight up your—"

"Just my joke. Do you think Slade would have allowed you to come if he thought we were going to hold you responsible?"

"Your Slav humour is a little heavy-handed, Oskar."

"Slade was ill."

"Rubbish."

"Yesterday, he stood on the window-sill outside his office on the top storey of the L'Enfant Plaza and called on the lightning to take him. It just took the sill from beneath his feet."

"I don't believe it. He was—"

"He's dead, Gaskell. Try that private number of his."

"How do you know?"

"News travels. The body count in San Francisco is rising. As it is in Moscow."

"Then what brings us here?"

"A good summer." Samov looked out on the downpour so gentle it was making frosted glass of the puddles.

"And motives?"

"They don't like you because you still house the major strength of Roman Catholicism—some of your cardinals-in-exile have been very outspoken. They don't like us because we were slow to help their struggle when we could not see it doing us any good."

"Then you're blaming the Italians."

"But who else? The mistake they made was ensuring their own comfort at the expense of ours."

"That's ridiculous. They wouldn't have the know-how."

"They would because we have given it to them."

"What?"

"Those pumping stations—they're only pumping stations in the same way that the purification plants at Baikal are pumping stations. They also house command relay buildings for our Cosmos satellite programme."

"I didn't know that."

"Martin Slade did. That's why he sent you to meet us here."

"Fine. But what have command relay posts got to do with our problem?"

"They transmit satellite firing instructions and firing releases ionised exhaust vapours. Time those right in an area of high conductivity like the Pacific and you can create lightning twenty-four hours a day."

"And these lagoon installations have the power to issue those commands?"

"They do."

"So close them down."

"We cannot. How do you think it would look? Only now we are beginning to have good relations with this country. Such a manoeuvre would do our prestige here irreparable harm."

"It's your problem."

"It's yours, too. You have seen how it is in San Francisco. Martin Slade appreciated that."

When he looked, Joe Gaskell had sunk half of the Trebbiano without a further cube of cheese. "What you are suggesting is that I close them down."

"I have been frank with you."

"By what means?"

"Your choice. But I would think demolition would be more positive than mere curtailment."

"Which are the relay stations and which the pumps?"

"I am afraid our circuitry has needed to be so subtle to avoid unauthorised recognition that the one is an integral part of the other."

"To save Frisco, I sink Venice."

"That is the dilemma. You can rest assured that we will do anything to help—"

"Outside of actually *doing* anything, huh?"

"I rather think Slade was expecting you to be a little more cooperative."

"Slade is dead."

"And you are drinking the wine of his killers."

Oskar Samov stood up and the rain stopped. Joe Gaskell had his commission, a task that would split his loyalties as the agony now split his head. Nobody had said he was going to like it.

This is how it is done.

Several of the three-hundred-range Cosmos satellites shallow down their orbits to forty to fifty miles high above the Pacific. The necessary correcting fire yields vapour into the heavily charged atmosphere, a readily ionized vapour.

A four-fold increase in the electrical conductivity of the atmosphere doubles the time constant in maximum-intensity oscillations, thereby increasing the number of lightning strokes before the oscillations decay.

The flickering at near-alpha-rhythm frequency pulls the brain into unnatural synchrony with it, degrading brain performance.

This situation in the earth-ionosphere cavity is not happenstance or valid experimentation. It is geophysical warfare.

Joe Gaskell took the lagoon tour with a score of visitors—a handful of Americans, a voluble Japanese family, a quiet French couple, the remainder Scandinavians.

But on Burano he paid scant attention to the lace, and on Murano his thoughts were not of glass. The Dutchess of Burano had always managed to hold him. No streets, just rows of houses scattered willy-nilly across a plain of paving-stones. Bicycles and old women and washing draped across the small transit canals. Now he looked instead for the new building, the vital installation. It should have stuck out like a sore thumb, but the Italians had been intelligent. They had chosen a spot encompassed by the walls of an old estate, reinforced them from the inside, set their killer equipment in the restored palazzo.

On Murano, they had been no less astute. The glassworks were on the quayside. That was where a pumping machine should be and that was where it was, in an old storehouse.

No extraordinary precautions, since there seemed little need to fear that such a sympathetic and essential function would be harmed.

His concentration was wandering so much that he almost bought a glass chamois at factory price. One of the Americans nudged him just in time. "Not here."

"What?" He was vague and afterwards apologetic.

"Here you pay the highest prices. These things are even cheaper by the time they get to the shops in Venice."

And of course he knew that. "Thanks," he said. "First trip."

"*Troppo, troppo,*" he told the hovering salesgirl. "Too much."

Close to the water at the stern end of the cabin cruiser which was transporting the party, he scanned the outcrops of land that dotted the lagoon.

Some were only big enough to bear a withered tree. Others showed tumble-down villas behind rusting, fluted-iron gates. Still others were just graveyards, locked up and left, the white weathering of time mingling with the pallor of death.

Venice. The more he saw, the more he suffered. Samov had spoken of a dilemma, presumably because his own sources were aware of Gaskell's deep feeling for the ancient gateway to the Western world. Dilemma was a poor word. To Gaskell, it felt as though he must kill one side of himself to let the other survive.

He ran his fingers over the surface of the lagoon like a caress and cursed his sentimentality. In his mind's ear, the cries of fishermen;

in actuality, the shunt and guzzle of the dredger fleet which worked day and night to keep Venice on a dry footing.

All this he would have to end and he wasn't convinced that it was worth the price. And then there was Martin Slade, his good friend for so many years, gone berserk upon a window-ledge and calling down the wrath of the elements on his head.

He drove his fist despairingly into the water, succeeding only in splashing the French couple.

"I'm sorry," he said. "The wind . . ." But they just smiled wanly and left it there, the woman blessing her raincoat.

What does a relay station look like? Gaskell, in his naïveté, had expected a display of aerials or at least some kind of visible link between earth and sky.

"Like lightning conductors?" suggested Samov when Gaskell met him at the Scuola San Rocco studying a Tintoretto.

"I have to take your word for it." Gaskell was in a bad position. "How many of these things are there altogether?"

"Murano and Burano—"

"Those two I've located."

"There's another at Chioggia, which is a bona-fide pumping station, and a fourth north of the beach at Lido di Jesolo. You can destroy them or leave them, as you will."

"You could be giving me the wrong two."

"It is possible. Why not blow them all? But don't forget when you're looking for deception that we built these things and we are being offended, too."

"I'll take them all."

"Feel free. If you consider that gives you more of a choice . . ."

"And I'll be checking back with my office—just to make sure they know what you say they know."

"I said Slade knew. I cannot be certain he told anybody."

"Sounds like a nice safe secret. All the more reason to check it."

Samov went away muttering. Gaskell returned to the Hotel Metropole-Suisse and tried a call to San Francisco.

He smoked out a three-hour delay and, having made the appropriate identifications, found himself talking eventually to Tom Pickard, Slade's number-two man.

"Tom?" The line was atrocious. "This is Gaskell."

"Who?"

"Joe Gaskell, Tom, in Venice."

"I didn't know we had a man in Venice—I'm sorry—my head is hurting. Your name again?"

"Gaskell. Damn it, Tom, I have an all-right name or I wouldn't be able to get through to you. . . ."

Fuzz and crackle and whine in Frisco. "Joe Gaskell."

"Right."

"Bear with me, Joe. I don't seem to be myself. These lights . . ."

"I know all about it, Tom. I'm here. In Venice. Where it's happening."

"Lightning in Venice?"

"No, Tom." It was tough. It didn't seem likely that Slade's deputy was going to be able to confirm details. "Where's Martin?"

"Dead." That much was incontestable.

"Dead how?"

"Out of the window. I'm just sitting here, Joe, looking at that window. Maybe I'll . . . sweet heaven—these flashes . . ."

"Look away, Tom! Turn your back on it and listen. You have to okay something for me. About the lightning."

"Right. I'm turned away with my hands over my eyes. My glasses are no good. I dropped them and trod on them. I seem to be getting that clumsy—"

"Don't worry about it, Tom. It's not for much longer."

"You said—okay."

"Correct. I want to double-check certain data with you. Did you know—did Martin ever tell you—anything about Venice?"

"Venice?"

"About . . . er . . ." Gaskell wondered how much guidance he could give. "About pumping stations?"

"The Russians helped build them."

"Good. That's good, Tom. Anything about any modifications?"

"They're not what they seem, he said. I remember that much."

"Did he give any hint about what they might be?"

"Tracking stations. No, not tracking stations. Something like—hell, do you know, Martin's polished cabinet here is picking up the pyrotechnics like a mirror . . ."

"Relay stations."

"That's right."

"Fine. Now—why am I here?"

"They asked for you."

"How?"

"Miamicon method. Using a book. Zelazny's *Nine Princes In*

Amber . . . It's a little better sitting this way, Joe. Things are clearer. Message was JUST PUT HIM WHERE WE CAN FIND HIM."

"Do you know why they asked for me?"

"Can't confirm it was you personally, Joe. Merely somebody known to them."

"But why one of us?"

"It was in our interests"—another phrase echo, noted Gaskell. "It was a job they couldn't do. It satisfied Martin."

"Thanks, Tom. Then it should be good enough for me."

"Regret I've been so vague, Joe—"

"I told you, I know the situation. Not for much longer. And look —stay away from that window, huh?"

"Make it soon, Joe. Those who weren't afraid to come to work are afraid to go home. We're getting a human detritus problem here. And it's the same in a hundred thousand other places . . ."

Then the voice of home was gone in static.

And Gaskell kicked himself because there was one key question he had not asked.

No matter. There were other and probably better means of securing a reply. The hotel switchboard connected him with the party he was calling.

With Chioggia, the problem is one of distance. Joe Gaskell takes a diesel rapido to Padua, changes it for a slower inter-urban to Rovigo, and then has to wait two hours for the last connection in his almost circular route to Chioggia. Once there, he is closer to Venice than he has been for some hours.

The pumping station has to be on the shoreline and he finds it facing inland to the Brenta delta. Imploders come in all sizes and Joe has a ready-made site for his device, housed in a quart of Vespucci industrial emulsion paint.

Joe is in black and so is the sky. Again, there are no guards where there is no recognition of hazard. The small dial gives him a twelve-hour limit and he sets it on eleven and a half, sweating while he avoids the "instant." A tin of paint can stand anywhere. Joe rolls it quietly down a pipe and into the belly of the pump. If they find it, they'll only take it out and keep it and the effect will be the same.

The haul back to Rovigo-Padua-Venice is more fortunate in train incidences.

At Lido the installation is as dark as the coastline is alight. The paint goes down the chimney just the same.

There is no attempt to make the blasts concurrent. Too much ground to cover. All will fall within a twenty-eight-hour period and Joe will have to rely on the fact that the several law agencies will still be arguing out whose responsibility it is—vandalism or security breach—to start concerted vigilance on like installations.

Joe picks a different time and gets a different boat for his second tour of the islands in two days. At Murano, he takes a drink from his vacuum flask as the party tails off its glassworks visit and then has to run to catch the cruiser, leaving his flask in the storehouse doorway.

There's going to be a lot of flying glass and he prefers not to think about results. The nighttime detonation is intentional, to limit injuries.

At Burano, with a two-hour stay including lunch, he lets his *passegiatta* take him through the convoluted gates of the old palazzo and consumes not a single sandwich from the lunch-box before he lifts a grating and drops the pail carefully into the sewer.

The reinforced walls surrounding the estate will absorb the impact here, at least.

Chugging back to the mainland. Lonely trees, crumbling villas, forgotten sepulchres, all bone-white. The Lido di Jesolo blast makes waves which pitch the cruiser alarmingly. Joe Gaskell screams and chatters with the rest.

The Corriere della Sera had made the usual mistake of calling the implosions explosions but it was only to be expected in the absence of fine detail.

Gaskell's Italian wasn't adequate to convey the total nuance of the news stories but the pictures were easy enough to understand. The pumping stations were in ruins. Naturally enough, no mention of their clandestine subsidiary role. Instead, the authorities were suggesting that the disastrous blasts were the despicable work of pro-Vatican guerillas—a theory that sat easily enough on the Venetian palate and in the designs of Samov and Joe Gaskell.

But the feeling in the arcades and along the domestic canals wasn't of anger; it was anxiety. Joe Gaskell picked it up like a scent as he crossed the Rialto Bridge and threaded his way through calle and casa to the square Napoleon had called "Europe's greatest drawing-room."

Samov, puffing on a black Sobranie at the water-bus terminal, picked up his approach and stepped well ahead of him aboard the vessel. Gaskell, in his turn, went past the open seating to the deck at the rear of the ferry and watched the sun on the water.

It added a dimension to his misery. Venice with its myriad cupolas and campaniles, was getting its colour back under the blue awning of a clear sky. It was the scintillating city of Canaletto and Guardi, dispelling the fitful aqua-tints of Howard Roberts and John Henry Wiggins.

But in Joe Gaskell's fantasy, the water was already inching further and further up the walls.

"You've done well." Samov at his elbow. "I must thank you. What is the word from San Francisco?"

"The fire-storms seem to be abating. The lightning goes on till the ionosphere is clear of vapour but the regularity of the strokes is falling off."

"No harm done, then."

"Depends what you mean by no harm. A lot of dead, a lot of walking wounded. We may not see the whole picture of damage for months. Even years. There may be people who will live in fear of a summer tempest for the rest of their lives—or die before they should because of that fear."

"But this is true of our people—"

"No, Oskar. Not quite."

"What do you mean? Lightning is the same for me as it is for you."

"You're blustering, Oskar. Your people knew—where it was coming from, what it was, how long for—that was most important, knowing when it would end."

"You're crazy. The Italians—"

"Don't keep it up, Samov. I told you I would check and I did. My man in San Francisco was in too bad a way to tell me anything about Moscow weather, so I called the Intourist office—as an intending Russian visitor. Not a word about the lightning because the man knew that by the time I got there it would be over. If the condition was going to persist, he would have told me—you Russians are scrupulous in small ways."

Samov was trying to smile. "I was about to tell you anyway."

"After the job was done."

"But knowing what you knew, why did you go ahead with destroying the pumping stations?"

"Because the lightning was no deception and neither was its effect. Don't worry, Oskar—your little experiment has taught us a lot and we're going to show our gratitude someday when you're not expecting it."

"And that's how it ends."

"Not yet."

Joe Gaskell showed Samov the hilt of the Borgia stiletto he had chosen for his task. The blade had gone long since, left in some Renaissance rib-cage. He had no stomach for bloodshed and the hasp was all he needed.

Samov's reaction upwards and away from the expected thrust put him off-balance. Gaskell's heavy-handed attempt to hold him helped him over the rail and down into the blue torrent flecked with off-white wake.

The Russian could swim like a fish but how long he could last underwater here was debatable. Gaskell rated his chances at better than good but it didn't matter. Samov was effectively removed from circulation.

He tried to go over the rail after him, knowing that hands would restrain him.

"Signore, the propellors . . ." The *condottore* was hanging on to his arm. "We will wait to see if the gentleman surfaces. If not, I am afraid nature must take its course. The canal traffic is too imperative to allow a proper search. Was he your friend?"

"An old friend," said Gaskell. "Not a good friend, an old friend— *capito?*"

"Si, signore. It is none the less regrettable. In five days, maybe, he will come . . . we will be able to arrange a proper funeral. Would you, by any chance, know if he had a religious belief?"

"Catholic," lied Joe Gaskell with talent. "A devout Catholic."

The silence was too sudden for mourning.

Rain falls and the Piazza San Marco is awash. If anybody can build a pumping machine, it is an Italian. But he does not have the money—and does not want it again from the Russians.

Joe Gaskell, drinking Valpolicello as bitter and red as the eyes of the string quartet at his back beneath their crow umbrellas while the cold brown lagoon flows about ankles, can offer only currency with strings attached.

One set of strings is much the same as another, he thinks, taking a melancholy glance over his shoulder at the perishing violins.

With a little luck, he will drown before the rain stops.

MARS PASTORALE
or, I'M FERTILE, SAID FELIX

Introduction

Being a journalist helps. Gathering information becomes second nature. And the way to project yourself as an expert (I thought when "Mars Pastorale" was written) is to treat the data with a familiarity bordering on flippancy.

One bonus of conscientious research is the startling regularity with which the facts turn out to support the idea—as in this case.

The story holds up so well after seven years that perhaps the approach wasn't so wrong.

Today, I couldn't tell you a single thing about poppy seeds or meristems because subsequent events and applications have buried the knowledge. Being a journalist doesn't help.

Two sepals dropped this morning. That is the sign. Lying here in the fitful sunlight of the gallery, scraping against my fellows, I know that soon there will be progress.

One senses it now, a tilting which causes us to bulk and tumble, the sudden admissions of mini-shafted brilliance that glint on my hard brown husk of a coat, a desire like an itch in embryo transmitted along funicular corridors to be out . . . right out . . . and away.

I check through my composition again, just for the hell of it, just to rout impatience. Here I go, from the skin in.

My outer integument is represented by the outer epidermis composed of tangentially elongated cells containing colouring matter and the inner epidermis of cells columnar in shape, with layers of parenchyma cells between epidermal layers. How's that for an introduction?

My inner integument—or outer epidermis, if you'd a mind to—is palisade-like and sclerified. The other layers have been crushed in growth and are papery. Do you think you'll know me?

Further in, I have materials stored in the endosperm—starch, polysaccharides, mannans, and hemicellulose. They are slowly being digested by the developing embryo in a complex series of processes that bring about transfer of food materials from old sporophyte —poor old sporophyte—to new. But all that comes later. Not yet. Not yet.

There is an axis (of course): two cotyledons above it which, I'm informed, are named collectively the hypocotyl. Then the axis, and below that, an apical meristem. Sounds like fun.

That is where it's all happening. At the meristem. Occasionally primordia. Maybe I'll be lucky and turn out to be a budding something before we hit the outer atmosphere. Patience, friend. There's plenty of time, plenty to do.

Felix Jimpson is large and shaggy—somebody once said he had the appearance of a Welsh poet and he has tried desperately to remain unchanged ever since. But above all, he is a one-dimensional man. He *needs* someone inside him to draw breath.

JIMPSON: A fertile mind, that's what I've got. Ideas growing like wild flowers under the hedges of my brain.

His handsome blonde wife, Velvet, offers no reply. She has heard the words before, or if not the very syllables, some so similar that the difference is negligible. In any event, there is no need for any reply. Jimpson is licking his lips to savour the phrase.

JIMPSON: That was a good one. I must remember that one.

He pushes himself off the vibrastool and searches the skeletal shelf system until he turns up one of his official creation sheets, still unused. Then he casts around for the means to write.

JIMPSON (muttering): Wild flowers . . . hedges . . . brain . . .

Velvet has been working her way through the newssheet diagaword with never-dry poised and darting. Jimpson twitches it from her fingers even as she begins to write, still mumbling, still showing her his back when she looks up to comment. He scribbles his phrase, leaves the pen on a shelf, and takes the phrase back to the stool to digest it in cold print. Feeling her gaze upon him finally, he looks up.

JIMPSON: What's the matter?

VELVET: My pen.

JIMPSON: Shelf.

He goes back to the phrase, with tongue busy and eyes slightly lidded as an affectionate parent might regard a child.

VELVET: My pen.

But Felix Jimpson has packed his mind and gone to another place.

JIMPSON: We must get out into the country more often. Wonderful inspiration for me. I swear I must be one of Mother Nature's favoured sons. I always feel that much more . . . powerful . . . among the greenery, as though the Muse were finding it easier to work.

He smirks self-consciously, happy in the literary jargon he is so fond of employing whenever the Mars Settlement Writers' Circle meets to marvel. Velvet abandons the puzzle, leaning back in her chair and closing her eyes.

VELVET: The greenery was a long time ago. Mother Nature doesn't know about this place.

But nobody answers her.

VELVET (thinking): This is how the conversation turns at some time or another every day. Felix Jimpson, founder-chairman of Mars Settlement (No. 3) Writers' Circle and Penmen's Guild; hero and champion to the not-so-young hopefuls who rode the perihelion to Mars as it swung within 137 million miles of Earth to find an inspiration that will start them churning out best-sellers; Felix Jimpson, whose kindly light leads local literati along paths of illusion where Nobel and Pulitzer and the Book-of-the-Month Club choices are milestones passed by walking; and unsaleability and sheer lack of talent, roots one can avoid merely by a raising of the foot. But a kindly light that soon disappears back under its bushel when the circle has dispersed after its weekly mutual-admiration session or when a member, inspired by who knows what source, makes a contribution too good not to have come from Felix Jimpson.

JIMPSON (breaking in on her thoughts): . . . as though the wind just breathes her secrets in my ear for me to write them down . . .

Velvet giggles and falls silent, much to the annoyance of Felix, who feels distinctly ill-at-ease when she laughs and gives no explanation.

VELVET: But why must you always be so deadly pastoral?

Jimpson doesn't like the question. By its very form it shows that his wife has been thinking before she asked it and she must be already suspicious of the answer. Probably she expects a platitude. He fumbles mentally.

JIMPSON: In Nature, one can find all the images, all the similes, all the metaphors one needs to cover any human state.

VELVET: A platitude. Not all states are human. What then?

JIMPSON (petulantly): Let me finish.

He has to finish. He is committed to say what is in his mind because it is all that is in his mind.

JIMPSON: Look at the great poets of earth. Look how they took the country and its seasons as the inspirations for their most beautiful works.

VELVET: All right, we'll stay on that level. They were misty characters, all of them.

JIMPSON: What do you mean *misty?*

VELVET: Poets in elegiac mood. Lacking in substance. Feather-light when they ought to be heavy with truth and purpose. Like the little parachutes on top of puff dandelions—see, I can do it, too. One good blow and they're gone. Now take a man like Charles Baudelaire . . .

JIMPSON (interrupting volubly): Filthy. Obscene. And such terrible rubbish. Perverse love, unholy friendships. A rhyming rubbish dump.

VELVET: Anyway.

JIMPSON: Anyway what?

VELVET: Is your John Milton any more suitable for this place than my Charles Baudelaire? We need new . . .

JIMPSON: But of course. This place is exactly like earth. The trees, flowers, insects are so . . . constant. That's why I came. I wouldn't have come otherwise, no matter how bad the other place was. . . .

VELVET: And the people—what about the people?

JIMPSON: They're the same. They're . . . well, they came with us, didn't they?

VELVET: Not enough. Be profound about them. Don't liken them to pretty petals or statuesque landscapes. Besides . . .

The curious suspicion comes back to her. She has not mentioned it to Felix because it seems so infantile when she is trying to impress him with maturity and make him acknowledge reality. But this vegetation—wasn't it just a little too ready to adapt to their ecological suggestions?

JIMPSON (echoing): Besides?

VELVET: I get a funny feeling about the plant life here.

JIMPSON: But it's perfect. Identical in every detail. It was a little isolated at first, admittedly, a bit wild to ensure survival. But the soil section did a wonderful job gathering it about the centre just to make us feel more at home.

VELVET: I don't feel more at home.

Velvet parades her defencelessness in the hope of attracting some warmth from him to end their cold exchange. But he misses her intention.

JIMPSON: Give them a break. They'd have a job reproducing nineteenth-century Montmartre. To conclude on Baudelaire—who needs him?

VELVET: To reconvene on Baudelaire, a world too used to seeing filth for filth's sake and not probing for goodness in the midst of it. A world like the one we got out of but never really left.

JIMPSON: You're too pessimistic about the new affairs of new mankind. We didn't like earth, we got out of it. Everybody's too busy being an expert up here to have any vices.

Sometimes his glibness, his easy acceptance, his blind, blind eye leave Velvet in awe.

VELVET: And you're a poet with nothing to say. Even up here with everything new and crying out to be sonnetted and celebrated in iambic lines. At most, in honesty, you're an amateur juggler with words.

She does not try deliberately to hurt him. She loves him or she would not have come with him. And because she cares, it angers her to see him constantly, habitually headed in the wrong direction, wasting a talent that only needs a purpose.

VELVET (thinking): Felix Jimpson . . . (she needs him so much she yearns to silence him with a kiss) . . . the original big fish in a fresh, small pool and loving it.

JIMPSON (desperately): Rubbish. You say I'm a fake because I like the sunshine and stay away from the dark. All right, tomorrow we'll go out into this little bit of collected countryside and we'll see how good a job Mother Nature and the soil section can do on your emotions.

VELVET: We shall see no more than we shall see. And I still say Mother Nature doesn't know this place.

It is done. We are toiling up the breeze now, away from the mother vessel. In free fall, I reflect.

Though we had expected the launch, it was still a shock when it came. A sudden tilt of the gallery floor, a precipitous rush, and then nothing—nothing to hold on to, no companions to antagonise.

Aloneness. And an all-pervading sense of colour—predominantly green and blue and with a dry rain falling out of the blue that excites the skin and flows inward through welcoming pores.

But what is this colour? What is this rain? I drift, seeking guidance from the hurried programming sessions in the chequered gallery. It will be like waking, we were warned, with a power and a sensitivity that we did not have before. But never having lived before, how do I know what is new and what is hereditary; what ordeals must I face in this new paint-and-paper world where dreams take suck like bees and we suddenly have the power to rule?

I bear downward as the impetus fails beneath me but am buoyed up again almost immediately by some ground current. I drift and am no longer young. For the first time I experience—fear?

So Felix and Velvet drive out along the ferroway, under the blue cupola sky, to meet the green lady. They eat a bulky, old-fashioned lunch from treasured polythene wrappers among the pines.

FELIX: You wanted strength—what about these?

VELVET: They're strong, but they're not going anywhere particularly.

Felix sighs deeply.

They drink traditional tea from an imported thermos as they walk along a dirt-camouflaged strip through a corn field. Quasi-life hums and pulses around them. A lark springs skywards.

FELIX (excited): There! Look at him go. Doesn't that speed, that song, suggest something?

VELVET: A bird. A song. No more. The poet who relied on that died—or should have done—when commuting was invented. These days, everybody has eyes to see everything. Poets should have had corneal grafting on their minds.

Felix swears so softly that Velvet does not hear. Had she heard, she might have thought it the most mature comment he has made all day.

FELIX (thinking): She's beating me down. Finally and irrevocably and mercilessly. Mother Nature, you're doing me no favours.

As it is, Velvet hears him cough sharply and wonders if, to give the afternoon some final irony, Felix Jimpson, Nature's number-one son, is getting hay fever.

I am—somewhere. A million soiled curses on my own inadequate vocabulary. It was light and now it is dark. I was free and now I am enclosed. A great portal tumbled shut behind me with a roar like thunder. I detect moisture. Its flow, it seems, is to be transport. Can I dominate from here? Now I must be brave. Now I must supervise my growth, stage by stage, with knowledge and purpose. I cascade to my destiny.

Between their car and the corn field lay a meadow, a patchwork quilt of buttercups, corn marigolds, and charlock. The micro-climatic hedgerows sheltered woundwort, hawkweed, and cuckoo-pint, and provided a foothold for the tufted vetch. It was a masterpiece of landscaping.

"And I suppose this," said Velvet, "is your mind. Well, it smells beautifully. But do you need a breeze to disperse your thoughts?"

Felix did not answer. He stood beside her, wheezing badly. He was looking at her, but not in any way that she recognised. It was as though he was giving himself over to her entirely, defeated by her sense and made needy by his own present physical discomfort.

Flaming countryside, she raged stupidly. False, cunning, beautiful countryside that may have given me my husband, I love-hate you.

Felix meanwhile heard a rustle like a new dimension sprouting. But it could have been their shoes through the grass as Velvet led him with some mysterious, sadistic smile playing around her lips, back to their teleported station-wagon.

Felix rolled down the window as Velvet struggled to unbutton his collar.

"We'll drive," he said. "The rush of air will clear my head." I hope, he thought. Why am I so wet?

The car bucked once on the iron road as the front near-side wheel went over an unlawful obstruction. Felix and Velvet walked back to the spot together, shyly hand in hand.

The hedgehog was crushed flat against the tempered steel with a red smear where the weight of the car had burst its body.

Velvet wept a little and Felix felt slightly sick.

They walked back to the car for a hand-shovel.

"I'm sorry about that," said Felix, but it didn't sound like an apology. "That's not an apology. I feel sorrow for what I have done, because that hedgehog might have been a family man, or on the verge of it, or necessary for it."

He took five minutes to dispatch the remains and when he returned to the car he was considerably shorter of breath. But he hadn't changed his subject. Even as he worked he had been sorting through his thoughts. Now he believed he was on to something, and he wanted Velvet to hear.

"Why did we have to bring the defenceless?" he asked her. And before she had a chance to answer, he added, "And if we had to bring them, was it essential for them to stay defenceless? Couldn't somebody have told them the rules? Hell, we have their communication patterns in stock."

Felix wondered why he had so much to say when he could scarcely spare the breath for it. But still the words kept coming. "It makes my own life seem somewhat futile. A great big car with a great big fool of a driver. What could a hedgehog do? Nothing. If only he could have yelled or something. . . ."

He checked himself. It was beginning to sound as though whatever had loosened his tongue had done a similar job on his brain. "I mean . . ."

Velvet silenced him with a finger on his lips. Even so, she noticed how he turned his head away quickly, either out of anger at being silenced or in some desperation to avoid any obstruction of his breathing process.

"And there you have it," she said, instead. "What else is a poet or any other writer except a hedgehog trying to find a voice to yell at oncoming death? With his yell he could have the power to make death stop, go back, or swerve on to the other side of the road."

She was aware that the words sounded pretentious and stilted, but she had to make best use of the moment, of the images available. Felix, his breath coming in tatters, heard the words from a great distance and had not the strength to be critical.

". . . my whole point, darling. Nature was fine for you, sure. But there's an awful lot of cannibalism below petal-level."

She kissed him lightly on the cheek and again he turned hastily away as though he feared suffocation.

"Tomorrow," she said, "you see the medic."

My downwards journey has ended. If I move at all, it is only in a leisurely, concentric course.

No light falls here, but as I investigate in my sensory, absorbent way, I find that it doesn't matter. Somehow, there is a trace element of nitrogen and—thankfully—more than enough magnesium. No light, so I will not be using much iron. Comforting to find that it is here, nevertheless, to act as a catalyst.

And sulphur. That means chlorophyll; and that means protoplasm. I can live here. I can live here. I drop my roots and throw out an arm.

Not a moment too soon. Already I am beginning to change symmetry. My beautiful spherical body, of which I have been so proud, is beginning to flatten at the head. Perhaps I should mourn the change, but it is all progress towards the final perfection, the fruition which is promised to us. Soon will come the cotyledons, then more cell division. Tissue systems are go. . . .

Felix examined the zig-zag trail of punctures down his arm. Even as he watched, two of them grew red, swelled, itched. He moved to scratch them instinctively. Vernon, the medic, stopped his hand.

He consulted a chart. "Pollen," he said. "Pollen and wheat germ. You're allergic to them. You have no anti-bodies to fight them. You might have had them, but they're gone now."

"And that means?" Felix already suspected the answer. He put the question only because he wanted to hear the fact from somebody else.

"Stay away from flowers," said Vernon. "Stay away from trees, grass, wheat fields, countryside. Stay among steel and concrete and dust-free urbanity."

"But . . ." There were no buts. What good was a but?

"Isn't there anything I could use? An inhaler? Couldn't I get into the country somehow?"

"Felix, I know the country's value for you. You're one of the few Aesthetes we have here. . . ."

Aesthete to asthmatic, thought Felix, in one simple unsuspecting damn lesson.

". . . Of course I could give you an inhaler—in fact, I will before you leave—but you have to remember that if you use it and then go back to the greenery, pretty soon you'll develop an immunity. And there's nothing else I can give you. Ruled useless, sent back to earth to spend the rest of your life wheezing. You can't afford that. . . ."

"We had trouble enough getting here," agreed Felix. "Food scarce as it is, breathing space a very real factor. I reckon we Aesthetes are here on borrowed time, anyhow. As soon as the testers chart our reaction to the new environment we'll be through here . . . back to earth, dumped on Deimos or somewhere." But my opinions have ceased to matter to me, he told himself. Why do I play on like a music-box after a room has emptied?

"Exactly. All the more reason for playing it very safe, Felix. Think about Velvet. Think about you."

Vernon fetched a box from his dispensary and pressed it into Felix's hand as he stood up.

"I don't give you this with any thought of comfort," he said, "but a lot of your friends have been in. What did you get up to?"

He began to laugh, but had to give up because he started coughing.

"I think they must have left something behind," he said eventually.

Felix was tempted to play for sympathy when Velvet met him out of the X-ray, but he concluded that any underlining of his condition was superfluous.

Instead, he tried a dedicated nonchalance, countering her first questions with comforting, meaningless clichés—"Don't worry, I'll live" . . . "Just a little bit of dust got down there. It'll pass . . . it'll pass. . . ."

But he was worried. His words conveyed less than the over-long pauses which separated them. Wisely, Velvet let him proceed towards revelation at his own speed. She knew he had something unpleasant to tell her and the longer he could stave it off, the better for himself. She would not have to wait long.

They let themselves into the chalet on the edge of the settlement and Velvet brewed tea while Felix read the instructions on the inhaler Vernon had given him and tried to make sense of the contents. He uncapped the mouth-piece, up-ended the cylinder, and pumped a little down his throat, sucking in air deeply.

For a while the aerosol relieved him but too soon the congestion was back. He used the inhaler again and his breathing became less laboured—until the congestion came back and he had to reach for the inhaler a third time. This time he set it down, remembering Vernon's warning that he must not over-use it.

"It's all finished," he said with a careful lack of emotion when Velvet sat down to pour the tea.

"As bad as that?" Velvet tried to sound as though she did not believe it.

"Medic warned me against the country."

Velvet's hand began to shake and she struggled silently to control it. "Against the country?" The nagging apprehension was back. "What's wrong with the country?"

"Nothing. It's me. Mother Nature's favoured son. I've developed an allergy to pollen and wheat germ. But where the hell did I develop an allergy? The medic said if I ever had anti-bodies, they're all gone now. . . ."

"Hence the allergy, then."

"But you don't run out of them, Velvet. The body is making new ones all the time. At least, it should be. . . ."

It was at this point that a crazy notion took Felix, a terrible, terrible suspicion that laid him weak and wordless back in his chair, his hands scrabbling round for the inhaler.

He steadied himself. At all costs, he mustn't pass it on to Velvet. "So there goes the fertile mind," he said. "There goes Felix Jimpson, Mother Nature's green-eyed boy."

"It isn't that bad. I knew it wasn't." Now Velvet was in the game, bolstering his confidence while she began surreptitiously to eat her heart out.

"Good grief, what do you mean, 'It's not that bad.' Only fatal." Felix embraced anger readily. He felt like screaming. At least anger gave him a chance to shout.

Velvet sat silent and let him go on until the congestion laid him low again. Then she said, deliberately callous, "What kind of writer are you, anyway? All right, the country's out of bounds. What is left?"

Felix had no ready answer.

"The sea," she said for him. "If it worked for Masefield and Tennyson, it'll work for you."

"Why?" The genesis of a memory caused Felix to pause, but there was no more. He would have to delve. "I was never inspired by the sea. What could the sea do for me?"

"You never gave it much of a chance. You were always too busy counting the minutes before you could decently say, 'Let's go the woodland way home.' We've never seen the sea up here. At least let's give it a chance."

Felix was leaning back in his chair with his mind packed away. Just like the old days, thought Velvet. The old days like yesterday. She watched Felix's hand move unbidden towards his spray.

I must be growing quite tall now, but the process has not been without complication. The acids—amino, nucleic, acetic, citric—have been present in heavy quantities and I have had to utilise the available alkali to balance them.

There has been a great deal of movement, too, though the fact that the host is not static does not seriously deter me.

I detect a new presence—calcium sulphate and a mess of other chemicals—amino-ethanol, hydroxide. This ethanol is a new one on me, but oxides and any nitrogen surplus ceased to present a hazard to my assimilation pattern many generations ago. I store the calcium and sulphate for subsequent use.

Meanwhile, there has been accelerated vacuolation of embryonic parts, as expected, and the less vacuolated tissues are forming the future primary vascular system. The meristems at either end of my axis are busy. Cell division continues apace.

The sea-line had been faithfully portrayed, even down to the salt-white driftwood that lay in a ragged barricade along the high-water mark.

The sea moved restlessly, small waves creaming momentarily on the sand and receding as though sucked through distant teeth.

Felix tried to look out towards a horizon but there was the sight-screen at cupola extreme, misty and noncommittal.

Sea-birds cried plaintively but when he looked for them he

couldn't see them and he suspected that they and their songs were long separated.

He tasted salt on his lips. Again the chord of memory shivered momentarily but the single reverberation was gone before he could grasp and hold. But if there was authenticity nowhere else along this rolled-out seascape, how was there salt? Some trick of the place-makers?

But . . . but . . . but.

"It isn't the same." Felix sat down heavily on a rock with his shoulders hunched and his chest pumping. "It isn't the same."

Velvet perched beside him and took his hand.

"You can make it the same," she said patiently. "The countryside is false, too. It's no different. You *wanted* the trees and flowers to be as you remember them, so you accepted them happily at face value. But it wasn't God or Mother Nature who put them there. You said yourself it was the soil section. And some queer culture before that."

Felix grunted. Any more expressive answer would have cost him valuable breath and he had to be content to listen.

"It was a matter of association. Recognition, inevitable comparison. But those are redundant motivations for real poets because they are second-hand.

"You have to look for something new here—something essentially Martian. You could even look within yourself. . . ."

Felix coughed to cover the shock. Surely she didn't know what he felt. How could she? Why should she?

"How do you react to the alien and strange?" she was asking. "What is it like having to call a lump of dusty rock home?"

Felix tapped her hand to attract her attention. His eyes were wide and his forehead running with sweat. He had been through his pockets hastily, and found nothing. She gave him the second spray she always carried in case he forgot his own.

He sucked at it hungrily and his breathing became fractionally less laboured.

"There's something I have to say," he started, haltingly. "It can't . . . wait. . . . I . . . I . . . haven't got the breath to be . . . gentle or subtle . . . about it."

Beads of moisture navigated the topography of his face and lay trapped in the skin water-sheds under his eyes. They could have been tears.

Velvet stroked his hand and waited.

"Us," he said. "Sleeping together. In same room. You . . ."

He stopped and turned his head away. Now there was no doubt that he was weeping. He tried again.

"You take . . ."

"Too much air," Velvet cut short his agony. "I'll move into the spare. I've been thinking about it, anyhow. Listening to the way you struggle, even when you manage to get to sleep."

He nodded gratefully. "It would . . . help."

She stood up quickly. "Do you feel like seeing any more?"

Felix shook his head. "Far enough," he said.

All the way back along the beach, he watched the water with an unconscious fascination.

At least it is wet, he thought. As if that fact alone should give him some kind of comfort.

He had bent for hours over the drinking fountain, trying to wash out the thing that seemed to choke his body, trying to flush out the dust or whatever it was.

He had constricted the jet until the water spurted with such force that it went straight to the back of his throat, making him gag and splutter.

He had tried to fill himself up, literally, with water, but he was always forced to the toilet before the experiment could be completed and he had to start the whole thing again. And again and again.

But the water—any water—still held its attraction as subconscious counterpoint to the terrible dryness that crept up on him.

"I'll make you a list," said Velvet, breaking in on his thoughts.

"What?" He abhorred the condition that prevented him from saying in his once-flamboyant manner, "I'm sorry, my flower, I didn't hear," or, "Your pardon, my love."

"I'll work out a list of subjects for you. I'll do it tonight when I've moved out . . . moved *in* to the spare. It'll give me something to occupy me."

Not that I'm short of occupations, she thought. Just company. Oh God, how I yearn to hear the sound of Felix Jimpson in the trees. . . .

I sensed sunlight. There is no doubt. My chloroplasts reacted positively. It is spasmodic, but it is sufficient to give me a definite purpose and outline for me a direction—a very necessary guide along these labyrinthine, yielding corridors where such a near-presence is easily missed among more chemical milestones.

The florical meristem is complete, and the latex within me throbs and courses with excitement.

The tales my children (beloved angiosperms) can tell at the next dispersal. My children. Such pride in their father-mother. Their potential thoughts rustle in my head as I nod in parental well-being. Their potential thoughts of expansion, of simulation, of eventual domination.

Felix Jimpson, chilled but unmoving at the window, could feel recollection—what damned recollection?—going away from him in a tidal drag.

No moon anymore but I still think of tides. No true seashores, yet my mind still goes paddling. Such useless words.

Get realistic, he ordered himself.

I will, I will, he pledged.

Velvet had gone away into her bedroom to work on the list. He wanted to call her in, to ask how it was going or at least to have her company. But she breathed and there was not enough of the precious commodity here for both of them.

Finally, sheer exhaustion drove him back to his bed, but he could not turn on one side or the other to sleep. He fought to organise his pillows so that they propped him in a sitting position and then slumped with the job half-done and a foul perspiration bathing his body.

Velvet, draped elegantly across her lonely double bed, wrote and then listened to the silence and wrote again.

"I am a pioneer," she wrote. "Elaborate!"

"A virgin land," she wrote. "In its pure natural state. A good old standby. On fishing in deserted canali."

She pushed herself up from the bed, moved to the window, and gazed out at the angular sky. Phobos and Deimos, the twin satellites of Mars, were away at their orbital extremes. There was only the settlement lemon-light, faithfully reproducing the liquid splashes of the distant moon but lacking its mystery.

She had carried the list with her. "No moon," she wrote. "Full empty sky. Mourn lunar death."

Gazing up on the new immensity of it all, she could feel her own loneliness tapering to a fine point of pain. Just when they ought to be sharing a revelation.

She read through the list, adding to it, making corrections. It remained inadequate. There was so much to be said, but they had to work it out together.

But perhaps this would help. She had read or heard somewhere that certain allergies had nervous bases. It was strange that Felix should now be physically at odds with himself; much more likely, frustration could be the cause, all tied up with the strain of the new life and the adjustment.

Perhaps, if Felix could be given a purpose . . . and if not, the hell with hell. They would go back to earth.

Even though it meant that they would land in autumn and never live to see winter, they would be together for the fall. Of leaves, of themselves. Death with each other was eminently preferable to this terrible, close apartheid.

Come out. I know you're in there.

Felix stood open-mouthed before the wash-stand mirror, pinning down his tongue with a finger while he peered into the reflected recesses of his throat for some sign of an obstruction.

He fancied something stirred beyond his tonsils, down towards the pharynx. He poked at it with his fingers, but the action caused him to retch dryly and then the battle for breath began again.

I'll get you, you little leafy. . . .

He flung himself back to the window and sucked again at the night breeze, blowing off the distant shore, rising off the imported sea.

The imported sea . . .

Felix tipped himself over the window-sill and landed eight feet below, on his knees, among the shrubbery.

He was thankful for his slippers as he moved out along the seaward track. The temperature, steadied at comfort level for the business of sleeping, did not bother him although his pajama jacket hung unbuttoned.

At first he hurried but the effort left his heart pumping and he slowed his pace for fear of collapsing before he could reach the shore.

But long before he felt sand beneath his feet, sweat was clouding his eyes and soaking through his pajama legs.

Up ahead, he could hear the vague mutter of the waves and he moved directly towards the sound. He picked up speed unconsciously and when he finally felt the water soaking through his slippers, he went down on his knees again, ploughing deep furrows in the wet sand.

He moistened his hands and cooled his running face with handfuls of sea. Then he began cupping the water in his palms and pouring it methodically down his throat.

His last recorded thought was of murder.

Now. It is now. I thrust myself over the last few fractions unfolding my scarlet banners. I have won. Daylight now and new life. Much new life. From the earth to me. From me to the world. I am the Creator out of the Created, the mother born of the child. I am triumphant.

A rain falls out of the sky to greet me and I turn up my face. A light rain that becomes heavy; a gentle rain that begins to irritate. An irritation that starts to *burn*.

MOTHER MOTHER MOTHER MOTHER A SALINE RAIN THAT HURTS HURTS HURTS . . .

MOTHER I

die. . . .

Velvet paused outside Felix's door with the list in her hand, listening for some sound of him. But there was no rattle of battle for air.

"Felix," she called. "How are you feeling?"

Silence.

She opened the door and saw at a glance that his bed was empty and the room deserted. Then she fled, calling, from the house.

The search party found Felix lying face down at the water's edge.

Velvet turned him over on his back, praying to find his face suddenly alive and his lips framing an I-fooled-you smile.

But his features were ashen beneath the crusting of salt and his eyes stared from his head. She backed away, whimpering.

The men took over. They lifted the body onto the collapsible litter they had brought and bore it back over their scattered, hurrying footprints.

Velvet fell in behind the cortège.

A dead poppy lay like a splash of hedgehog blood on the sand. Shortly, the breezes found the wilted flower and picked at it, sifting the tough little seeds and carrying them off along the shore.

THE GLOOM PATTERN

Introduction

If you have been writing for years, grab a good giggle at my naïveté. If you merely read, pass quickly to the heart of the matter. If you are still my kind of novice, perhaps the shared experience will do you some good.

This is not a hair-raiser about clashes with publishers or cash that never came or sole misrepresentation, it is just a word or two about raw materials.

The science here is bunkum; the people fare rather better. At the time, I was more closely acquainted with the latter. And the lesson to be learned is: always work with what you know.

Technique is only a gradual acquisition. The best quality you have to bring to the literature right from the outset is your *self*. Sculpt it, be frank with it, be critical, but preserve it.

While you find your *modus operandi,* be careful not to become a *corpus sine pectore*—a little Latin can get you classed as an intellectual, you know, and they are *much* better paid.

"The Gloom Pattern" is an early, early story. In one sense, it should have been rewritten. In another, it is more valuable as it stands. So take it.

They slept on the run, ate between brainstorms, moved everywhere as though autumn was pushing.

Charlie and Nicholas were both at the eavesdropper age and drawn like opposite poles to an idiosyncrasy or a hint of something that might be a challenge to fourteen-year-old's stock of credulity.

They looked to and listened at Gregory Birtle but there was nothing to copy and nothing to ridicule. Just Birtle, shifting his feet, inhaling his air, going his way with an expression of—detachment.

At night, when he emerged from his furnished mausoleum on the edge of town, they took to following him, hungry for a glimpse of some humanity lighting his eye or straightening his back.

Charlie kept always a little ahead, Nicholas always lagged a little. They shot like bunnies from cover to cover along the byways. They blew like conspiratorial paper wrappings along the neon thoroughfares, the breeze dropping miraculously when Gregory Birtle turned or stopped or looked as though he might have guessed.

This night, they tumbled themselves into a doorway as Gregory Birtle paused to examine the still photographs outside the Roxy Manual Bioscope.

"If he goes in, he's got to laugh," said Charlie. "How's your pocket money?"

"Still there," said Nicholas. Saturday night. He was trying to make it last—at least until Sunday.

"Two tickets?" queried Charlie. "You'll have it back. In the interests of science. Experiments cost money. Feel noble about it."

Nicholas wavered before his friend's flood of rhetoric.

"What do we want him to do?" he asked, not for the first time.

"I keep telling you . . ." Charlie was exasperated in his enthusiasm and then tolerant, remembering the pocket money. "We want to see his face move. We want to hear him be amused."

Charlie could feel a grandiose pronouncement coming. He squeezed back against the wall to allow it room. "I crave that man's happiness more than I crave my own," he said. "Phew!"

"He's gone," put in Nicholas.

Charlie was up and out of the doorway, running desperately for the cinema.

"If he laughs and we're not there . . ." he shouted, as no paper bag should shout.

Nicholas loped a little way behind, fumbling for coins among the dust-jammed, rust-jammed pen-knives and the year's bus tickets.

"Our uncle," Charlie panted at the woman in the glass box. "Just went in. Which way?"

"Two halves," added Nicholas, just to show Charlie he understood the urgency.

The slotted top of the woman's desk spat forth two tickets. The woman pointed, tore the tickets.

The boys scaled the stairs.

"She's another," said Nicholas, still trying to impress.

"Nah." Charlie dismissed the observation. "She's just working. No, gloom people don't sell tickets for entertainments. That would be more than they could bear."

"But Mr. Birtle came in here . . ."

"Tactics. Subtlety."

Nicholas concentrated on the stairs. Charlie charged the door and passed through into the darkness and the Mel Blanc voices.

Nicholas, spurting to catch the swing of the door, proffered the ticket-stubs to an invisible usherette and waited for the power of sight.

One man sat alone in the middle of a row in the middle of a block, his face occasionally illumined in the fitful sunshine from the animated screen.

A small figure moved in the row behind him. A seat bounced. A small figure sat down.

Another figure. A second seat bouncing.

"Quiet," said Charlie. "Quiet."

"What's up, Doc?" said Nicholas, Bugs Bunny fashion.

Charlie screwed up his face.

"What's up, Doc?" said Bugs Bunny on the screen.

Nicholas laughed but Charlie was watching the face in the row in front.

"Not a flicker," he said, unbelieving.

"Quiet," said Nicholas. "Quiet."

"Not a flicker," said Charlie at intervals throughout the evening.

They rustled after Gregory Birtle all the way to his angular house on the edge of town and retreated only when an inspection of the heavy drapes revealed no chink.

The town-hall clock chimed as they sped home.

One . . . two . . . three. They paused to listen.

Four . . . five . . . six. A sudden compulsion sent them racing for home as though home on the chime was nowhere near as late as home ten seconds later.

Seven . . . eight . . . nine. They counted in flight, Nicholas getting mixed up with his paces, reaching thirty without realising.

Ten. No, never ten.

"Ten?" asked Charlie.

"Never," comforted Nicholas.

Boy choreography took them up their paths in matching strides, made them reach through letter-boxes for keys, seize, turn in unison.

"See you," called Charlie.

"Hear you," called Nicholas, who knew Charlie better than that.

What if Gregory Birtle never smiles, wondered Nicholas, filing away the events of the day to make room for dreams. What does it mean except he's miserable? And why waste finance and experiments on a miserable man?

Down to five-p on a Saturday night, in the cause of science. Crazy. More than that, stupid.

The battle-scarred radio-telephone at his bedside buzzed like a glassed-in mosquito.

Charlie.

"They sent me to bed, too," he said. "Vegetable parents. Listen, I had a thought."

Nicholas, receiver in hand, sat up in bed and peered across the width of two gardens to Charlie's window. No skin-flash, no Charlie looking the other way.

"Get up," he said. "Look out the window."

"Why?" asked Charlie. "Why, when we've got the RT?"

"I prefer to see you."

"Nuts. Look, I've got a lot of talking to do. I'm lying down to be comfortable."

"A lot of talking?"

"Yes. I KNOW WHY GREGORY BIRTLE NEVER SMILES," Charlie said in capital letters.

Nicholas settled the pillows behind him. "All right, why?"

Across town, a house with quaint turrets went blind in one eye, then another, then another, then altogether.

Niktar, Superemedial Agent to the Sad Sometimers. Joy made

Animate, Prince of the Inner Smile, propped his great laughing belly in a more comfortable position and surveyed his minions.

"Chuckle some more," he ordered.

They shook to his request.

"More."

They bellowed. They howled.

"More."

They rolled about the floors of the Tinkling Palace until the festoon ceilings rippled and sighed in the draught of their laughter.

Niktar flung out a hand. Silence fell as though he had thrown it.

"Remember," he said. "This is how we are now. We are a good place to be. We are the happy land, far, far away."

The happy land spun peacefully in its sun-coloured universe, lazy and lovely among its hazy blue planets.

"We are sweetness and light," said Niktar. "You hear? You hear? It is an order."

His creatures beamed obediently.

"And now you are to witness the final briefing of our secret weapon."

The strangelings cackled.

"No laughter," snapped Niktar. "Definitely no laughter."

The cackling subsided.

"Our secret weapon, our aid to the import drive . . ."

The festoons fluttered in felicitous currents.

"Enough!" screamed Niktar.

"But, Master," pleaded a grotesque, "you are so humourous. How can we contain ourselves?"

"You must try," said Niktar.

He amended the statement.

"You must do more than try. You must succeed. Otherwise . . ."

He let the sentence hang. The gathering was silent.

"Now . . ."

The girl came forward and he watched her spectacular progress, marvelling at the work that had gone into her, the carefully pendulumed swing of her hips, the precise detail of her figure, the mould of the features. Perfect.

"Master?" Her voice was all marshmallow and moonlight, the lips framing it full and red as bursting poppies. He let her see that he was pleased with her.

Behind the curled lashes, the china-blue eyes, the isotope mind felt the warmth and reacted accordingly, pumping blood into the cheeks, manufacturing a blush.

"Perfect." He spoke out loud this time and then forced himself to become business-like.

"You have been fed your instructions?"

"They are fully digested," said the girl. "I am to—"

"Wait." Niktar stopped her with a gesture. "I want you to turn to face my people. I want you to show them all how well we are prepared."

The girl turned and directed her gaze to the frondescent roof above the bobbing heads. She felt no fraternity with any of the varied life-forms who inhabited the mellow planet, united in the common bond of happy servitude.

She chanted:

"I am to take up residence at the Bay of Emotions until our glorious technicians have located a sadness track. Then I am to descend the track, which will be immediately negatived and reversed. My purpose will be to cultivate to ecstasy level the subject who put out that track. Meanwhile, the technicians will maintain the location and wait for the subject to attain sufficient ecstasy to reopen the track and allow progress in the opposite direction. Then, I am to bring the subject to you."

"For what purpose?" prompted Niktar.

The girl paused. "For no bad purpose," she said.

"For what good purpose?"

"To see whether this unfortunate person may be educated to our level of happiness in an environment where joy is the order and the law."

"Precisely."

Niktar felt for his throne. He could stand no longer, his aspirations outweighed by his physique.

"You are indeed a credit to our body-builders," he said with limp gallantry.

The isotope recorded, the blood pumped, the cheeks reddened.

"Thank you," said the girl. She began to walk away from the throne.

"Remember," called Niktar.

She turned back, the perfect brow furrowed. What else was there?

"You must keep him happy. Otherwise the track will fall apart and we cannot know what may happen to you."

Keep the subject happy. Could anything be as simple as that? Niktar managed it by force of arms but she had no such power.

Sometimes she pondered whether the master's proud creative process might not be without its shortcomings. What was her creation, after all, but a mixture of seeds, a chemical preparation? He called it new. She knew he had copied it from his observations at the Bay of Emotions, moving from track to track, building up a peeping-Tom knowledge of elsewhere life by its static electricity, its chameleon properties.

Quitting the throne-room, she reflected on existence in the happy land and was unhappy at the constancy, the monotony of fun.

It was a traitor feeling. She concentrated hard on the Bay of Emotions. And she was there.

"Are you prepared?" asked the senior trackman.

"I believe so," she said. "My mood is suitably flexible."

"The track has been fixed in place," said the man. "You merely have to become downcast."

He laughed at that. She found it made misery that much more accessible.

She entered the track and let herself fall heels over head, immodestly. Who could see, anyway? Revelling, but not too much, in the freedom of movement, spinning, twisting, assuming stop-still positions as she moved, almost laughing with the abandonment of it. Then, when she felt herself slowing because her buoyancy hampered progress, making herself sad again, falling stiff and uninteresting . . .

"It's bound to happen," said Niktar, watching the object that was the girl tacking across the radial screen. "Let's face it, falling without getting hurt is fun."

Falling at attention, falling with hands flat against sides, dull, dull falling . . .

Contact. Satina, undishevelled, shivered as grass tickled her unaccustomed legs and moved out of the woods towards a house with quaint turrets on the edge of a town.

"Charlie . . . Charlie," said Nicholas into the radio-telephone. "That's incredible. When did you dream up that fairy-story?"

Charlie fumed at the other end of the twenty-yard connection. "It's no fairy-story. It's a *fact!*"

"Come along, Charles. A little sobriety . . ."

"I'm not kidding you, Nick. I didn't ask for it. I wasn't even think-ing about it. Suddenly it was just there. You know theories—you know the way they sneak up on you tasting of toothpaste and toilet soap, grammar books and good-night drinks . . ."

"Sure, sure."

"You know they come in all sorts of unlikely places. Hang it, Nick, didn't you ever have a theory about anything?"

"Of course I—"

"Well, don't step on it."

Nicholas permitted himself a superior smile and was immediately ashamed because his friend could not see, could not argue.

"I'm sorry," he said, and meant it. "Is there more?"

"Is there more? Nick, you'd better give your pillows a punch."

The house with quaint turrets did nothing. Absolutely nothing. What can a house do?

Satina had selected simplicity for her approach to her subject.

His name, she had been told, was Gregory Birtle. He was, to acknowledge earth statistics, thirty-nine years old, of serious visage, and unmarried.

His invalid mother had died a year earlier, leaving him too old to learn how to chase girls and too shy, anyhow, to try. He was tied to the house because he had gathered his scant ration of contentment in its dark, atmospheric rooms and in scenes of joy observed from the arrow-slit windows.

He was weighed down with a permanent sorrow, a bodily con-coction of malheurusement.

His track was constant and unwaning. It had been simple for the sensors of the happy land to locate his aura and to knit in the dimensions necessary for a composite picture.

Gregory Birtle, unpractised in mood camouflage and intrigue, was a wide-open, straightforward, right-down-the-middle character who shouted the truth about himself every time he showed the world his face.

It was no miracle that Niktar's trackers had managed such a rapid and easy fix. In the second any person took to pass Birtle on the street, that person knew it was suddenly October and as suddenly July again.

Birtle attracted Charlie and Nicholas like a scatter of russet leaves, to be built into a mountain shape and flattened by falling boy-bodies tougher than diamond.

Most of this, Satina sensed as she stepped onto the cold sidewalk and winced. Cold elements beneath her feet were unfamiliar. Not frightening but uncomfortable.

Satina's own personality was hyper-styled to catch moods and match them. She was an early empathist, very much an unknown quantity except to herself. And in the happy land, where nothing was ever too meticulous because ingenuity meant a furrowed brow, she had soon learned to say no more about herself than her makers and her masters already knew.

She left stone, mounted boards. They were warmer beneath her feet, better retaining the heat of the sun.

She approached the flaking iron gate which gave onto the path leading up to the Birtle door.

Then something sharp thrust itself into the ball of her foot. She screamed with the shock of it.

Perched on her right leg, leaning against the gate, she examined the base of her left foot and found a splinter protruding.

Discomfort aside, it was something of a phenomenon. Wood, she knew from her study of basic earth elements. But wood that came up out of the ground—was it some kind of weapon?

Seeing it there, knowing it should not be there, watching the area turn pink and then red as the blood navigated the broken skin, she felt sick. It—well, it did something she had not been taught to expect, caused an unpleasant sensation in her foot—she could only describe it in such general terms.

When, with her stomach churning, she forced her attention away from her foot, she saw that Gregory Birtle was advancing cautiously, alightly stooping, down the path.

"Did you scream?" he asked, though nobody else moved on the tea-time street.

"I—cried out," she said.

He paused at the gate without opening it.

"A piece of wood in my foot . . ."

Still he paused, indecisive. Then his eyes were attracted, by virtue of the raised skirt hem, to the foot she cradled. He unlatched the gate, passed through it, and took the foot gently in his hand.

"A splinter," he said. "Nasty. Does it hurt a great deal?"

Hurt—was that the word?

"Yes." She played safe, shuffling the words. "It hurts a great deal."

"I have some bandages and iodine in the house," he said. "I'll . . ."

Again he faltered. "No. You'd better come in. I mean . . . I'd like you to . . . I mean . . . Please come in."

He held back the gate and waited for her to pass.

Balancing on one leg, Satina tried to hop, using the wrought iron for support.

But up the path, there was no support. She felt light-headed and close to nausea. She stumbled and had to put down the injured foot to keep from falling. She cried out with the . . . the hurt of it.

"I'm sorry," he said. "I'm not very gallant. But . . ."

He scooped her up in an impulsive, clumsy movement and carried her none too steadily up the path.

He was aware of her closeness, aware that she seemed to mould into his arms and that, as a woman, she was heavier than he thought women to be, trained on the empty, verbose husk that had been his mother.

Borne waist-high, Satina crossed the threshold and was instantly conscious of the drop in temperature. First contact with the dark interior of the house struck her blind.

She blinked the carefully curled lashes but irises new to the process were slow expanding.

The man was meandering along passages. She could hear his slippers slapping on bare stone and once a beaded curtain brushed her arm and face.

He set her down finally on a heavily brocaded settee and placed a pillow for her back.

She met dust for the first time and it tickled her throat. She coughed.

The chestnut staining of the ancient furniture, the intense wall-covering, the absence of direct sunlight, all combined in an almost physical impact. She felt she had been dropped into a shrouded jar and a cover screwed on. She must have moved involuntarily against the feeling.

Gregory Birtle said: "Probably it's not what you're used to."

Smothered as she had been, she had forgotten his presence.

"Forgive me." She smiled to cover awkwardness. "No, it . . . is not what I am used to."

"I can't seem to make it bright," he said. And then, in mitigation, "Something to do with the architecture. A century ago, they thought gloom was a necessary part of respectability. Sunshine was a red light."

She could not follow the conversation. He was talking of a time she did not know. Niktar, and she through Niktar, had heard references to Victoriana. But the word was widely used and elusive in meaning.

She did not want him to get too deep into the subject or she would be expected to answer in context. Besides, her foot throbbed.

"The house seems . . ."—she searched for a word—"lived-in."

Hollow laughter as he plundered the drawers for bandages.

"It's been that all right," he said. "The iodine is upstairs. Will you be all right while I fetch it?"

"Yes."

He left her. She could hear him pattering back along the passage, his hurried ascent of the stairs.

Now that he had gone, the room seemed to close in unashamedly, snatching at her breath, betraying murderous intentions. Or it could have been fever.

She cried out again.

An avalanche down the stairs. Gregory Birtle clutching a bottle. "What happened?"

She was very pale. Strands of auburn hair clung to her brow. "Not thinking, I put my foot down."

He wondered if she could genuinely have been so careless. A young woman who came walking barefoot out of the woods—he had watched her progress from one of the slit windows before her demise. He had heard of the sensual effect of grass among toes. He had read about it in illicit excursions to his mother's H. E. Bates collection. But even such woodland nymphs as those had to have shoes somewhere. Or sandals—almost always sandals, carried over the shoulders. Dangling from fingers by straps. A persistent image.

Perhaps she had dropped her shoes. He would go to the gate and look when he had tended her foot.

"It wasn't the room, was it? It is a bit dreary but there is nothing to fear."

How do you know what I fear? she wondered.

She noticed the instrument in his hand with sudden alarm. He caught her concern.

"It's all right," he said. "This won't take a second."

"What does that—do?" She forgot caution.

He paused in the midst of his activity and searched her face. He opened his palm to show her the complete utensil.

"Tweezers," he said. "You know—*tweezers?*"

"Yes, of course. Silly of me."

But it was another little point that raised a question. First the shoes, then the scream, then the unfamiliarity with tweezers.

"You're not from around here," he ventured, dabbing at the wound with clean linen.

"No."

"From away?"

"Far, far away," she said.

"A happy land?"

She wondered how he knew.

"There is a happy land, far, far away," he sang. "Like the song we learned in school. Remember?"

She looked blank.

"Well, maybe you didn't," he said. Point four.

"I was wondering about your shoes. Now this may hurt a little."

He caught the splinter in the tweezers and pulled. Her stomach somersaulted. Her face felt clammy. She moaned.

"There we are," he said, and dropped the piece of wood into the bowl of warm water. "You look a little grey. I'll fix you a drink before I put the iodine on. You should feel better then."

He crossed the room to an ornate sideboard, opened a bevelled cupboard, took out a bottle, and poured tawny liquid into a glass.

The brandy lighted the way to her stomach and then some. Tiny needles pricked her cheeks. He saw the colour returning, the grey giving way to peach. "Feel better?"

She managed a wan smile. "I'm sorry."

It was a recurring theme, right back to those first words over the gate.

Why are you sorry? he thought. Why am I sorry? Why do people spend so much time saying sorry and so little time doing things they ought to be sorry for?

He saw she was watching him. "I'm sorry, too."

"It is really quite simple," she said.

"What is?"

"Humans have this inherent uncertainty. Whatever they do, they wonder about alternatives. So they are always ready to be apologetic, always half-suspecting that they have done the wrong thing."

Had his thoughts been out loud? Surely not. And why "humans"? His word had been "people."

"You seem quite the philosopher," he said. "But—detached."

Satina had never once considered deceit. To succeed in her mission, she had to make the subject want to go with her and she could do that only by making her happy land sound appetising. Besides, for better or worse, there was some simple charm of this man that demanded honesty.

"I am detached for this reason," she said. She wriggled to make herself comfortable.

Gregory slotted the movement away as kittenish and was surprised to find that it disturbed him. He had never cared much for cats.

"The reason," he prompted.

"I don't expect you to believe this," she began. "Not the first time —and perhaps not ever."

"Stay there," said Charlie. "I'm going down for a drink of water."

Nicholas stared at the receiver in his hand. Charlie surely didn't expect him to believe all this "happy land" rubbish. He found himself muttering, "There is a happy land far, far away . . . Where all the . . ."

The rest of the kindergarten song evaded him. He tried to improvise, making ridiculous rhymes, finding them getting more and more coloured as time went on and Charlie, presumably, filled the sink and sucked at it.

"There is a happy land . . ."

"Okay," said Charlie suddenly in his ear.

"Listen," said Nicholas in his best no-nonsense tone. "I've been trying to work this thing out. I mean . . . I believe most of what you say to me most of the time. But this is ridiculous. It's a great story for New Worlds SF or somebody, but . . ."

Charlie pressed his lips against the mouth-piece and spat cusswords into it. "I hope they wet your ear."

"Impressive," said Nicholas, hurt that his suspicion should have produced such a violent reaction from his friend.

"Then believe me."

"I'm sorry, Charlie. But keep talking. I never said I wasn't entertained. . . ."

"Hang you, Nick. It's the truth I'm telling you."

Something about Charlie's insistence, his reluctance to admit that he had been fooling, left a reasonable doubt.

"All right," conceded Nicholas. "I'm with you, Charlie. But you've got to admit it's a bit way-out."

Charlie crowed with satisfaction.

"Now listen to the rest of it," he said.

"And now I don't want to go back." Satina was thoughtful in one corner of the settee.

Birtle watched her. The whole concept was a little beyond him. He wanted to know more before he tried to be constructive.

But Satina had become silent. She gazed into the middle distance, the china-blue eyes clouded with carefully sustained worry.

"If you should move—" said Birtle.

She looked up.

"If you should be somewhere else, could they track you down?"

Satina pondered.

"Not right now," she said eventually. "They are too busy waiting for me to be happy. They could follow me, certainly, visually, but they couldn't get a track to me. Not yet awhile. Not while I don't know how I feel."

Birtle waited for her to explain. If he could offer no solution he could at least let her proceed at her own pace.

With his eyes on her, she reddened.

"I want to stay," she said simply. "Here. With you."

"With me?" Birtle couldn't accept the fact. There had been too much misery in the past to be countered with any sudden exultation. The slow response saved him.

Satina, who could read his every thought, uncurled from the settee, hopped to his side, rested a hand on his arm. "Remember—it is too dangerous for us to be happy here."

"But how can I help it?"

"By keeping in mind that as soon as you get too happy, you'll be transported."

"And what about you?"

"The prospect of returning to the happy land makes me very unhappy. So I can't go unless I find joy with you."

"It's too much. I can't believe—"

"Don't try. Just stave it all off until we get away from this place. And be natural. They know your timetable. Keep to the routine. Otherwise, suspicion."

"Perhaps . . ." he started to say, "perhaps in the Mediterranean or the Paraguayan pampas or the Asian steppes, I could—kiss you?"

He hovered. "There's something I ought to do, then," he said reluctantly, discarding his slippers. "It being Saturday night, I am expected to go to the cinema. Alone. Believe me, it *is* routine. There are two young followers who will be most suspicious if I break the habit."

While he was gone, leaving all the lights in the house ablaze, Satina had no trouble staying miserable.

The distress bulb on Niktar's vanilla control panel glowed like a strawberry. He slapped at a switch. "Proceed."

"Emotions," said a strangled voice.

"Emote," ordered Niktar and chuckled to himself. He had little faith in his minions' interpretation of an emergency.

"I hardly know how to tell you . . ."

"Use words," said Niktar. "Wiggle your tongue."

He settled back in his swivel chair and propelled himself first this way, then that way.

"Our earth contact seems to be behaving oddly."

"In what way oddly?"

"Her motivation charts seem to be going haywire. She is neither one thing nor the other, neither sad nor happy. When she impacted, we recorded a distinct flicker of—relief."

"Safe landing," said Niktar. "Successful transportation. It's natural."

These benighted technicians. They knew only machines. If somebody behaved in any way contrary to their expectations, it must be a mechanical failure. So buzz the Ruler.

"There was something else."

Niktar spun his chair once to the right, once to the left. "Well?"

"There is a hostility build-up."

Niktar wished himself at the Bay of Emotions and was immediately there. "Show me."

The trackman led him to the manner-scanner and fed him the readings, a fold at a time. Niktar traced the erratic course of the marker. At intervals, it veered alarmingly close to the edge of the roll. He pointed out the meanderings. "What are they?"

"An urge to get away from us altogether, I would speculate," supplied the trackman. "I can't be sure. We have never had anything like it."

"Why not?" demanded Niktar unreasonably.

"With the greatest respect, Ruler," returned the trackman heavily, "up until now we have scanned only minds which were ignorant of the process. They were not hostile to it. We did not expect our own people would act any differently. We are, after all, of one accord, are we not?"

"We are *not*." Niktar flung the man to one side and looked for a seat. "Obviously we are not or I wouldn't be here doing your job for you and you wouldn't be whining. The prime concern now is our next move—how we get her back."

The trackman looked uneasy. "Her continued stay on earth is governed by several considerations."

"Quiet!" Niktar did not enjoy having anyone provide solutions for him. The answer should be common sense. It should therefore be accessible to him. "Find me something to sit on."

The trackman pushed a stool towards Niktar and the Ruler let himself down gratefully upon its meagre surface, his bulk overlapping on every side. He shrugged into the least uncomfortable position. He settled into thought.

"If she gets happy, she comes straight back here," he said. "Right?"

The trackman nodded. "We have already reversed the track. Everything is ready for her return. . . ."

The considerations were all creature here. Why was she hostile? Or was she even hostile? The man had already said these were circumstances without precedent. Perhaps these were emotions without precedent, also, creating freak readings.

The possibility was far from remote.

And why the sadness? Because she had been disappointed in her subject? Because she had found it impossible to satisfy him? Because, that being so, she was now stranded on earth with no hope of returning while the track was tuned to ecstasy level?

That, too, seemed feasible.

In any event, she was not happy. The apparatus showed that clearly and definitely.

If the track was reversed again, the way would be open for her. It could do no harm. If there was no reaction in an hour—a fair time for a compass of emotions—the track could become ecstatic again.

If she still evaded the trackers, they would operate the random element and suck up anybody in the right state of mind.

"Up-end the track," he said decisively.

"But . . ."

"Do it," said Niktar. "That is the Ruler's decision. If that shows no response in an hour, reverse it again. Still no reaction, randomise. Snatch up any happy person in the catchment area."

He wished himself back to his apartment, well-satisfied.

Gregory Birtle had used the cinema darkness to make plans, aware of but undeterred by the attention of his two young followers.

In fact, that had done no harm—because it gave him a better idea of how Satina felt with the scanners on her at all times.

Back at home and free of the boys' attention, he was trying to be practical. "Then I'll sell up and we'll go," he said.

Satina was unrelieved. "How long would it take?"

"I'd have to contact the agent. I don't know how much you appreciate of this world, but it must be a universal fact that you cannot do much without the power to buy. We need money. I shall have to put this house on the market. I have a little money. I never had cause to spend it. And an old Rolls-Royce that runs on love . . ."

"You see," said Satina gently, "I don't know how long it will be before they decide to send somebody after me or use the randomiser."

Gregory sat down, stood up, sat down again. "Randomiser?"

"A disturbing little element that sucks up anyone at correct frequency who happens to be near track bottom."

"And where's that?"

"Out there on the fringe of the woods. A pretty wild area, I would say. Thankfully, I don't suppose many people go there."

"Do me a favour, Charlie," said Nicholas patronisingly.

The line went dead.

"Charlie?"

Nicholas swung his legs clear of the bed and peered out the window. The moon, late risen, hung heavy. The sky bowed with the weight of it.

On the opposite wall, a four-feet-ten-and-a-half-inch lizard clung, then dropped.

"Charlie!"

The lizard stopped in its tracks.

"Charlie, let me get my pants on and I'm with you."

Nicholas struggled. Foot in wrong leg, foot in right, foot in seat, jerking trouser-tops from his fingers. Nicholas fumed.

Up zip. Down drain-pipe.

They ran, Charlie a little ahead, Nicholas slightly behind.

They turned the corner, bouncing like tennis-balls away from their houses. The street, the roofs were washed silver with the moonlight.

The sun bakes, the moon washes, noted Nicholas. Just Creation doing its housework.

Charlie, his eyes set purposefully ahead, was lengthening the distance between them, unconcerned with his friend's philosophising.

But Nicholas liked to get a composite picture of mystery. Here they went to witness something barely credible. Nicholas wanted to savour the tilt of the sky, the mood of the trees, the sound of the silence.

The strawberry glowed, the communicator buzzed, the alarm wave broke and creamed across the Bay of Emotions. Niktar flicked a switch with one hand and cleaned out an ear to listen with the other.

"Sir!"

"Sir!"

"Sir!"

"Use one medium," he snapped. "There is only one of you and you only have one message, presumably."

The communicator went dumb. The alarm wave went into ebb.

"Sir," said the strawberry voice.

"So you said."

"The girl's track has run off the roll altogether."

"And what does that mean that we don't already have provisions for?" Niktar was growing ever more intolerant of the trackman's easy panic.

"It must mean . . . it means something . . . well . . . in between. Not sorrow, not ecstasy, nor any degree of either. . . ."

"But surely she must be feeling something."

"It could be indecision of some sort or—apprehension."

"What's that?"

"A sort of scared happiness. Sick-in-the-stomach excitement."

"Don't struggle anymore. It is an unnecessary emotional complication. Why were we not prepared for it?"

"Because it is nothing we have encountered in great detail before. Mostly it shows up as atmospheric. This is the first time anyone on a line from us has registered it."

"In other words, we have lost her."

"*No*, sir! No. Only while she feels this way. As soon as her pattern settles, we shall have her."

"And suppose she changes location in the meantime. We have the track nailed down."

"I . . . I . . ."

"Exactly. I'm not pleased. I'm not—happy."

"Oh, mercy, Master . . ." The trackman's voice rose in throbbing appeal.

"You have ruined my mood."

"Please, Master, it wasn't my fault. . . ."

"Then you will want to restore my good humour."

"Anything, Master, anything at all."

Niktar settled back in his chair and built a cathedral with his fourteen fingers. "First," he whispered along the fleshy nave, "adjust the random pick-up. We must not dwell too long on our failures."

There was a grumble of shifting kinetics, a wet-dry sound as the channel began its permanent swallow.

The trackman came panting back to the console.

"It's done, Ruler," he breathed. "It's functioning perfectly."

"Good. Now, do you still want to please me?"

"Eternally, Ruler."

"Then die . . ."

They slowed to a walk as they drew near the wrought-iron gate, retrieving their breath and searching the house for lights. Robbed of perspective, the building had flattened itself against the night. No chink showed. No shutter moved.

The gate was a lone voice as they passed through it and considered their next move, squatting beside the path.

"We'll have to knock," said Charlie.

"Don't be stupid. It's the middle of the night. They'll go spare."

Nicholas watched Charlie's face for a faltering of resolution, a hint of deception.

But Charlie had his eyes on the front door, willing it to open and the whole house to spring into illumination. "We'll have to knock. We've come this far."

"You knock," said Nicholas.

"You still don't believe me," countered Charlie. "You reckon I'm fooling you. Some friend. All right, I'll . . ."

He moved towards the door.

"No," Nicholas called after him. He ran to catch up. "If being believed means that much to you, I'll knock."

Charlie looked momentarily relieved. Or did he? Nicholas could not be sure in the darkness.

They stood together on the porch, trying to peer through the ancient stained-glass panels. They pried open the letter-box but the gloom within was like dust on their eye-balls and the stale odour of the yesterday world filled their nostrils. They let the flap fall.

"Well," said Charlie, straight-faced, sincerity beaming darkly from his eyes. "There's always the sportsman's way. . . ."

"My coin," said Nicholas. "My last five-p. We'll spin that."

"Is it—all right?"

The doubt stung Nicholas until he realized that his insistence had evidenced a similar suspicion. Charlie was only taking payment. Nicholas placed the coin carefully and flicked it into the air. "Tails," he shouted. He caught the coin in his right palm, slapped it onto the back of his left wrist. Then he took away his right hand.

A woman's head.

"Tails it is," he said, and struck the door a mighty blow.

Gregory Birtle had scoured the house for something to put in the suitcase he carried open and empty in his hand. But there was nothing he wanted to take anywhere with him.

"Perhaps I ought to take it empty," he said on his return to Satina. "A symbol of complete divorce from this place."

She peered at him curiously. "Symbol?"

"Then again, perhaps a symbol is a connection in itself," he amended. "Forget it. I'll scribble a note to the estate agent and we'll post it through his door as we pass, running."

Satina rose from the settee and tested her weight on her foot. Instantly he was at her side. "Do you need support?"

The physical contact would have made him happy.

"I think I can manage," said Satina. She saw it even if he did not. He felt vaguely embarrassed. He changed the subject.

"Whom would they send?"

"Anybody," she said. "Anything, so long as it has the emotional power to travel."

"Have moods, will travel," he said nonsensically.

And the front door shivered under a mighty blow.

When Nicholas turned back from the door, Charlie was gone. Not down the path. Somewhere. Into the undergrowth. Lost in the garden shapes, not breathing, not touching the crackling ground. It was as though Charlie had never been there.

Nicholas was poised to flee when Gregory Birtle opened the door with his hair tousled and his eyes half-lidded.

"Did you knock?"

Nicholas wondered momentarily whether he could get away with saying no. Then he decided that even Gregory Birtle was not that deeply immersed in autumn.

But what else could he say? He did not know why he was here. Only Charlie knew that.

"Why did you knock? Who are you?"

"We . . . I . . . we . . ."

"Is there somebody else with you?"

"Yes . . . there was . . . no . . ."

"Where are you from?"

Gregory Birtle used the question like a whip. Not only miserable, thought Nicholas, but nasty with it. And then . . . It was, after all, the middle of the night and the man looked as though he had been sleeping.

Now the tight set of the features, the furrowed brow, showed something more than anger. More like caution. Didn't it?

Nicholas posed the question and knew he could not give the answer. How can I think straight now, here, right in front of him? He cursed himself roundly and silently.

"I asked where you came from."

"Across town," said Nicholas hurriedly. "My friend and I . . ."

"Then there *is* somebody with you."

"He's gone now. Don't ask me where. He left me."

"Some friend."

"That's what he said."

"Why? Why should he say that?"

"No reason. Something else . . ."

Gregory Birtle opened the door wide and came out onto the porch. He ran his eyes over the garden.

Charlie, away in a distant corner, bellying down behind an azalea bush, began to perspire.

"You see . . ." began Nicholas.

"You'd better come in if you've something to say."

"It can wait till morning," said Nicholas in a forlorn hope.

"No. Come in."

Gregory Birtle stood back and waited for the boy to pass him and enter the house. Nicholas made no move.

"Charlie had this—theory," he said instead, lamely.

"Charlie?" Gregory Birtle folded his arms and considered the night temperature. Then he sat down on the porch rocking chair.

"He ran away," said Nicholas.

"This theory," Birtle prompted him.

The theory was unutterable in its stupidity. How could he ever have been taken in? It was taxing friendship too highly. That was the end of it, Charlie. Humiliation laid a latch on Nicholas's lips.

"About me?" Birtle was prodding again, rocking slowly in the chair, observing the boy's discomfort.

"Yes . . ." The latch was holding.

"Well, go on."

"It seems so stupid now."

"Nevertheless, tell it. I think I have a right to hear it."

"We were wondering why you never smiled." Nicholas gave up the struggle. Birtle gave up rocking, but said nothing. "Charlie had this idea that you might have a reason for keeping your face just so."

Birtle stood up suddenly and stepped to the top of the path. "Charlie," he shouted. "Come on up here. Don't leave your idea fatherless."

Charlie lay paralysed. Only the wind moved among the bushes. Birtle returned to his chair.

"There was this girl," said Nicholas.

"Girl? Another one of you?"

"No, not us. You. She came from the happy land to see you."

"The happy land?" Birtle forced a chuckle. He looked hard at Nicholas. "You're a bit old for fairies."

"Space travel," said Nicholas. "There was this chief called Niktar and this happy land was a planet."

Birtle grunted under the paling sky. "Space travel," he reminded himself. "Go on . . ."

"It's too . . ." Nicholas stumbled again and then the latch lifted completely and the words flooded out like a kitchen light. "This girl descended in a sadness track from this happy-land place. She was to take you back with her as soon as she made you happy. It was an experiment. The idea is, these people tap your emotions and make them some kind of transport. Sadness brought her down. Happiness will take you up. The track is out there, near the woods, waiting for you. . . ."

"It figures," said Birtle, straight-faced.

Nicholas wondered at the reply.

"But tell me," said Birtle, "what was my reason for keeping my face—just so?"

"The girl. You love her and if you look too happy, you'll be transported."

"How long has she been here?"

"I don't know. This afternoon . . ."

"I went to the pictures tonight."

"I know," said Nicholas before he realised it. "We followed you." He hesitated. "We—wanted to see if you would laugh."

"I went to the pictures," Birtle repeated, as though it were important. "Would I go to the pictures?"

Nicholas thought for a moment.

"To keep things normal," he said. "You go to the pictures every Saturday night. Someone might have noticed a change in routine. You didn't stay long. . . ."

"There was nothing to laugh at. Cartoons bore me. And you think I would have left this girl in this gloomy old house with a splinter in her foot?"

Nicholas bent his head and watched his battered shoe scuffing at the wood of the porch. "I told you it would sound stupid."

Birtle's laughter was prolonged but as hollow as an echo. He should have stopped, thought Nicholas. It isn't that funny. . . .

The laughter grew more restrained, altered its rhythm. It was a while before Nicholas recognised sobs. Birtle was leaning forward in the rocking chair with his head cupped in his hands. Nicholas looked with some panic upon the man's shaking shoulders.

"I'm sorry," he said, wishing he knew the words to comfort. "It was—cruel. We should have minded our own business. If you're lonely, perhaps we could . . ."

"Get out of here!" Birtle pushed himself up viciously from the chair and flung himself through his front door, slamming it hard behind him.

Nicholas could hear the slap of his slippers down the long, dark corridors for an age. The rocking chair slowed its tempo and fell still as Nicholas went on hearing the dry flutter of the slippers like butterflies trapped in a tomb, like a tattered flag a long way behind the procession.

Charlie bobbed up beside him.

"Hobo!" said Nicholas succinctly.

Charlie giggled. "You have to admit—"

"I have to admit," countered Nicholas, "that I don't like you and I don't like myself much either. We made him cry."

"You *lie*. I heard him laughing. We finally made him laugh."

"Yes. Then we made him cry, just to pay for the privilege. Why are we so cruel?"

He turned and walked quickly down the path and into the woods to relieve himself. The incident had sabotaged his bladder.

Charlie followed him, chuckling.

Nicholas finished the function, zipped himself up. Something tugged at his memory.

"Now laugh," Charlie challenged. "Now you feel better, laugh."

"Get knotted," said Nicholas without steam, as though his mind was elsewhere.

Charlie guffawed. "Take it, Nick. Confess it was a great story. You said so yourself. Good enough for a science-fiction magazine, you said."

He screamed, he jabbered, he took great gulps of air. He fell about, laughing.

Memory heeded tugging. "Who said splinter?" asked Nicholas. "Charlie, *he* did. He *must* know something. . . ."

Charlie was exultant. He rolled in the grass on the edge of the wood, howling with happiness.

"Charlie . . ." Nicholas, of an instant desperate, tried to get a hold on the wriggling Charlie, but the boy kicked him away, went on laughing.

"Charlie . . ." Nicholas, winded, begged from the brambles where he had fallen. "Charlie, he *knows*—"

And then.

Flattened grass but no rolling Charlie. A sound like last bathwater.

"Charlie . . ." Nicholas called hesitantly. "Charlie, where are you? Come on, enough's enough."

He heaved himself out of the brambles and battered through the undergrowth, unmindful of the roots which tripped his feet and the branches which clawed at his face. He reached the pavement, still shouting, and broke into a run. "Charlie, don't fool me anymore. . . ."

The old Rolls-Royce passed him at the bottom of the street. The mournful face of Gregory Birtle peered at him through the driver's side-window. A shadowy figure occupied the passenger seat beyond. Then the car spun round the corner, braking hard.

"I crave that man's happiness," Charlie had said, "more than I crave my own."

With the dust from Birtle's exhaust stinging his face, Nicholas slowed to a walk, broke his pace, and collapsed. Weeping like no paper bag should weep.

WELCOME TO THE LAND OF SMILES

Introduction

A couple of hundred yards south of my home lies Victoria Park, which, in summer, suffers from that greatest of all setbacks—people. People are pigs. On an evening after a sunny day between May and September, you may cross the lawns without once touching the grass, stepping from sandwich bag to ice cream wrapper to morning tabloid, all the while skirting dog-dirt.

From the gate I enter to the gate closest to the bus-stop, a straight line of walking cuts across paths and sward (but no flower-beds). Early morning is the time to do it—prior to people, that is.

But I cannot dismiss the inland flotsam entirely. One 8 A.M. I found my curiosity downcast and my thoughts in a rare state of eloquence. If this were the seaside, I ruminated, I would be a beach-comber. So what of the here and now? A grasscomber? A *green-comber!*

A couple of miles north of my home stands Castell Coch (that's Welsh for "Red Castle"), overlooking the main trunk road to the South Wales valleys. It is a folly, created in the nineteenth century by an eccentric architect, William Burges—but a fairy-tale castle so imposing that it featured in the late Alan Ladd's one mediaeval adventure epic, *The Black Knight* (or was it The Shortest Knight?). I don't think that Ladd or his damsel in distress, Joanne Dru, ever came near the place, but when the film went through post-synch and the major release circuits, it found its way to our local in Cardiff —and there, sure enough, was Castell Coch, with a Black Knight (not *the* Black Knight) heading up the wooded trail to the draw-bridge.

Now you have as much of a beginning as I had.

Satin had been saved from a genetic shipwreck. With her father on acid and her mother on Mexican thunderweed, the chances of her seeing reality at all were poor.

For the dubious reward of survival, she could thank a team of chromosome engineers at what had been called the Karolinska Institute, Stockholm, before British sulphur dioxide, Russian DDT, and Scandinavian exhausts combined to form a hybrid which even the local denaturation techniques could not negate and which buried Sweden in a fall of soot.

The team had escaped to this crazy place. While they went on with their RNA/DNA trifles they came into possession of the Satin mixture, and by translocation, inversion, and deletion, all plotted with quinacrine fluorescence and Giemsa stain, they had produced a cell worth tubing.

And here she was. From a cell to a cell, she would say in her simplistic, five-year-old way.

The songs had it differently. But to Satin, if the words sounded the same, indeed *were* the same, there was no more to be said. Or sung.

> Half a pound of soya bean
> That's your allocation.
> Eat it where you can't be seen
> Pop-goes-ulation.

Ben had no recollection before this place. Sleepfeed had taught him all he knew. Which was plenty, taking account of the fact that he was six. The songs said he was six.

Sleepfeed had told him that, left to his own devices, he would have soon been persuaded that his presence on the mortal coil was superfluous and more than that, a criminal irresponsibility on somebody's part. Not his part: he would just bear the stigma and the blame.

He couldn't take a breath without squandering oxygen that would not be replaced now that the trees had gone. He was gnawing his way through a dwindling food-pile and for what return? Some more fluid ounces for the detritus dump. Recycling? It cost too much. Better to stop people relieving themselves. Better to stop people.

Sure, they would have made him welcome outside.

That was the message of the songs and it was a big message for a small brain. So the experts worked on the brain, a neural enhancement that would render Ben coherent to adult considerations.

And adult manipulations, added Ben quietly to himself, for you cannot heighten activity in the right lobe without building up performance in the left.

> Singer was born, as if it mattered,
> On the day the mirror shattered.
> The glass pane cracked from side to side,
> The black cat spat and tried to hide.
> Singer was born.
>
> Singer's windows, they never have a view.
> Singer wears her luck like a built-up shoe.

It was beautiful. It had long auburn hair and green eyes and a voice formed in honey comb and spun out like an Aeolian string.

Even allowing for so many talents, so many outs of the way, it remained wholly functional. For this was the control animal and the singer of songs. The messages were channelled through this creature as surely as lithium carbonate flowed upon the water conveyed to Ben and rubidium traces marked the outfall from the tap in Satin's cell from a cell.

The lyrics made some kind of sense when you were blessed with reasoning power. It was not. Reasoning meant the ability to argue and that was a dangerous luxury in the vehicle of consent. It could not think, could not fight, could not look in a mirror (could look in a mirror, but . . .) and say, "I am beautiful."

It just delivered its didactic couplets and then went quiet at its window. Rapunzel with her hair pinned up and no white charger coming out of the oxide mists.

> "I am,
> You are,
> He,
> She or
> It is . . ."

What? Three third persons screaming in their singular way. He, she, or it is *what?*

The Red Castle crouched upon a hill like an Arthurian joke. That was a fair description because the citadel, all turrets and ravens and shades of Grimm, had been started in a decade of excess and then forgotten and then built again during the nineteenth century as a monumental folly.

It sat on the unlunatic fringe of a moon landscape paralysed and powdered by mercury thinking and bad vibrations, nestling among pines which would have contradicted fact by their very existence if they had not been responsible for a little tocsin of their own in the clay which bedded their roots.

Coniferous ancestors, struggling to make time on small coal and fly-ash and smears from smelting had learned the spell and passed it on in their juices. It was nice to see a bit of green.

> The other day upon the lawn
> I picked a flower which had not gone.
>
> And as it bled into my palm,
> It just said: Why? I did no harm.
>
> I've lived through dust and DDT
> —What made you do this thing to me?
>
> Believe me, I was going to thrive
> If you had just left me alive.

Satin saw green. She stood on her toes and thrust her head into the narrow window-crevice. Beyond, something verdant was moving and a cold blowing came upon her face. The blowing inside was something to do with the movement outside. Wind, said her lyrical informer. Leaves.

Satin got back on her bed and wished she could see the voice. Straight away, she knew she had made an inconsistency. You do not see a voice. You hear it. You see a mouth, a face, the maker of the voice. All right—she wished she could see the face that made the voice.

She tried to visualise such a face and knew it must be beautiful. But she found that the only face she could picture was her own because it was the only face she had ever seen. If there were other faces in other places, perhaps they were fairer than hers. Perhaps she was not beautiful at all. What is beautiful?

Ben saw green, too, and by design. Leaves, he knew. Leaves on branches and branches on trees and if there were still trees growing he had been told an important lie.

Or rather, he would have been told an important lie if he had been in the world where the sayers of sooth pretended such things. Fortunately, he was here, peering out on visible proof of that lie and friends were looking after him.

That must be so. Whoever was putting him straight must be regarded with warmth. They practised love, otherwise what? His food came by mech through a panel that operated at no other time. When he had eaten, he drank water and enjoyed it. An enclosed cabinet in one corner of the room was equipped for all his other needs.

He had no criterion but sometimes when his mind wanted to lie down his body did not, and hair-springs in his knees and spine reacted. It made him think he slept rather a lot for a boy of six.

The Singer could look out upon a coastal plain depressing in its entirety with skyblocks blackening like rotting teeth and the rest of the development coming to ruin. The view was not vital to the Singer and messages of doom registered no differently from tidings of great joy on the workings of the throat. It was functional.

Not that doom had much to say. Optimism was the cliché. Optimism can become a cliché? When expectation founders on lack of fruition, you can accept the inevitable or scale down the expectation.

Censor hope, remove dreams, and you have a Singer with a view that doesn't matter.

Here is Snoopy, the Mad Scientist, pacing his laboratory. And lest that should place too great a strain upon credulity, ask what else one might call the last of the Karolinskans, a pure figment of his own imagination.

The equipment is good in this installation—far better than a comic-strip rendition needs to be—and Snoopy's flying friends have truly lost out to the Red Barren. Sweden took too much out of them by leaving too much in them. Woodstock has walked south for the last time.

Snoopy, then, was Wolf Hochbaum, a man who claimed that his vision was not impaired, an experimenter in the classic tradition of Auschwitz who just happened to have the kind of facilities available to him now that could produce a solution.

Hochbaum was too young to remember Adolf, but history had been unkind enough to state that the man had perished through his own powers of self-destruction, quite apart from anything of a military nature.

Wolf wasn't going to see his creatures come to that state. Hitler had been set in his ways before anybody could work on him. Ben was a different proposition—young, pliable. And the girl? She was a just-in-case. Hochbaum had great faith in iron maidens and if Ben didn't dominate, Satin surely would.

It didn't make a lot of sense, taken objectively, but Wolf, as stated, was quite mad. An unwilling and unrepentant victim of the trace-metal plague.

As bad luck would have it, the facilities available to him included two perfectly sane children and a beautiful woman so scarred intracranially by many losses that she had withdrawn from the touch-logic of her senses. She would have been a zombie but for the songs. Even so, she might just as well have been. She did not know she sang.

Satin rocked on a stool, nursing her elbows as she would cradle a doll.

She crooned a tune she might have heard from the Singer, but thought not. She was still missing a definition of beauty and an awareness of her position in that particular design. She could see herself in the mirror, rocking, cradling. "How will I ever know?" she said aloud.

"One question," said a voice from the wall. "One answer."

She was not shaken. Disembodied voices were familiar to her. The chance to communicate was not.

Where do I begin? Who am I? What am I doing here? How long must I—? Why? What is beautiful?

"It doesn't matter," she said eventually.

"One question, one answer."

She considered herself, rocking on the stool with an imaginary baby. What is a baby? Why do I hold my arms so? What am I pretending is in them? Why do I rock?

The room was big and empty and only a part of the whole. She was small and cold and feeling slightly foolish at being spectacle and spectator all in one.

"Am I alone?" she asked, because the matter had attained a prominence.

"No. That is your answer."

"Who else is here?" Satin, so excited, didn't grasp the significance and the finality of the response.

The wall was mute.

"Why won't you tell me?"

Silence.

"When can I ask again?"

Silence, except for the big wind moving beyond the window and the frondular greenery dancing.

"When can I? Please?"

Nothing. Satin threw away her baby and cried.

Ben woke up shouting.

"How? How do I get a question answered in this place?"

It was still daylight, or was it already daylight; the same with a minute gone or new with a night gone?

"One question," said a voice from the wall. "One answer."

Ben jumped. "Why only one question?"

"That is your ration. That is also your answer."

"But I didn't mean . . . It's not fair."

The wall was saying no more.

"When can I ask the next question?"

Silence. Ben kicked the grey stones and hoped it hurt them as much as it hurt him.

I want a happy ending, breathed Satin.

A happy ending is out, said Ben, just to himself, away across the battlements, unknowing. Out of this place.

The Singer trilled "stay put" stanzas.

Greencomber was down on his luck. It had ever been thus, when his ancestors had toured the high-water line and found their tidal bounty being replaced by a residue that was rich in octane and nothing else.

The move had been made inland to summer parks and pop-festival grounds—strawberry fields forever. But the pickings deteriorated, as did the grass. Inland again to picnic grounds and forests going tattered at the edges.

Now Greencomber had been a long time without shade, let alone reward.

And suddenly there were trees and a castle or schloss or Camelot. He headed towards the mirage at a gallop and found it not to be so. The shadow which cooled his brow and came like a wet flannel to his red-rimmed eyes was real. The rough grey stone which exalted his fingers was too solid for hallucination.

For a while, he made a squirrel pantomime among the trees with his feet crunching on the browning needles scattered over the hard clay soil; dodging hither and thither, hider and seeker.

Then he turned his attention to the castle. No immediate access presented itself but on the south frontage, overlooking the ravaged plain he had left in his wake, he sensed a movement at a window.

The situation was all wrong. The trees he might have climbed for a closer scrutiny were at the back. Instead, he had to take his chance on the parched earth.

A flash of pink, a sunset glint. A face of a woman with auburn hair. And such fairness. Even as he registered this, Greencomber absorbed, too, the pain that went with the beauty.

And yet . . . He looked long at the face, until its owner must surely feel the warmth and the weight of his attention. And still she did not look down. She was neither noticeably happy nor visibly upset and it was the absence of either of these extremes or any state in between that gave eloquence to the tragedy.

It caught and held him impaled.

He shouted, "Rapunzel, Rapunzel, let down your hair."

No flicker of life from the face.

A doll, maybe. And if so, whither Dr. Coppelius?

"Excuse me, pretty lady . . ."

Nothing.

"I am a traveller lost and weary. Can you give me shelter for the night?"

The eyes did not move. The lips twitched.

In the failing light, the Singer poured forth another blackbird melody.

A last pull into the window-crevice and Satin looked down upon the man standing among the pines. He was very tall, it seemed to her, and quite young in her sparse understanding of the word. There did not seem to be many more lines on his face than there were on her own.

"Are you the Singer?" she asked.

He laughed and the voice was different.

"Do you answer more than one question?"

More laughter. "I answer any number—as long as I am able to answer."

"Why am I here?"

"I don't know," said Greencomber truthfully. "Is there anybody there with you?"

"I'll ask the questions, please. There's the Singer and a voice that comes from the wall. Who are they?"

"I don't know."

Satin bit her lip. "You don't help any more than the wall voice."

"I just got here."

"From where?"

"From the plain. And before that, another plain and prior to that, a ruined city."

"I don't believe you. The Singer says such things are myths."

Greencomber shifted his weight from one foot to the other. He was beginning to feel the weight of the implements in his belt and he knew the day was ending. His neck was aching from the effort of looking up. "Does she talk to you, then?"

"Sings for me. Why do you say 'she'?"

"Because it is a woman."

"A woman?"

Greencomber was stumbled momentarily, not knowing whether the girl did not understand the word "woman" or whether she was just showing surprise.

"A woman. A—a grown-up version of yourself."

"How do you know?"

"I have seen her."

"What is she like?"

"She is—beautiful."

"A grown-up version of me."

"Yes . . . not exactly like you."

"But she is beautiful."

"Yes."

"Then I am beautiful."

"Of course."

"What is beautiful?"

Ben heard two voices and recognised neither one of them. They were of a substance with the breeze and the rustles beyond the window.

Left side of his intellect argued against dismissing all such happenings beyond his vision as beyond his understanding. Get up there and look, said curiosity. If only he didn't feel so tired. . . .

And maybe there was a logic in that. Tired boys don't look out windows. What happens when tired boys *do?*

He *did.*

And saw Greencomber and heard a small voice of the timbre of the singer and yet not the Singer. Too light, too high, too—young?

He didn't know what to say but he had to make a noise. "Hi!"

Greencomber turned. "So there *is* more than one of you."

It was an exciting statement.

"Is there another?" said Satin and Ben together. "What is he/she like?"

Greencomber, dappled by the green, made jaunty by the descending twilight, cocked his head, looked at Satin and then away along the wall, looked at Ben and then back along the wall.

"He is handsome," he said to Satin.

"She is beautiful," he said to Ben. He could have said "lovely" or "pretty" but he knew the word Satin wanted to hear was "beautiful." Plenty of time for synonyms.

"Who are you?" asked Ben. Satin had forgotten that she did not know. She waited impatiently for the answer.

"I am Greencomber," said the man in the woods. "So called because I seek my fortune among the greenery as my forefathers once grew rich on pieces of eight and ambergris awarded to the faithful by the sea."

"What does he mean?" There was more to Satin's question than mere inquiry. She wanted to see whether he along the wall would co-operate, whether he thought enough of her to attempt an explanation.

"Beachcombers." Ben wasn't too sure himself and he didn't appreciate Satin's many motives. His idea of their togetherness was rather different. They were in, Greencomber was out. That was what they had in common. "Once upon the time there were men —and women, too, I suppose—"

"My mother," assured Greencomber.

"—who used to walk along beaches after high tide to see what they could find. If there had been a storm at sea or a shipwreck . . ."

Shipwreck. Shipwreck. Why did that ring with Satin like a race memory?

". . . they might find valuable things. Tins of food. Ambergris comes from whales. It is used for perfumes. It is expensive."

This time Satin directed her question unmistakably to Greencomber. "What is a mother?"

Ben's unuttered data turned to ersatz in his mouth. This he couldn't answer. Did it mean he was no longer of use to she unseen at the other window?

"A mother is the one from whom you learn love," said Greencomber. A teacher, then. A being not vastly different from the media within the children's experience. "I thought perhaps the lady on the other side of the castle was your mother."

"The Singer?" Satin sounded enchanted with the idea.

"No." Ben was firm. "The Singer is a teacher but not of love. I am not sure I would know love if I saw it."

Greencomber's voice had gone brittle, as though he doubted its strength. "You don't see it or hear it—you feel it. Do you mean to say you have never—felt—such a feeling?"

"How can I tell?" Ben was irritable over what he might have missed.

"What do you feel about the Singer?" The light was fading fast. Greencomber wondered how best to keep himself within their compass.

"It has a function," said Ben.

"Not it—she. The Singer is a woman."

"I feel," said Satin, who had been out of the exchange long enough, "that I would like her to be my mother."

Then her arms could bear the strain of her weight no longer and she fell back into her chamber. Greencomber could hear distant weeping. Ben, too.

"A woman." Ben was too sick with his own disappointment to feel for Satin. "But are there no men?"

"You and me," said Greencomber. "Maybe one other."

"Then will you be my—teacher?"

"You could have a mother, too. It's not impossible."

"The same mother?"

"You would have the same right to her."

"But how?"

"We must see how." Greencomber had decided the way to keep their attention.

He would get inside.

Wolf Hochbaum, as a scientist, came from the line which had begun in the medical block at Buchenwald, weathered Groote Schuur Hospital and the gas-shops of the Moon, his curiosity geared not so much by the will to understand and build upon as by the will to tamper. A pathological vandal was Wolf Hochbaum.

He had it in his mercurial mind that he could produce people for the conditions now prevailing. But there the reasoning split in classic schizophrenic tradition.

The only way to fashion humanity to face the outside world was to be honest with it from the outset.

The only way to make humanity look forward to that prospect was to give it something other than the truth.

The dilemma resulting could be extrapolated thus: the only way to make people want to go outside was to keep them inside.

Hochbaum was fortunate enough to have Ben and Satin inside, the former dosed with lithium to keep him amenable to suggestion, the latter fed on rubidium to heighten her initiative.

What he had done to the Singer was nobody's business but in fairness to him, he had stopped short of frontal lobotomy and in fairness to her, she had been glad of the oblivion he offered.

The airy nature of the instruction, the talkative nature of the cold grey walls were parlour tricks of octophonics. It suited him to have the children think in terms of magic if the tuition was rendered desirable by mystery.

Someday his charges would be ready to play their parts and the Singer could be given back her consciousness and the world would hail his supreme normality—the only man who kept his head when all around were losing theirs. If . . .

Some day. It was a good job there was nobody around to ask him when.

Came a knock at the great wooden door.

Greencomber knew his heavy-handed summons must yield the fourth occupant, if there was one. The boy and girl looked, talked, and acted as though they were restricted to their chambers. The Singer seemed not to move at all.

The person who opened the door must be the one in charge of the situation, or an underling of that one.

It never crossed his mind that the overseer might decide not to grant him access.

After all, a knock on the door in this day and age, an actual stranger, a person whose appearance, whose conversation, whose very body smells were *new* to you . . .

There would be a response or there was no fourth person.

The door swung wide. The clinic-bright lights sabotaged Greencomber's pupils.

"What do you want?"

He blinked, trying to focus on the speaker.

"Now is that a fair question?" he said. "I've come a long way on a lonely road. I want company."

"I'm sorry but we're not—"

"Hospitable? I'm no trouble, I assure you—"

His eyes adjusted. He was getting vision as well as sound now, a vision of a medium-sized man with receding hair or high forehead, and reptilian manner.

"I was going to say we are not equipped for overnight guests," said Hochbaum. "I have some people here in a rather distressing condition. I am their one source of comfort. It is not possible for me to entertain—"

"I've spoken to a couple of them." Greencomber got a boot over the threshold and braced himself to take the swing of the door. But the door didn't move. Only Hochbaum's face moved.

"You've—?"

"Through their windows at the back here. Two children. They didn't seem very distressed—"

"Not distressed," Hochbaum put in uncertainly. "Distressing. They have lost touch with reality."

"Is that the way of it? I'm sorry—I had always thought that was the whole idea of childhood . . . staving off reality until it was inevitable. And the poor lady who looks out over this hellish landscape. Some overwhelming bereavement, perhaps? And yet she sings. Like a bird, she sings."

Late in the day, Hochbaum was realising the need to bar this talker from his stronghold. He had got the door to Greencomber's shoulder and that was as far as it would go.

Then the visitor pivotted and while Hochbaum was off-balanced by the door continuing its swing, he stepped into the hall proper and started looking for stairs. "Perhaps they would all welcome a new face."

"Believe me, they wouldn't. You don't seem to realise that I have a duty to see these hapless people are disturbed as little as possible. Now, if it's food you want, I dare say I could find you some in the kitchen. Or money—I could let you have some money."

"My, my." Greencomber unbuttoned a hand-ax from the belt at his waist.

"I just don't want them troubled." Hochbaum could not take his eyes off the blade glinting from the hasp in Greencomber's hand. "I don't see the need for that."

"It's to smash locks."

"What?"

"If you don't open them."

"I've got no intention of allowing you to roam free and easy around my home. You must be mad."

"Not me."

"Look, I've tried to explain—"

"I don't believe you. That's all. It would be a waste of time trying to convince me otherwise."

"Then how can I satisfy you?"

"Show me."

"And you don't care how many people you hurt. The situation is most delicate."

"I don't intend to hurt anybody. As far as I am concerned, the harm has been done."

In a corner beyond the throw of the light, Greencomber had seen some steps leading upward. He moved towards them.

"You're making a grave error of judgment," said Hochbaum, but he was on the stairs barring the way before Greencomber could cover the distance.

"Out of my way," said the woodsman.

"At least listen to an explanation of my work here."

"Unnecessary. I can get past you, you know."

"I know. You could do whatever you set out to do. But without knowing the whole of it, you could trigger consequences you would not want. That's why I am asking you to listen to what I have to say."

Greencomber backed off three paces. He turned his attention to a doorway ninety degrees around the circular hall from the stairway.

"Kitchen," prompted Hochbaum. "I'm sure you could use something to eat. They won't go away."

"I take it you feed them."

"But naturally. I have plans for them. Naturally, I keep them in good health."

Greencomber went through into the kitchen. Hochbaum motioned him to sit before a dish of cold meat, with bread on a side-plate and a glass of wine to hand.

"That's your meal," said Greencomber.

"There's more. I'll eat when I've explained."

So Greencomber ate. It was worth taking a chance on the food being harmless because Hochbaum had had no notion of his coming.

And Hochbaum said:

"You know what it's like out there . . . you've seen the misery and the desolation. You're a strong man or you would have cracked, perhaps. Now, you consider—how do you prepare children for a world like that? Can you tell it all to them with words? Can you supply it to their brains by other means? Their limitations are great and would remain so in normal circumstances for a great number of years. Do they have that much time? Does anybody? The answer must be somewhere in between—a subconscious awakening, an early-warning system, a tempering of body chemicals so that they are ready to accept things as they are right now. At the same time, don't rob them of their dandelion days. Give them the magic of songs and the sleepfeed of reality, the food of legend and the drink of pharmacotherapy and when they're ready—"

Greencomber wiped the crumbs from his mouth daintily and sipped the wine. "How do you know when that is?"

"I don't. It hasn't happened yet."

"Then how can you be sure it will, or that you will recognise it?"

"That is the chance I take."

"That is the chance you make them all take with you. Tell me—why do the children face the greenery when the woman faces the scorched terrain? Does she not have as much right to the restful as they have to the real? What's the matter with her, anyway?"

"She is at the other end of the spectrum. They have seen none of the devastation until they are prepared. She has seen as much as she was prepared to see."

"But she still looks out."

"Without seeing."

"You mean she's blind."

"She might as well be. Don't worry. It's safe enough stationing her there because she has a specific occupation. She is my nursery spokesman. She teaches the children what they should know."

"From afar."

"I don't understand. The other side of the castle—"

"No physical contact."

"It isn't necessary." Hochbaum stood up, anxious to have the man finish his business and be away.

"Huh." A small smile played at the corners of Greencomber's mouth but failed to ignite his eyes. He heard Satin crying again for a mother.

He regained his feet, recovered the ax from the table. "What's your name?"

"Why?"

"Professional curiosity. I have a smattering of science. I thought perhaps you might be a household word—if there were any households left."

"This is a household. My name is Hochbaum—Wolf Hochbaum."

The ax glinted. Greencomber laughed heartily.

"Is it funny?" asked Hochbaum, on his dignity.

"Okay . . ." Greencomber had to stop for breath. "Only that in all the best nursery stories, the woodsman cuts off the wolf's head."

Ben woke shivering and knew by the state of the sky beyond his window-slit that there was something out of order with the day.

His throat was inordinately dry, as though he had been sleeping with his mouth open. He swung himself off the bed and trod carefully to the wash-basin.

But the tap would not turn. As he pitted his six-year-old strength against supposed air trapped in the pipe, the small metallic noises of the struggle raced like mice along the castle plumbing.

The wall said: "Ben."

It was a new voice. A voice half-recollected from the night before when he had gone to sleep in despair hoping to wake in joy.

"Ben. This is Greencomber. Are you well awake, would you say?"

Ben's teeth were chattering by this time. "Yes. But so cold."

"Press the wall behind your closet. You will find it becomes a door. Don't bother with anything else. Once you are in the passage beyond, you will know which way to come. I've got warmth here for you."

Ben was so chilled that he had to use the closet before he pressed the wall. Once out in the corridor, he could feel the woodsman's warmth increasing upon his face and under his feet.

Satin broke reluctantly from the embrace that wrapped her dormant hours, saw by the stars that the night was not over, and wondered at the cruelty which had cut short her slumber.

Her eyes were still sore from the last bout of weeping. Her nose was full.

She found a handkerchief, blew her nose, and woke up the wall.

"Satin?" In the wall, the voice from the woods. What next?

"I am here."

"Where I am is much better for you, Satin. It is warm and light and I think you have some friends here."

"The boy?"

"More than the boy."

"The Singer?"

"Come and see. Press the wall behind your closet."

Satin pressed stone and ran towards the embrace.

A sudden peace had come to the Singer. Something moved now at its door, picked it up and carried it down flights of stairs to love-colours and soft breathing.

Something sat it before a bright fire and gave it hot sweet drink with spirited lacing.

"You can come back now," said a new voice; not the one that dictated the songs. "You have been through shock and agony and you have moved inward away from life. But that is over now. Old things are past. New things are better."

More of the vivacious drink and now small bodies thrusting themselves alongside, picking up its arms and winding them round waists.

"You are soft," said a boy's voice.

"You are beautiful," said a girl. "Like me."

Their warmth was pricking with pins at its fingertips, penetrating, flowing along veins. The sweet libation moved to meet it.

Green eyes unclouded. The clouds loosed just one retrospective raindrop which formed on lid and wandered down marble cheek.

Three third persons becoming first and second, second and first.

When the sun was high enough for travelling, the castle door sprang wide and ushered forth four figures.

They walked out from the stronghold a little way and turned.

Greencomber pointed at a window. "There is where I saw you and loved you."

They made a quick half-circuit until their feet were damp with dew in the grass where Greencomber had stood to talk to the children. "That was Ben's window. That was Satin's."

Then came the worst part. They returned to the front of the castle and Greencomber set them to gaze at the moon landscape through which they must travel.

He felt the Singer's hand tighten in his own and knew fear. When he looked at her face, she was already regarding his own.

"As long as I keep seeing you," she said. "That was my desolation —the people going away."

The children were straining to step further into the derelict scene. "Ben?"

The boy knew Greencomber wanted an assessment and an assurance. "I can see it and touch it and doubt it," he said bravely. "My impressions will be my own."

"Satin?"

"It's all right. Not terrible. It's nice being able to hold a hand."

They took the downward track, moving more surely as their feet became accustomed to the exercise. Ben, mulling over contact so far with Greencomber because it was precious as a record, remembered something the woodsman had said the previous night. "Was there anybody else?"

"Yes."

"What happened to him?" asked Satin.

"Nothing bad. We couldn't start off with something bad, could we?"

"Then what?"

"While you were sleeping, I got the hang of the place and the person. He persuaded me that he wanted to stay there."

"And he was the one who—controlled—us?" asked Ben.

"That's right." Greencomber was expansive in the fresh day. He could afford compassion—would have to learn to afford it often. "But his only reason was that he was trying to save you from what he thought would disturb you."

"If—" The Singer was still unfamiliar with self-expression. "If he has no-one to safeguard, what now?"

The breeze was coming down off the hill. A sudden tension, a prickling of anticipation set up the ravens and cast them looping in skeins across the battlements.

"Four blind mice," sang the nasal octophonic voice of Wolf Hochbaum. . . .

"Four blind mice,
See how they run,
See how they run . . ."

In reality, only Wolf Hochbaum lived happily ever after.

THE POST-MORTEM PEOPLE

Introduction

"The Post-mortem People" is the first conscious science-fiction story I ever wrote . . . that is, the first work styled in protest at a particular facet of medical technology and using research to qualify that protest.

It had a very warming success for me. Its first outing was in New Worlds for Michael Moorcock. From there, Judith Merril liked it and sought it for her SF12. Judy was patient enough to allow me to rewrite it in a major way and even change the title—to "Beyond the Weeds." The title change was a mistake. The reference to widow's weeds was too obscure by far for a professional communicator. So when Leo P. Kelley wanted the original NW version for his "Themes in Science Fiction" contribution to the McGraw-Hill Patterns in Literary Art, I was able to restore the old title to the new version and thus it stands.

I am grateful to all the above-mentioned for succouring the child over the years and though Judy and Mike did me a tremendous amount of good (as they did so many others) it is the tribute of selection by Leo that keeps me comfortable on cold nights. To think of the work actually being discussed and analysed in places of learning all over the United States is—well—so cosy.

I would like to make one minor didactic point to that dissemination. The story belongs to the time when I believed (and this is the opposite of a boast) that futuristic characters should have names that were vaguely mid-European. That is still an extremely widespread belief within the genre. It requires no particular insight to note that Berke and Hejar are variations of Burke and Hare, the infamous Edinburgh body-snatchers. The origin of "Jolo Trevnik" continues to baffle me, unless blue cheese or bad ale may stand the blame.

This time, Anton Hejar came by chance upon the event. He heard the shrill gathering of locked tyres and was running before any sick-soft sound of impact. The car could be skidding, no more; but one could not afford to stand and wait. One had a reputation.

He shouldered a passage through the lazy-liners on the rotor walk even as a bundle with flapping limbs and thrown-back head turned spitwise in the air. He was at curb-side when the body landed close to his feet.

Hejar placed his overcoat gently to retain a little of the man's draining warmth.

"Somebody get an ambulance," he shouted, taking command of the situation while women grew pale and lazies changed to the brisker track and were borne smartly away.

The man's eyes flickered. A weak tongue licked vainly at lips grown dry as old parchment. Breath came like a flutter of moth's wings.

"How are you feeling?" asked Hejar.

The eyes searched for the speaker, blinked and blinked again to bring him into focus. The man tried to speak, but there was only a rattle like too many unsaid words fighting for an outlet.

Hejar sniffed the air. His nostrils, finely attuned to the necessities of his calling, could pick out death like hollyhock or new-made bread. Yes, it was there, dank and acrid as stale perspiration.

"No need to worry," he told the man. "You'll be all right."

He took off his jacket to make a pillow for the man's head.

"My . . . wife . . . she . . ."

"Don't concern yourself," said Hejar. "Let's get you settled first."

He's kind, thought the man in his mind full of moist pain. Perhaps he just isn't trying to fool me with sentimentality. I feel so cold. . . .

The siren of the approaching ambulance rose and fell on a scale of panic. Hejar moved the man's head gently, looking for marks or a telltale run of blood from the ear. He found nothing. Good. The brain, then, the control center was undamaged. Great.

He went through the pockets of the overcoat covering the man. From one he produced a small tin and opened it, exposing an inked pad. He manoeuvred digits on a rubber stamp.

The man moved feverishly beside him. "You'll be fine, old son," he said gently. "Help's just arriving."

Then he brought the rubber stamp down right between the man's eyes.

Doberman Berke, a morgue attendant of intermediate stature, humbled through life in constant awe of the ubiquitous Anton Hejar. Where death stalked, there, too, walked Anton Hejar, hat pulled low, hand on stamp.

Berke paused in his work to examine the insignia between the corpse's eyes. It was not elaborate, a mere functional circle with script around the outer edging and the characters "A.H." tangled in some written state of intercourse at centre.

"Item and contents property of . . ." read the circumferential legend if one cared to crane one's neck and bend kiss-close to the poor dead face to see.

Berke did no such thing, nor had he ever done so. He knew Hejar's function, knew the language of the snatchers from careful study. Instead, with a curiosity he compared the time on Hejar's stamp— 1434—with the report that accompanied the cadaver. The ambulance men had put the time of extinction at 1434.5. Hejar's professionalism was uncanny.

He detached the item and placed it in a refrigerated container. Then he pushed it to one side to await collection.

Invariably, Hejar came himself. If he had any juniors, Berke had never seen them. Certainly, they never came to claim their master's bloody bounties. Hejar knew Berke's routine. He had already checked the attendant's volume of work. He would be here very shortly.

And even as Berke acknowledged the fact, the door swung wide and Hejar was walking towards him, smiling and beneficent, unfolding a spotless receipt.

Berke took the receipt and examined it closely, though he knew full well it would contain adequate authority from Coroner Gurgin. Dealing with Hejar, an expert in his own field, Berke endeavoured to appear as painstaking and conscientious as Hejar's patience would allow. And Hejar had a fund of patience. Hejar had so much patience he should have had a long face and a penchant for squatting on desert cactus plants to go with it. Instead, he just smiled . . . and in that smile lay a chill warning that if you didn't move fast enough to prove you were alive, then Anton Hejar would take you for dead.

Berke handed back the receipt. "Any trouble this time? Sometimes sector centre gets a little old-fashioned about dispatchment at speed. Like sympathy for the dependents."

"Sympathy is out-of-date," said Hejar blandly.

"Absurd sentimentality about a piece of stiffening flesh." He showed his teeth again, setting up laughter wrinkles around his blue, blue eyes. "Gurgin knows where his steroids come from. He gives me no complications. A little blind-eye money for his favourite dream pill and he is always prepared to write me a rapid registration marker. Now, is this mine?"

He moved towards the container and identified his designation, humming busily to himself. He caught up the container by its handle and started for the door.

"Wait."

"Why?" Hejar spat out the word with a venom that made Berke writhe, but his face, all the while, was mild, his manner charitable. "Why," he said, more reasonably.

Hejar was no stranger. They met elsewhere and often and dialogue came far more easily where surroundings were no more indicative of the one's vocation than the other's.

Berke felt foolish. There were always questions that occurred to him moments before Hejar's arrival at the morgue, and each time he lined them up and rehearsed a conversation which, he hoped, would impress Hejar with its depth and insight.

But when Hejar came, it was as though he dragged the careful script out of Berke's head and bundled it into a corner. Berke was tongue-tied. Hejar, as ever, was sunny. Today was no exception.

"Why?" Hejar asked again, patiently.

Berke stumbled. "Isn't . . . isn't there anything else you want? The trunk isn't spoken for."

"No wonder."

"I'm not with you."

"The man has been struck by a car," said Hejar with exaggerated diction. He might have talked thus to a retarded child—if he had ever spared a little of his surface warmth for a creature who could do him no good. "Digestive chemistry, kidney system, circulation . . . they're all finished. At most, there may be a dozen organs worth salvaging, and we don't have time for that. Besides, our clients pay more money for bits and pieces."

"Uh-huh." Berke slotted away the piece of business acumen. Sooner or later, he would have to take his chance on the outside—he was fast running out of apprenticeships. And he was determined to sample the lush pastures of the thoroughfare section, with its easy pickings and its first-come-first-served credo. There was small reward, by comparison, in industrial accidents or domestic mishaps.

"Now," said Hejar, "is there anything else?" He made it sound like a polite inquiry, but Berke knew that he delayed the man further at his peril. He didn't want to leave his room one morning and find Hejar waiting to follow him. He shifted from one foot to another.

"Oh, yes. Forgive me." Hejar reached in his pocket and tossed a handful of notes across to Berke. They fluttered on to the separation table. In the time it took Berke to wipe them clean of tell-tale stains, Hejar was gone.

Jolo Trevnik locked the weathered door of his downtown Adonis League and wondered, as he wondered every night, why he tried to carry on. Once, his culture clinic had been definitely uptown and well-filled with rounded young men who slung medicine balls at each other and tested their biceps in crucifix poses on the wall-bars.

Ironic how, when you had survived everything else from social stigma to national laziness, finally location turned against you. The people had moved away into apartment blocks on the town periphery, leaving the centre purely for business and only that which was conducted in skyscraper settings.

These days, Trevnik exercised alone, moving slowly from one piece of apparatus to another, not because he had himself slowed up, but because now only time hung heavily on the wall-bars.

His suit grew progressively shabbier and his fortune, body-built in the days of blind, rootless activity that followed the tobacco ban, grew correspondingly smaller. As did his steaks and his health-food orders. He was still in fine shape . . . and frustrated as only a man can be whose sole talent has become redundant.

He turned away from the door and walked towards the main rotor quay. A shadow in a doorway down the street moved to follow him.

Hejar had made only a token attempt at concealment and Trevnik knew of his presence. It was part of the new fatal system that had emptied Trevnik's clinic and all others around the town, and all football grounds and all places where excitement or over-exertion might bring unexpected eclipse. The body that had once been so envied in life was now attractive only in terms of death.

I guess I ought to be honored, Trevnik thought. But I feel like a cat in heat. I'll make the pink punk work for his money.

At the rotor quay, he selected the slow track and moved quickly along it. He wanted to put the idlers in his pursuer's way and they made no protest, silent, turned inward with the seashells in their ears filling their minds with hypnotic rhythms and whispered words.

Above the whine of the rotor and the passing traffic, he heard the man stumbling after him, heard him cursing, and laughed.

At the next junction, he transferred to a faster track, still walking rapidly, weaving neatly between the younger mutes, with their frondular arms and snapping fingers.

Hejar was less adept and less gentle. Once, he jostled a young man so violently that his ear-piece slipped to the moving pavement.

The youth recovered it and pursued the pursuer long enough to tap his heels and send him headlong before returning to his reverie.

Trevnik heard the resultant tumble and allowed the pavement to bear him along until the dishevelled Hejar regained his feet. Then he back-pedalled until the man drew level, still dusting himself down. He raised the pitch of his voice a deceptive shade.

"I hope you didn't hurt yourself," he said, fussily . . . too fussily. "Perhaps we should walk a little more slowly."

Hejar eyed him warily. "I'm quite recovered now," he said. "Thanks for your concern."

If the guy knows why I trail him, he wondered, why doesn't he show it? Why this spectacular concern?

"Perhaps I should walk with you in case you feel suddenly faint," said Trevnik. "If you're shaky, you ought to get to bed. Are you sure I can't help you?"

The attitude jarred on Hejar's sensitivity. He began to notice other things about the man. How he moved—almost mincingly. The breeze that played on their faces as they were drawn along the track brought a musky aroma to the nostrils grown acute with death. Hejar swallowed and looked at the man again.

"Really," he said, almost defensively. "It's all right. The next quay is as far as I go."

"As you please," said Trevnik. His lips tightened with a hint of petulance. "But if there's the smallest thing . . ."

"Nothing," said Hejar, savagely.

Trevnik rode beside him, barely glancing at him but carrying the smug conviction of a man who has done a good turn only to meet an ungracious response.

Smug? Hejar, sneaking glances at Trevnik from the shelter of his hat-brim, became even more apprehensive.

Trevnik's finely developed limbs and torso were bound to fetch a good price. Or were they? Trying to sell internal organs marred by chromosomatic complications or a brain whose motivations were neither particularly masculine nor blatantly feminine but in some twilight in-between . . . that had definite setbacks.

At the quay closest to his office, he disembarked. "Thanks for everything," he said.

"I hope we meet again," said Trevnik. He waved until the rotor bore him out of sight.

There was no doubt Trevnik had a physique rarely seen among the squat inhabitants of 1983; a body which, if properly marketed, could still prove profitable despite . . .

Hejar chewed his sensual lower lip. Despite nothing. He had kept observation for weeks now, at first unnoticed and lately unheeded. In the beginning there had been no such doubts proffered. It was just today? Hejar could not be sure that the disturbing traits had not been there for some time. Certainly, they had not been apparent when he began his vigils. And that was it—a device, dated from the time Trevnik first noticed that the snatchers were on to him, or at least some time subsequent to that . . . when he thought of it.

Hejar felt better. The fall had shaken him, had made his heart pound alarmingly. But now he had rumbled the man, his good spirits returned.

Any fresh measures to protect the remains after death intrigued him. There was, after all, no pain, no occupancy, and post-mortem activities were unlikely to disturb the main participant. But the sanctimonious sprouting of the sixties and early seventies still persisted though even the government had officially classed them out-of-date. There remained in certain circles a horror of disturbing the corpse. Hejar had long ago shouldered and forgotten the inferences of obscenity and laughed all the way to the credit pile when somebody called him a ghoul, a cannibal, a necrophile.

"I do mankind a service," he would tell people who questioned his motives. "The burial grounds have been used up, built over, defiled in asphalt. The crematorium has a use, but it is a great leveller. How do you identify ashes? Items that could be vital to the living are wasted in the flames. Far better, is it not, to have a scroll stating that even in death, your dearest are unselfishly helping those who continue to suffer. I aid medical science. I am trained to the task and my spirit is right."

"If I can help somebody," he crooned raggedly as he entered the block where his office was situated, "as I pass along . . ."

He boarded the elevator and pressed the button for the eleventh floor.

"Then my living shall not be in vain. . . ."

The elevator wound upwards. Head bowed, Hejar was engrossed in the half-remembered song.

"Then my living shall not be in vain . . . Oh . . ."

The elevator shunted him into the eleventh floor berth. He opened the door of his office.

"My living shall not be in va-a-i-i-n-n-n . . ."

The woman in the guest chair had red-rimmed eyes but she watched him intensely.

"Good evening," he said calmly. He was used to finding such women in his office. One pair of red eyes looked much like another.

"I've been here for hours," she said.

"I didn't know you were waiting," he said, obviously. He did not concede the necessity for an apology. Instead, he smiled.

"You are . . . Mr. Hejar, the . . . reclamation . . . man?" Hejar's smile had disconcerted her, as it had been meant to do. The smile therefore broadened.

"I've been sitting here, looking at your . . . pictures," she said, gesturing vaguely at the Ben Maile skyline and the Constable pastoral. "They're not . . . what I . . . would have expected."

Hejar hung his hat and coat carefully on the old-fashioned stand. He took his seat behind the desk and built a cathedral nave with his fingers while the smile lay dozing on his face.

It was always best to let them talk—as much as they wanted to, about whatever they wanted to. Gradually they would work their way round to the inevitable plea.

"What had you expected, Mrs. . . ." He deliberately left the sentence hanging in the air.

"An office without a single rounded edge. No softness anywhere . . . everything sharp and cold and soul-less."

She would tell him her name and the reason for her presence in her own time. He would not prompt the revelation because it was important to maintain a singular lack of interest.

"I think pictures add another dimension to an office," he said.

"Constable had a way with water, an eye for minute detail. I often think he sketched every leaf. Maile, now . . ."

"You're probably wondering why I am here," said the woman. She was fortyish, plump, not unbecoming. She was in pain, with her loss, with the alien circumstances in which she now found herself.

"Take your time. I know how it is. . . ."

"I'm Elsie Stogumber."

Stogumber. Hejar switched on the audiostat which unscrambled the data from the long-winded secretary computer.

"Stogumber," he said into the feeder piece.

"There would hardly be anything recorded yet," said the woman. "Today?"

The woman twisted her gloves in her lap.

"He asked for you," said Hejar.

"Small comfort to me now." The woman seemed mesmerised by the anguished play of finger and nylon. Hejar waited.

"They say you—you had his head."

"That's right."

The woman watched his face for perhaps five seconds. Then she went back to her glove play.

"You wouldn't still have it?"

Hejar's stomach churned. His vocation was bloody enough, even viewed with the detachment he brought to it, but . . .

"Why?" he asked. The smile had gone.

"I suddenly couldn't remember my husband's face. It terrified me. If I could just . . ."

"I no longer have it. My clients demand prompt delivery."

"Your—clients?"

"Come now, Mrs. Stogumber. I'm sure you realise the complete situation. You already know exactly what came to me. You also know why and that I am only an agent in this . . ."

She screamed once, sharply. But her face was unfrenzied. It seemed impossible that such a sound had uttered from her.

"Who has it now, then?" she asked. Her voice was controlled, but only just. "Who has it?"

"My dear Mrs. Stogumber . . ." Hejar found another smile and slipped it on. "Will you not be satisfied if I say that your husband is beyond any inconvenience or pain and that his last thoughts, to my certain knowledge, were of you?"

"No. It is not enough."

"What would you want, Mrs. Stogumber?"

"Ideally, my husband. Or at least, some part of him."

"But he's *dead*, Mrs. Stogumber. He's gone. He is nothing without the spark of life. Why prolong the parting? Why mess up your pretty dress, Mrs. Stogumber?"

The woman crumpled visibly in the chair. Her shoulders shook and she took in great gulps of air.

"Don't you have any movies of him? No threedees, maybe?"

"He went out after breakfast and I'll never see him again. You—you buzzards chop him up before I can even . . . identify him."

The fight for breath became less laboured as tears began to flow. Hejar let her cry, thankful for an escape valve. He wondered what he could say when she came out of it. Evening edged a little closer to night. Her sobs softened to an occasional sniff. She blew her nose and then looked up.

"It usually helps if I explain," began Hejar. "You see, when in 1973, the Central Committee rescinded the Anatomy Act of 1823 and the Burial Act of 1926 . . ."

"I've seen you," she said. "All of you. Waiting at busy road junctions, chasing ambulances, trailing feeble old men . . ."

Her voice was close to hysteria. He rose, walked round the desk, and slapped her hard. She fell silent.

"You might feel different if you understood our mission," he said. "We are not buzzards. We play a vital role. To benefit the living, we make certain adjustments to the dead. Nobody suffers by it. The Salvage of Organs Act of January, 1974, gave us the full power of the legislature. This was tantamount to a declaration that the racket in kidneys and heart valves and limbs that had thrived up to that time was accepted as inevitable and made conventional. We have new thinkers now. Wasting precious sentiment on a pile of gone-off meat was not progressive. Surely you can see that."

The woman took a deep breath. For a moment she teetered on the verge of more weeping. Then she struggled on.

"I accept it in theory," she said. "It seemed to make good sense at the time. Things like that always do when you are not involved . . . But I've seen the way you work. You salvage men don't just wait for death—you prompt it. Surely, if you are the public servants you say you are, you shouldn't have to compete with each other."

Hejar swung his feet up onto the desk. Now the situation had resumed a calmer plane, he could pick and choose his words. He clasped his fingers behind his head.

"Now there, admirable Mrs. Stogumber, you have hit upon our problem. This is a living as much as a vocation. I must play as others shape the game. If there is a certain—over-enthusiasm, it is not of my choosing. But I have to absorb it if I am to continue in the practise. As long as there are people who deplore this trend, there is a chance that it will be thrown out. You see, there are so many new people trying to make out. As yet, we have no control over membership. The dignity that once went with this calling . . . the pathological training . . . well, you know how it is. You open a door and all manner of undesirables flock through it."

"I'm sorry," she said. "For acting like that, I mean. It was childish of me." She tried a wintry smile.

"I am sorry, too, Mrs. Stogumber, for having to resort to such extreme measures. Your present composure impresses me considerably. Perhaps you find the situation a little easier to accept now."

She smiled again, a little more like autumn now.

"When somebody takes the trouble to explain, it helps," she said.

"The 1974 amendments to the Human Tissues Act of 1961 . . ." said Hejar. She stopped him with a raised hand. "Now, Mr. Hejar. I fear you are trying to blind me with science."

High summer shaped her lips. Hejar swung his feet off the desk, stood up, and came round towards her. "Not at all, my dear lady . . ."

But Elsie Stogumber was clear of her chair and through the office door before he could reach her. Her summer was not for Anton Hejar.

Hejar stood on the permanent walkway opposite the gymnasium and made no attempt at concealment. Such intrigue became ludicrous with repetition, particularly when all parties were aware of the charade that was being played out. Now, he did not veil his intentions even out of courtesy.

He was too little of the hypocrite, he told himself, but even in that, he lied. He stood so because he liked to watch Trevnik's dark face as the man noticed him, to see the nostrils flare and the eyes go suddenly wild as if in fear of an old superstition, and then just as suddenly narrow and normal and carefully averted.

He heard a descending thunder on the stairs. Trevnik must have seen him, given the advantage of darkness looking out on light, because he simply showed his back as he locked the door and started down the street.

In no apparent hurry, Hejar crossed the road and fell into step about twenty yards behind the giant. Today, he saw nothing suspect in the man's gait. Trevnik, presumably, had given up any pretense and walked now only in a way that exhibited the disciplined thrust of hip and leg.

Elsie Stogumber, cramped from her unaccustomed sojourn in the narrow doorway once occupied by Hejar, emerged into the mid-day brilliance and watched the two men down the street.

Berke took a final wheat-germ sandwich and pushed the remaining pile along the bench to Hejar.

Though he had long since ceased to be troubled by his occupation, his appetite had never returned. Each day he prepared more sandwiches than he would eat.

And each day, still feigning surprise at the meeting and hungry from his hunt, plump Hejar joined him on his bench at the leisure zone and waited politely until Berke had shown himself fed to sufficiency and offered him the surplus.

Berke washed his mouth out at the nearby drinking fountain, spat, and sat down again.

Hejar chewed, his attention riveted to the children's fun-run, watching for a collision with the spinning chairs or a fall from the helter-skelter.

"We could, perhaps, fill in the loop-holes," said Berke. Hejar grunted.

"The way into this game is too easy," said Berke. "If we study, it is to be eventually better at our job. There is no ruling. It is a labour of love. Amateurs, opportunists can always make inroads. Perhaps we should form a union, or get some recognition from the Central Committee."

Hejar shrugged. He was uninterested in Berke's theorising, his verbal attempts—in his incompetence—to make the living more secure for himself.

"The amount of money the amateurs make, the volume of business we professionals lose is negligible," he said. "What do they get? A relation dies at home. Natural causes. Who pays for natural causes? The bodies are worn out, anyhow. A murder victim is discovered on a rubbish dump in an advanced state of decay. Where's the money in that? No, myself I don't mind who gets the stamp. I can always keep myself well."

In his sudden silence, he indicated his doubt of the other's ability.

"Me, too," said Berke hurriedly. "I was thinking of the less fortunate members of our calling."

Atop the fifty-foot slide, a jostled child screamed and clutched
with vain fingers at the air. Berke and Hejar moved with speed towards the gathering crowd.

The Minerva no longer pretended that the health foods it served
were any more than politely fashioned simulants or, at best, sal-
vaged from some overgrown delicatessen. But at least the cafe still
retained certain of the musty odours that had once given herb stores
an impression of geography contained within three walls and a display window.

Jolo Trevnik avoided the glassed-up, crowded planktonia. His
stomach, accustomed to a balanced carbohydrate intake, turned on
the lead oxide that came with every boxed cereal these days, a
legacy of the brightly painted free gift needed to sell any competi-
tive product.

His system revolted against battery lamb and the beef and
chicken, he knew, contained sterilizing agents. Not that he was bothered particularly about potency. The unborn were the lucky ones,
he reasoned.

A shape above his table cut out the light. Momentarily, he
started, his mind still fixed on the snatcher with the Santa Claus
face.

Then the woman sat down opposite him and he noted the carefully highlighted features and the over-bright eyes with a measure
of relief.

He took a sip at his acorn coffee to steady his nerves. When he
put his cup down, she said, "Mr. Trevnik?"

He nodded.

"I saw the name on the door of your gymnasium."

"But that's a long way away. What . . . ?"

"I followed you," she said quickly. "I couldn't help noticing I
wasn't the only one."

Trevnik dropped his eyes and considered the grey coffee. He felt
—unclean; a curiosity, a freak. All the more for having someone else
notice his humiliation.

"I'm sorry for you," she said, and that made it worse.

"You don't need to be sorry, lady," he said, almost angrily. "It
doesn't bother me. I look after myself. I avoid accidents."

"My husband was the same."

"Should I know your husband?"

"I think he came to your clinic a few times—Harry Stogumber."

"Stogumber."

His echo of the word chilled her with a memory.

"Tall man," he said. "Not too fat. Not much meat on him at all, really . . ."

"Please." The woman laid her gloved hand across his fingers.

"I'm sorry," said Trevnik. "Did I say something . . . ?"

"A phrase. It has associations. . . ."

Trevnik went over it in his mind. " 'Not much . . .' " He bit his lip. "I am beginning to understand," he said. "I didn't realise. Forgive me, ma'am. Maybe I should . . ."

Trevnik freed his great legs from the meagre table and turned his seat at an angle to allow them access to the gangway.

"I hope you're not going," the woman said. "Please don't go."

Elsie Stogumber was running her eyes over the breadth of his shoulders, the width and density of his hands. The frankness of her inspection began to embarrass him. "I was going to ask you a favour," she said finally. "That man who keeps following you. He was there when the car hit my husband. He . . ." She swallowed hard.

"Don't trouble yourself," said Trevnik. "I can work out what happened."

"I want to hurt him," she said. "Really physically hurt him. But what can I do?"

Trevnik looked down at his hands, saw how the tendons moved under the skin.

"So you want me to hurt him for you. . . . Do you know that I have never in my life used my strength to hurt anyone?"

"I could offer you money," she said. He looked up angrily. "But I won't. I can see that you would do it only if you wanted to do it."

"Lady, that man is only waiting for me to die so he can tear me apart. I *want* to do it *now*."

"Then what is stopping you?"

Trevnik clasped his hands to stop them from moving of their own accord. He rested his chin on them.

"It is against the law," he said.

"What law? What human law could possibly deny that I have a right to hurt that man?"

"You, maybe. Not me."

"You could plead self-defence . . . if you said he tried to push you into the road or trip you into the rotor plant, you would have provocation."

"Lady . . . Mrs. Stogumber, ma'am. How could I plead self-defence. I mean . . . I mean . . . look at me. I *look* like an attacker. I *want* to help you, Mrs. Stogumber, but . . ."

"It's all right," said Elsie Stogumber. "I'll find somebody else."

Trevnik found himself on his feet. The woman said no more. All she wanted was for him to stand still while his thoughts progressed. She allowed perhaps fifteen seconds to pass while Trevnik hesitated, towering above her. "Of course, they wouldn't have to *kill* him," she said quietly.

"Maybe if I . . ." Trevnik sat down again. "Maybe if I told them how he'd been following me and all and . . . and . . . taunting me, they'd understand."

Elsie Stogumber let him talk on, convincing himself, committing himself.

"I am sure nobody on earth would blame you," she said eventually. "He is trying to—well, interfere—with you. That's almost an offence in itself."

Trevnik smiled happily for the first time in a long while. "You're right, Mrs. Stogumber," he said. "You're sure as hell right."

Again the plump man waiting on the far pavement; again the thunder down the rotting wooden stairs. Jolo Trevnik emerged and turned to lock the door. Hejar shifted his weight from one foot to another, anxious to be away.

Trevnik turned from the door and looked straight at Hejar. Then he started across the road. Hejar was suddenly afraid. He sought desperately for another purpose to give to his presence.

"That building," he said before Trevnik could reach him. "Doesn't look too safe. It could fall down any time."

"Is that why you keep following me?" Trevnik mounted the curb. "Because you're afraid I'll go down with it? I'm not much use to you crushed, am I?"

"No . . . no. We—my department—we wanted to find out where you live, where you eat, your transportive habits, so we can site your replacement office accordingly. . . ."

"Rubbish," said Trevnik.

"No, I assure you . . ."

Trevnik hit him first on the nose, drawing blood. "See a little of your own," he said pleasantly.

Then he sank his right fist deep into Hejar's solar plexus and followed it with his left. He began to enjoy the way the stout man yielded and swayed before him; the way the flesh gave beneath his knuckles.

He began a methodical destruction, aware that he was going beyond his brief, but somehow no longer able to call back his massive fists.

He chopped down on the nerve centres inside Hejar's collarbones.

"Grave-robber," he said without expression. "My, how you little pink people love to get blood on your hands."

He hit Hejar twice more in the stomach and the man was there, jackknifed in front of him.

His knees spoke to him. Use us. Smash him. But he controlled them. If he used anything but his fists in this, it would no longer be fair, would no longer carry a justification.

Hejar folded slowly to the ground. Trevnik's feet spoke. Let us finish him. Please.

"No," Trevnik shouted. He turned Hejar face upwards then, and with tears streaming down his face, he walked away.

Hejar, his senses reeling, his mouth salty and crowded, saw roofs tipping at him and tried to twist out of their downwards path. But he could not move.

A shadow lingered above him. His flooded nostrils barely caught a woman's scent before a smell he knew only too well, a smell of ancient perspiration.

The woman pushed back his damp hair and then seemed to be going through his pockets.

Hejar closed his eyes. Get on with it, he thought through a blood-red mist. Take my wallet and go.

The woman spoke. "Mr. Hejar." The voice had a familiarity but it defied identification as the torrents of imbalance raged against his ear-drums.

He opened his eyes. The woman bent towards him. Something glinted in her hand.

He tried to scream but choked on his own blood, his own overpowering smell.

"A widow has to make a living somehow," said Elsie Stogumber. Then she brought the stamp down right between his eyes.

SEAGULLS UNDER GLASS

Introduction

This is a true story up to the point where the family finds refuge in a warm, friendly hotel with thatched roof and fantastic menu. Those Siamese cats, thick teacups and mouldering tarts, pork chops and poor rich old people are straight from memory—though rascally Mr. Zachary and his decrepit Cliff Hotel obviously do not use those names.

In truth, I wrote "Seagulls Under Glass" to get Zachary out of my system . . . and found the narrative making excuses and explanations for him. You're supposed to have more control over your creations than that, you know. So those mental somersaults of James Calvin are as much my therapy as his.

But I never went back to *my* Cliff Hotel. Then, I was too determined to enjoy that Hampshire autumn. Now, I am too afraid of what I might find. . . .

The travellers never did above forty miles an hour down through Hampshire villages with domesday names and the flames of autumn licked at the car the whole way.

Exhalations of wonderment took the place of words until Avril, the wife, said: "Trees make death so spectacular."

James, the husband, laughed and changed gear and laughed again. "The fall is to be encouraged," he said. "Leaves shouldn't have to waste time just hanging around."

Avril punched him in the side at the same time as their back-seat son, Anthony, dug him between the shoulder blades. "Don't make fun." Like a chorus, the pair of them. So close in body and mind.

"As a matter of fact"—Anthony enjoyed biology at school—"our teacher said autumn shouldn't be looked at like that at all. Autumn is survival. The tree withdraws its energy from the leaf extremities and just—sort of—sleeps on it for the winter. In spring, it's back at the game again. It's called apical growth. Meanwhile, conservation . . ."

"I think that's a bit of environmental propaganda," said James. "Conservation . . . Look at these little corpses drifting onto my windscreen—"

"Depending on what you mean by life. A snake sheds its skin. You wouldn't call that dying. A tree drops a little of its regalia, hardly extermination." Avril turned back in her seat to wink at the boy.

"Well, you started it," James reminded her, "with all your talk of death and spectacle."

And then the scene was taking on a drier aspect, the trees were spreading out and a lick of the lips was salty.

"We're nearly there." James found a sign and swung off the road and followed a winding lane. Skeletal beeches branching overhead turned the sky into a stained-glass window.

Past a field of stubble, rounding a barn corner, and here was the coast road.

Ahead, a neon, pallid in the dwindling daylight but weak in any event, pinpointed the Cliff Hotel.

As James brought the car to a halt before glass doors almost too narrow to admit a man with a suitcase, the light went out altogether and the evening seemed the brighter for it.

"Just like the brochure," he said. "Only older."

Avril was thoughtful, examining what little she could see of the hotel. There was some kind of courtyard at the back and the seagulls were down at the bins filching their evening meal.

"Well, the food seems to be all right," she said.

They all laughed and the sensation served to bring the life back to their legs.

On the seaward side, a long glassed-in verandah followed the line of the ground floor. Vague figures stirred within like aspidistra spears before a breeze.

"They're watching us." Anthony was quick to give reality a sinister slant. "They're weighing us up."

James depressed his safety belt, opened the door, and thrust himself out. "We won't surrender without a fight."

Anthony came behind, courageous in his father's lengthening shadow. Avril skirted the bonnet and stood at James's left side. Then they set off in step for the entrance.

"I'll come back for the cases," said James. "I don't suppose there's anybody strong enough to be a porter."

"Don't make it worse." Avril's tone was slightly edgy, slightly cautionary.

"I'm sorry." James held the door to let his family pass. When he followed them into the tiny foyer, he almost choked on dust, depression, and ancient urine.

"I—" Avril hesitated, biting down on a first impulse. James knew what she had managed to keep to herself.

"I think," he said, "that we ought to have a pot of tea and take our bearings."

A thin man of delicate features and years indeterminate between fifty and seventy was approaching them with hand outstretched. "Mr. Calvin and family," he said with authority. "It's no trick really. I'm Mr. Zachary and you're the only guests we have arriving this afternoon."

Or this century, thought James. Another fine mess I've got us into, Stanley.

"I can show you to your room now and then perhaps you would like some tea."

"Tea would not go amiss," said Avril bravely.

"Yes." Mr. Zachary smiled, male-conspiratorial. "The ladies don't like to miss their tea."

He led them aloft on stairs which sloped inwards to the walls. On the first landing, they passed an old and unseeing fellow-guest who clicked more in her motion than the adjacent grandfather clock.

Tea in the sun lounge was traumatic and this was how James observed it.

Thick porcelain cups that would not break when they proved too heavy for befeebled fingers; thin arrowroot biscuits which would not make too much of a demand on aging digestion. And for a contrast, wrapped chocolate wafers and flat-bottom tarts that must have been on their way to the supermarket waste pile before the Cliff Hotel intercepted them.

See the ancients suck and swallow. See them enjoy. Sweet Lord, the terror of knowing what was going on.

A draught at the neck. Prompt appraisal of the lounge fittings revealed inches between roof glass and frame, open inches stuffed with yellowing newspaper.

A brush at the leg. One Siamese cat—no, two Siamese cats . . . tracking each other between scrawny brown stockings and dangling Fairisle wool.

The place stank of them. James was almost relieved to discover that it wasn't just his elderly neighbours falling away inside their elderly clothes.

Red sun was immersing itself in the mist that had risen on the October sea. Coastline was made harsh with the complexion of blood and James was the one man to see the nightmare.

The long-term residents were warm and lost in their refined yesterdays and glorious past campaigns—Marie Corelli or Red Letter or Blackwood's Magazine. They nibbled and sipped and thanked villainous Mr. Zachary, who must be a nice man because he was kind to his mother.

Now he takes their twenty-five pounds a week and makes them all pay for the apron-strings that garrotted his good nature long, long ago.

A smile here, a laying-on of hands there, a deft adjustment to a vagrant shawl.

"A nice tea, Mr. Zachary. You can't beat Glengettie—I remember having it with Mama when I was ever so small."

Please keep giving me the things of my childhood, Mr. Zachary.

Limbs wither and synapses perish and nobody sees this as captivity, thought James. Years scale the eyes and the person is satisfied with less than the best.

Only we in our young and middle years who came for an off-season holiday on our favourite coast see the treachery here, the easy money, the dark side of Zachary.

A fiftyish couple called for their relative. She had been sitting, humming quietly and tunelessly for an hour, secure in the knowledge that they would be here and that if she was waiting, she must be early—silly her—and they couldn't be late or unpunctual or reluctant to the task.

They stepped out of the lounge and onto the springy, moistening grass, and disappeared round the side of the hotel, making for the road.

James wondered if they had seen what he had seen and how they could be content to leave a mother in this place. He wondered anarchically whether twenty-five pounds might not be a small price to pay for keeping somebody out of the way.

And when he had wondered that, bent shadows were at the lounge door and the party was back, replacing mother in her basket-chair.

"Thank you so much for coming," she said, and meant it. Five minutes in all—to their car and back, perhaps. Money changed hands, hers to theirs.

Hell's tears, thought James, they're *all* in the game.

"But we can't stay here."

The bedroom light was dim, not more than a forty-watt bulb. There were unmentionable stains upon the linen and there must be more cats in the bathroom.

"I'll lose my mind," said Avril in a voice controlled with difficulty. "One night in this place and I'll be as nutty as—"

She bit on more words. She was getting accustomed to the taste of her lower lip. As nutty as they are but they don't know how nutty they are. Everything is relative.

"You can't stay," said James, "and I can't go."

"What?" A flurry of panic, a beginning of hysteria.

"I can't leave them here. Not now that I've seen them."

"But it doesn't bother them."

"It bothers me. I see the man taking their money—I know how

much because he quoted me a week. . . . And I suspect he weighs them all up before he tells them the terms."

"Well, I'm telling you, James, I can't sleep here—so it's up to you."

The time-honoured trap. "Don't make me choose."

"If you have to think about it, don't bother." The time-honoured retort.

"Please," said Anthony. "We're on holiday."

James sought refuge in the obnoxious bathroom, beating open the tiny window with little regard for casement or hands.

With the fresh air came the strident reminder from the courtyard below that the sea-birds were still at their dinner.

I know why I am troubled, James told himself. I'm troubled because I am thirty-four years of age and now I can do something about these people.

Twelve years ago, my maternal grandmother was ill at her lodgings and the landlord complained she was making a mess with her incontinence. She said he had pushed her onto her bed. He said no. She went to hospital and died an hour after I left her for the night and they never bothered to call me. I was twenty-two. I let it ride.

My paternal grandmother was in an old-people's home. The staff there was pilfering her clothes and her money and I didn't even know about it until years after.

Too soon the first instance, too late the second. The third has to be right on time.

But try explaining that to—

The seagulls had long gone before James quit the bathroom.

The dinner plates came from the same heavyweight set as the tea cups. They were running with gravy, packed with yellow greens and honoured by the semblance of a pork chop.

"Chops," said James. "For crying out loud, how can old people stomach this?"

Avril scanned the dining-room, saw activity among the mashed potatoes and busy jaws dripping juice. She broke her silence.

"Their appetites are better than mine," she said, pushing her plate away. "Give me the car keys and Anthony and I will go and find some food. Don't try to eat this muck, son . . . I'll get you something nice . . . I can't understand you being so selfish, James. I'll never forgive you—"

"I've *tried* to explain . . ." Her husband got so far and then realised that voices were strangers in this grim dining-room and gnarled heads were turning. "Believe me, I don't want to be selfish. . . ."

"Then *remove* us." Reptilian eyes were lidding, heads nodding, tongues clicking at these loud young people.

And with a wrench, James did. He packed the cases and then the family in the car and went back to confront Zachary.

"I find we are going to have to leave," he said with resolution. "My wife has spent the last year nursing her mother through a terminal condition and I am afraid the presence of these elderly people is very upsetting to her. So I will pay you whatever is proper and we will be gone."

"But what about food?" shrilled Zachary. "This is no time of the night to be looking for another place, you know. It's the end of the season. Most of them have closed up."

"All the same"—James pressed money into his limp hand—"I have to look."

Zachary examined the loot. "Thank you," he said. "I hope you understand this is the very minimum. I had put aside your room for three days."

"Three days you don't get," said James, heading for the door.

There, a man and woman and two girls entering.

"We're looking for a place for tonight," James heard the man say.

"You're lucky—I just have a cancellation," said Zachary.

James was too annoyed with himself as a fool to issue any warnings.

But he found a place with almost supernatural ease—a thatched cottage set in a garden and bright with strong lights. There, he and Avril and Anthony ate as though their lives depended on it and he even tried the wine and found it good.

That first night in soft beds and surrounded by good, dark oak with the scent of care, Avril was apologetic.

"When I think of that other place," she said. "Thank you, James, for taking us away from there. I know what it cost you."

"The price of the meal we never had." James knew she wasn't talking about money. "And a night's lodging. Zachary made a quick million."

"He ought to be reported."

"He ought to be more than that."

"Surely we could contact the people who produce the brochure. Or the A.A. and the R.A.C. They recommended it."

"*Listed* it." James was fastidious, for no good reason. "And good-ness knows how many years ago that was."

"All the same, we could give him a lot of trouble."

"I'll give him trouble."

"Now, James, don't be impulsive."

They chuckled together because it could hardly be impulsive to serve fair warning.

"You know what I mean," amended Avril. "Nothing you would regret."

"Nothing I would regret," confirmed James, safe in the private intelligence of his bathroom revelation.

"Those poor people," said Avril drowsily.

"What?" James's thoughts had been elsewhere and yet in the same spirit.

"I—what?"

"You said something."

Avril tried to remember her words but failed. Shutters were com-ing down on her mind. Shortly she slept.

James was alone with the primeval bellow of the Needles light-house and his visions from the afternoon.

James was up when the first thrushes patrolled the tiered lawn of the cottage and away before his family could make objection.

A stiff wind from the west pressed his clothes to him as he crossed the sea-front road, reminding him that this was indeed October going on November and not the day for morning strolls taken lightly.

The dew at his ankles started a shiver right through his body and distracted him from the ceaseless rerun of yesterday's scenes that had coloured his dark night.

But his course was unfaltering. His steps took him back to the Cliff Hotel.

In any event, the pandemonium might well have led him there.

The gulls were down to the bins, attacking their contents with something like frenzy. Except when you thought about it and real-ised that they were merely shrill and that the phenomenon which now held James's total attention was common to many such hotels along this and any shore, to fruit markets and dumps in coastal cities, to all places which offered food within the compass of a sea-bird's hunger.

Even so, the voice of reason had little place in James's fascination.

He watched how the gulls strutted the courtyard, was shocked by their size, saw the merciless action of their necks and bills and found a peculiar parallel.

It seemed that the pork chops of last night had been no culinary success. The birds were making up for that now. From this distance he could see that the bones were still heavy with meat and fat, but they were tossed aside or transported from the spot by successive waves of gulls.

The greens were going, too—bound for the dunes along the beach or across the eight miles to the Isle of Wight. Zachary didn't need a daily refuse collection. These scavengers cleared his waste—and for nothing.

In fact, the shrunken stomachs and meagre appetites within financed the service. Somehow, that made it all a bigger cheat than ever and in so doing, underlined the parallel that James had drawn.

The five-minute visitors were no different from these regular callers. They came because they wanted. They fulfilled their needs and left.

And all the while, Zachary was go-between, safeguarding the sources and seeing that they didn't dry up. Except that the greater scavenging was done indoors. Seagulls under glass.

James turned away and headed for warmth, content that he had made the observation. Knowing that if he thought about it long enough, its significance would become clear as now the mist retreated and the day grew wide before him.

Morning in Lymington was splendid.

At the quayside, tanned men who plied the Solent and talked of the deep sea were unloading nets of grey pebbles.

Anthony went to investigate and was there so long that his mother had to call for his return.

"They're oysters," he said, breathless with discovery. "From here, they go all over Britain. Do you think they have pearls in them?"

Avril waited for James to instruct, but his eyes were cast far away across the reed-banks of the estuary. "James?"

"I'm sorry," he said. "Did you speak?"

"Your son," she said, "asked a question."

"The oysters," supplied Anthony. "Do they have pearls in them?"

"Some do."

"Some of those?"

"I don't know, Anthony. I don't have X-ray vision."

"You can't tell from the outside?"

"Well, apart from the label."

"What label?"

Avril took a hand. "Your father's teasing you. I don't think he knows."

"I said I didn't know."

James's mood was brittle this morning, she thought. She hoped it wasn't going to spoil these precious days. He might improve if they left him alone. "British oysters don't have pearls," she said. "It's all to do with tropical water and a grain of sand. The oyster puts a kind of hard gloss around the sand that is irritating it and that is the pearl."

"Thank you," said Anthony. "That's about right."

"You knew all the time." She chased him over the pebbles of Captain's Walk.

James did not know which way they had gone until Avril shouted. He was watching a gull balanced on the top-sail of a craft put up for winter and wondering why it seemed so alien from the creatures that clamoured in his head.

Lunch in the forest was idyllic. They had parked and locked the car, walking in among the tall green-grey trunks of beech and picking their way past pony spoors decorated with pink toadstools.

Sometimes they would stop and draw in their breath, waiting for the woods to speak. There would be silence, windless and sepulchral, until a branch fell, glancing fellows in its descent.

Severed leaves had lodged feet above the ground in holly bushes of persistent green and would stay there winter through or until they came to dust.

Anthony gave a short, sharp bark once, like a fox, to hear the way the sound died only by degrees, as though the trunks bounced it to and fro until they were tired.

"This," said Avril, "is why we came. Three times a year we should be here—spring, summer, autumn—and I wouldn't say no to winter."

"I wouldn't say no to living here all the year round," said Anthony. "Great."

"Not so great," corrected his mother. "If this was our commonplace, where would we go for our special?"

"We wouldn't need it, Mum. We'd have it."

Ahead of them, a toppled tree lay like a beached whale. Avril passed out meat sandwiches as they sucked at soup from the vacuum flask.

"You're quiet, love," she said, knowing that there would be no answer.

Anthony was more optimistic. "What's your idea of paradise, Dad?"

But James was lost and hopeless on his plain of desolation.

They came to Lepe in the late afternoon with the sun falling and the mist rising like a cushion to catch it. The guide at Beaulieu had said that if they timed it right, they could see the *Queen Elizabeth II* coming down the Solent from Southampton at the start of a New York run.

The guide had reckoned without the haze. Now two men fishing from a row-boat a hundred feet out were just vague silhouettes and the first beacon buoys were glimmering.

The beach facilities hadn't changed much in more than thirty years. The shore was a mixture of shingle, small pebble, sand, and the concrete debris of gun emplacement turned archaeological record.

But the high-tide mark was a joy. Avril had not seen driftwood in more years than she could remember. Here it lay in a profuse ribbon yards across, sculpted by the sea in infinite wisdom and cast up for humanity to varnish and respect.

Here lay a giraffe salted smooth, there a tortured figure, there a witch's face. She and the boy waded into the pile and did not stop until their arms were loaded.

James had tried to join them, knee-deep in drying wrack; had found a piece that drew his attention.

Had cast it from him and gone to sit in the dunes above the search. His driftwood had looked like a bird with wings outspread and head drawn back to strike.

The sense of the morning's vision, it seemed, was pushing very hard for comprehension. James wished he had the understanding of it and then suddenly wished that he did not.

With the car-boot full of flotsam and his family restrained, he drove towards another night.

In the small hours, James was talkative. Avril, coming out of sleep with resentment, had to grit her teeth while natural response was replaced with artificial calm.

"I love you," he said. "Please believe I love you."

The words were passionate only in the sense that they desired to be accepted and absorbed.

But there could be no understanding unless she, too, spoke of what she felt. She would try to do it moderately. "Then why aren't you enjoying yourself? You're—somewhere else—the whole time. How do you think Anthony and I feel, leaving you out? It makes things unpleasant for us, too. We can't really enjoy ourselves without you. What's the matter?"

And James was only too anxious to reply. "Forgive me. It was that—place. It upset me. It set going all kinds of emotions I didn't think I had . . . regrets from way back, buried sadness, sorrows I should never have forgotten."

"But you had them at the time."

"No. That's just the point. At the time, I was too young or too stupid or just too distant to feel what I should have felt."

"All the same, James, you can't start grieving now."

"I can't stop. As long as that place is there, as long as Zachary does what he does, it is a bereavement for me."

"But, my darling, there are people living like that—Zachary *and* his ancient guests—right up and down this coast and lots of other coasts. It's a fact of human nature. There's nothing you can do about it. People don't change. People *won't*."

"Then I have to make them."

"Now look, James. Don't be—impulsive."

But this time the giggle didn't work.

Another tack. "We're your responsibility now, James, not long-dead relatives. You should be working to make *us* happy. Now how about it in the morning?"

"By all means," said James easily. "After breakfast, we start this holiday all over again."

As simple as that. After breakfast, the debt would be paid.

He must have slept because he dreamed.

In the early morning, with the mist lying like a blanket close against the shingle shore, James walked on the cliff-top.

Today was beautiful, not just in the natural sense but in the notion of an answer and a direction for the feet.

The whole of the water-line for miles along the coast was clear, as though this were not the drop-off between land and sea but the one side of a ravine, with the fog-bank as the other.

Small waves creamed across the floor of this ravine in a contradiction of flow that mattered very little to the man in a hurry.

James moved fast and already he could hear the gulls calling, began to see them circling high above the Cliff Hotel.

Any time now they would be down for their *petit dejeuner* of scraps from the abortive dinner of the night before. Meat for breakfast—James shuddered at the prospect and his stomach turned in agreement.

Off the cliff-path, across the springy turf, and into the back of the hotel, with the great birds dropping ever lower.

Zachary was in the kitchen, measuring oats into a pot. There was little resistance as James rendered his solution. Perhaps the man was even too ready but that was not a consideration to stay this feverish hand.

James donned an apron and worked fast. When all was complete, he took himself off to the cliff again to wait and watch.

The first gulls sheered away from the bins as he passed but by the time he walked a chosen distance and swung round, they were already back at their meal.

They seemed to have passed the word. If a sky could be black with white birds, here it was, with the sun blotted out and the clamour incredible. Somebody must surely hear and suspect.

They came west from Christchurch, east from Lymington, north from the Isle of Wight.

They swooped, they took, they veered away with their scraps. Fish-heads, vegetables, and morsels of a meat rather darker than pork. Raw meat, sweet and freshly killed.

In the midst of their cries, a new voice. It was a voice so weak that the effect was strange. A voice and then another, faltering. Pale humans at opening windows.

"Mr. Zachary, you forgot my tea."

"Mr. Zachary, my hair won't curl."

"No shaving water, Mr. Zachary."

Zachary, Zachary . . .

"I can't move my legs."

"My head hurts."

"Keep giving me the things of my childhood, Mr. Zachary."

Voices that put the gulls to flight and flung James back like hammer-blows. Getting through at last. Putting daylight in his mind and air under his feet.

Not all old life but one new truth James saw as he toppled towards the sea. The long-term residents cannot choose their autumn. They only make the best of what they can afford.

Now waking intervened.

The grey dawn of an uncertain day lay beyond the windows and James took himself, moist with night fever, to the cushioned sill.

The dream had provided a realisation that persisted. Zachary offered a service. From James's cosy, young middle-aged, family-surrounded point of view, it was unsavoury, even immoral.

But if you were old and alone and glad of any small attention you could buy, what then? Zachary took their money. Well, maybe he earned it. The reluctant relatives who sponsored his good works obviously thought so. And if there should be no money and no Zachary, what then?

All manner of needs going unanswered. The whole curriculum of hungers unrelieved. There had to be a Zachary and perhaps this present gentleman was doing the best he could with the flock of aged albatrosses he carried round his neck.

That was fine, the day dawning inside and out. But the needle sharpness of the vision stayed with James and made him anxious for the man's welfare. Suppose . . . suppose he *had* done something to Zachary. Suppose, in the night, under the influence of the melancholy that had haunted him all day, he had gone to the Cliff Hotel and settled his account.

Unlikely. His feet were unmuddied, his clothes were as he had left them on going to bed.

Even so . . . Perhaps he had to see the man and the place again to get his perspective right. And then he could forget it. Creating a situation where the matter could be discarded, surely that was part of his promise to Avril.

The day was yellowing now. He dressed quickly and left the cottage. All too soon he was on the cliff-edge and looking down at the way the fog sat like an opposite side of a ravine, with the waves flowing from that side to this.

When the gulls began their strident circling, he had to pull himself up short in the conscious knowledge that everything so far was identical to his dream.

He deliberately dragged his steps. He willed the creatures down upon the bins before he could reach the courtyard and in that, they obliged.

True, they scattered at his approach but he was moving towards the Cliff Hotel and not away from it.

No window sprang wide, no plaintive voice accosted him with painful truth—and the kitchen was empty.

Sounds came from the store-room.

Zachary was bent over the deep-freeze, selecting the victuals for the day.

He had already put aside the meat.

It was a no-more-cash, elderly human torso.

Avril awoke to find that James had gone for his walk without money or keys. She searched out Anthony and saw him washed and dressed. Then they went hand-in-hand downstairs to wait for James and start the holiday afresh.

THE DAY THE WIND DIED

Introduction

This title and the names of the two main characters are all that survive of a heavily derivative venture from days when storytelling was more like wishful thinking for me.

It is the first (there are a lot of firsts here for a lot of reasons but this is the only first for this reason) story to benefit from a by-no-means infallible policy of mine never to throw anything away.

After small success with other stories and large dollops of ego-boost from those professional encouragers Merril and Moorcock, I put my three-published-works maturity to the task.

The happy result was, I finally managed to produce something good enough for Ed Ferman.

I said hanging on to rejects doesn't always work. When I want to be sure to make my agent laugh, I just say: "Felicemare—The Inside Story."

Meanwhile . . .

Grandpa was up on the roof again. He watched the milk float moving down the street and saw the mailman come and go.

All the while, he kept his left index finger erect, well-licked and waiting for the wind.

He had climbed out the dormer window which shadow-lit his attic before the others were stirring and edged along the sill and onto the roof parapet, mouthing his tune.

> "I'm an airman . . . I'm an airman
> And I fly, fly, fly, fly, fly
> High in the sky,
> See how I fly.
> Sparrows they can't catch me
> No matter how they try.
> I'm an airman . . . I'm an airman
> And I fly, fly, fly, fly, fly . . ."

The song was with him now and he flapped his arms experimentally, as much beating time as testing his buoyancy.

The breeze caught his shirt and plastered it against his meagre shanks. He remembered his mission and licked his finger again, thoroughly.

The mailman had caught the movement, shielding his eyes against the roof-level sun. He waved.

With his free right hand, Grandpa waved back.

"Have you brought my wings?" he shouted, though he knew full well the mailman had only delivered—would only ever deliver—the perennial round of circulars, bills, and letters to other people.

"Flew out of my bag," called back the postman. "That's the trouble with these air-mail packages."

I wasn't cut out to be a comedian, he apologised to himself continuing down the street, or I'd be delivering my own lines instead of everybody else's. Humour the old guy, that's all I'm trying to do.

"Watch out for the helm wind," he called back over his shoulder.

"Hey!" Grandpa's excited yelp caused him to turn back. "What helm wind?"

Now for it. Perhaps he had said too much. Well, now he had to go on with it. The mailman sorted the pigeonholes of his mind. Helm wind?

"Due today," he shouted. "Wind from the hills. Light close to the ground and lively up in the air. Just your style."

He watched the old man wet his finger again; watched him turn like a Father Time weather vane in search of the helm wind.

Breakfast time. A good time, thought Charlie Parkwood as he lathered his face and slipped a new blade into his razor. A bacon and toast time of full stomachs, warming bodies, and new-day optimism.

With the window half down to freshen the air and the bright bathroom fittings close to him, this was the time of day, the place in time, when Charlie took stock of himself.

Face young and pink beneath its soap beard. Eyes protruding slightly. Like goldfish, thought Charlie, with a head like a bowl to match. Lots of little golden ideas swimming round. Likely today, one of them will come up for air.

I'm a bright young man, and Beth and I and the kids, we're going places. Prosperity looms . . .

He shivered in his vest as a breeze puffed itself over the window and goose-pimpled the room. The first faint nagging of reality came with it, a starting sap to his bouncing but brittle high spirits.

Bright young men, confessed Charlie to his image, were not going grey at the temples. The mirror swayed slightly in the wake of the retreating breeze.

Those ideas are there, he reassured himself, as he did every morning. All they need is somebody other than Beth to listen to them.

Beth, he thought, and the warm glow set in. Beth had listened to him until she knew his vain boasts better than he did. Even corrected him at times—that made him see sadly just how futile it all was.

Was it that the big boys at the met bureau weren't listening to him? Or was it that he wasn't making enough noise for them to hear. Let's not fool ourselves, Charlie boy, he spat at his reflection. When you talk to anybody outside, you're as ineffective as a pint of automat tea.

Breakfast time. A time when Charlie Parkwood took stock of himself—and was sickened by what he saw.

He was cutting a swath down his cheek when the window rattled violently. Suddenly the mirror was off the wall and coming towards him, with his face climbing crazily out of sight above its upper rim as it fell short, bounced on the edge of the washbasin, and landed glass down on the floor, scattering slivers.

Charlie, looking down on it with his hands shaking and his heart pumping, felt a warm trickle along his jaw-line. He brushed his chin and his fingers came away red.

"Beth," he yelled. "Beth, where are you?"

The mailman entered the telephone booth, inserted his credit disc, and dialed a town-centre number briskly.

"Eccentricities," he said, when the connection was made.

"File your report." Eccentricities wasted little time on the trivia of polite conversation.

"There's an old man on Acacia Avenue," said the mailman, undeterred. "He is nutty about flying and about the wind. Stands up on the roof waiting for it. Asks me every day about wings. He's an eccentric, if ever I saw one. Harmless, maybe, but . . ."

"The assessment isn't yours to make," snapped the metallic voice at the other end of the line. "We examine the latent hazards right here. Good of you to call."

"Think nothing of . . ." said the mailman. But the line was dead.

Grandpa joined the family for breakfast, humming furiously. He ran a rheumy eye round the table, resting his gaze perfunctorily on the strip of plaskin which lined one side of Charlie's jaw. He made no inquiry.

"Wind coming," he said and applied himself to his cereal.

"There are always winds," said Charlie, impatient at his father's apparent lack of sympathy. "Too many damn winds."

Beth made a remember-his-condition face at Charlie. Grandpa went on eating.

"Mailman told me," he said. "Knowledgeable fellow. Knows as much about winds as you do, Charlie."

Charlie sighed. "Expect he does," he said. "Computers, they're my field. I might be able to tell the mailman a couple of things he doesn't know about systems analysis."

"You *ought* to know something about winds," said Grandpa. "You work in the weather bureau."

"On *computers*," said Charlie. "I just *feed* them with *statistics*."

"Ought to be able to run a few winds past the window occasionally for your own flesh and blood. Seems stupid to me, working in the weather bureau when you don't know the first thing about weather."

"Like trying to fly without wings," said Charlie callously. "Like climbing around the roof in your nightshirt."

But old Hiram Parkwood was back in his own sweet world again, taking pot shots at a Zeppelin, coming out of the sun on the tail of the Black Baron.

"That aileron trouble seems to have fixed itself," he said.

Charlie bowed his head. "I'm sorry," he said, though he knew his father would not hear.

The children came down the stairs in a scattering of thunder.

"I heard a crash . . ."

"I heard a tinkle . . ."

"How'd the mirror get broken?"

"Now children," said Beth hurriedly. "Get started on your breakfast. You don't have much time."

"It was an accident." Charlie was anxious to preserve the status quo and end any speculation. "And stay out of the bathroom. There may still be pieces of glass on the floor."

The children fell to examining their father's battered countenance.

"Is that where Mummy smacked you?" asked Mark, avidly.

"Don't be silly," said Amanda. "Mummy only smacks the backs of your legs. The face is naughty."

Charlie and Beth exchanged amused glances. The children's unconcerned rapport had the effect of steadying Charlie's taxed good humour and restoring lost optimism.

"It was an accident," said Charlie again. "Nobody gets smacked for accidents."

"Not even daddies," said Beth.

"Not even mummies," said Amanda.

"Not even Grandpa," said old Hiram, back from the blue. "Good morning, children. Have you seen the wind?"

"We didn't actually see it," said Mark. "We saw where it went. All across the gardens. It looks like a good one today."

"That's what I thought," said Grandpa. "A very good one."

He was silent, listening for some rattle of the latch, some whistle down the drainpipe.

The house was still. Out over the hedge and down the street, he could see the leaves of the plane trees lightening before the blast.

He settled back against his chair and eased his imaginary Sopwith into a victory roll.

Charlie kissed Beth on the door-step, boxed with the children, and then headed down the garden path. The night wind at autumn strength had brought down dozens of leaves from the garden chestnut, and they lay scattered like big, soggy corn flakes across the lawn.

He looked back over his shoulder, pointed at the rollicking children and then at the leaves. Beth nodded.

There was little if any wind now, although Charlie could hear it, far off beyond the boundary hedge. The roar seemed to grow as he approached the gate.

Stout hedges, thought Charlie. Stout, brave hedges that keep out the weather and keep out the row. He ran his hand almost caressingly through the foliage as he opened the gate and caught the faint ammonia smell of cats on his fingers before he closed the gate behind him and stepped out on the pavement.

A gust caught him and hurled him bodily against the wall.

Then it carried off his hat, laughing triumphantly as he gave chase, howling wild insults in his ears as it kicked the hat further and further ahead of him. Until an unseen hand sewed a painful stitch into his side, and he was brought up short, gasping for breath. The hat grew perspectively smaller in the distance and disappeared.

Charlie, one hand against his side, tried to keep moving as he re-filled his lungs. He was only halfway up the steps to the local monorail stage when he saw the cars pulling away and knew he would be half an hour late for work.

Hardly sheltered by the meagre framework of the stage, he began wondering how his hedge—no thicker than it should be, in truth —had managed to shield the house completely from what must surely be a Force 9. And anyway, the herbiage didn't grow *that* high. What of bedroom windows that didn't shiver in their sockets and chimney pots—his carefully preserved chimney pots—which failed to sigh the passing of the wind?

For the chilling thirty minutes, he thought hard, and by the time the next monorail train hove into view, he was still no wiser.

The children, meanwhile, were stockpiling the last of the fallen leaves where they could dive into them when they returned from school.

In ten minutes, they cleared the lawn completely and stood close together admiring their handiwork.

"It's funny," said Amanda suddenly. "There's something very wrong."

Mark tried to follow her thought. "What?" he said eventually.

"Well, cleaning up leaves is like digging a path through snow. Even while you're digging the path clear, there's more snow falling from the piles you've made at the side, isn't there?"

Mark pictured the instance, had to agree.

"So where are the leaves that fell while we were clearing up?"

"No wind to blow them off," said Mark, proud of his observation.

"Yes there is—listen."

They listened and heard the currents breaking like surf on the town beyond the hedge.

"It's like I said in the bathroom," said Amanda. "We've scared it off. We've killed our little bit of wind. And that's a good way to start the day."

They were skipping round the garden singing, "We've killed the wind, we've killed the wind," when Beth called them to be inspected for school.

Old Hiram fussed over his post-breakfast cup of coffee, blowing on it, sipping at it, grimacing when it stung his tongue, anxious to be up the stairs and away.

With monotonous regularity, he hauled out his ancient watch, scrutinizing it with his tongue moving over his ever-dry, thinning lips.

"I don't hear it," he kept saying. "I don't hear it. It is due. It is due."

Beth, clearing up the dishes, took little notice of the performance. Until, quite suddenly, the old man caught her wrist as she passed and looked up at her beseechingly.

"You don't think Charlie will stop it, do you? After the way I spoke to him this morning?"

"Stop what, Grandpa?"

"Why, the helm wind. You don't think he'll send it somewhere else?"

Beth got herself a cup from the cupboard and filled it with coffee from the nevercool. "Even if he could—which he can't—he wouldn't do a thing like that to you. He loves you, Grandpa. We all do."

"That's as may be. But it is supposed to be here and it isn't. That bureau could have . . ."

Beth put her hand over the old man's gnarled fist.

"I'll tell you something about that bureau," she said. "It is a conceit to say they can control the weather. All they can really do is to forecast what is likely to happen and in some cases, take action to prevent it, like . . . like . . ."

She faltered, unfamiliar with the terminology of Charlie's calling. "Like, for instance . . . imagine a forest fire. A sudden switch in the wind and the fire changes direction. Hundreds of men who thought they were safe are trapped. All sorts of unexpected tragedies.

"Now, where Charlie works, they take readings from weather satellites that are in orbit round the earth. These satellites can keep them informed of the winds they are likely to meet and the hazards. And that way, they can think ahead of the fire. Do you know what I mean?"

It was an imperfect and probably inaccurate illustration, Beth knew. But she knew, too, that old Hiram would know no better than she did and would accept her example as an assurance.

"Don't believe in them satellites," said old Hiram. Beth tried deliberately to look hurt.

Hiram winked. "I believe you, my dear," he said. "If you say it's all right, I'll take your word for it. But I don't allow for those satellites. Heck alive, when I was flying, you couldn't go no higher than a couple of thousand feet because you started choking and getting ultra-violet poisoning and all sorts of things. They say there's men living in those things. I don't believe in them. Anyhow, I know Charlie isn't in a satellite because he comes home every night, so I guess he couldn't do much anyhow."

Beth had given up trying to follow the old man's logic, but she seemed to have cleared Charlie, and that was the main objective.

Hiram found the coffee had cooled to his taste. He sank it so fast a little spotted his shirt front, and then he was gone out the kitchen door to continue his search in the garden.

On schoolyard duty, Miss Alsop found Amanda Parkwood weeping bitterly in the corner reserved for return milk crates and bins heavy with the scent of old school dinners.

Amanda was a member of her class, and so there was no need for the preliminary of introduction as she bent down beside the child.

"I . . . I . . . looked through the railings and they w-w-were hitting Mark," said Amanda with difficulty. "F-Five or six of them all dancing round him and then hitting him."

The yard of the boys' section was divided from the girls' yard by a high railing, surmountable at no point.

It was an old school, like most of the kindergartens in the town. The focus of education had settled on the eleven-to-thirteen age group, the stage when a pupil began thinking seriously about a career and selecting the most meaningful curriculum of studies to that end. The kindergartens and elementary schools had been neglected in the enthusiasm to provide the best equipment, the finest facilities to the children of this group.

In many places, the segregation born of ancient adult taboos still existed in a contradiction of the new understanding of children and their educational needs.

And this was segregation—a little girl who had seen her brother harmed and had not been able to do anything about it.

"Are they still doing it?" asked Miss Alsop.

"No. One of the teachers came and stopped it. He took Mark inside. I shouted, but he pretended not to hear."

"Perhaps he didn't hear, dear."

"He heard. I shouted, 'He's not a liar, honestly.' But they just don't want to know."

"Had they been calling your brother a liar?"

"Yes, jumping round him and shouting it. But he isn't honestly. We *did* kill the wind."

"I'm sorry." Miss Alsop was taken aback. "You said . . ."

"We killed the wind. At least, we scared it off."

Miss Alsop laughed lightly. She pointed at the way the breeze was wrapping Amanda's dress about her knees. "It's blowing now."

"Not here," said Amanda. "At *home*. The mirror fell down and Daddy cut himself and he made a noise and the glass made a noise and now there are no leaves on our lawn. We've all scared the wind off."

"And that was what Mark was telling the boys?"

"Yes, but they didn't believe him."

Miss Alsop had to choose her words carefully.

"Well, it's not every day a thing like that happens. I guess they were jealous. I'll make some inquiries about Mark now on the telephone. You can come and watch me. I think there's a spare bottle of milk round somewhere."

Miss Alsop entered the school's public phone booth and dialed. She smiled comfortingly at Amanda, perched out of earshot with a second bottle of milk and one of Miss Alsop's lunchtime cookies.

"Eccentricities," she said, when the connection was made.

"File your report."

"Well, hello, anyhow. Nice to know you're there."

"Your report," echoed Eccentricities.

"Two children, Mark and Amanda Parkwood, Acacia Avenue, Helm, report they have—quote—killed the wind—unquote—alternatively—quote—scared off the wind—unquote. Apparently, freak climatic conditions are in evidence at their home."

"We shall check," said Eccentricities. "Good of you to call."

"Don't mention it," said Miss Alsop. But the line was dead.

She left the booth and beckoned to Amanda.

"It's all right," she said. "Mark was a little upset, but he's not really hurt. The man teacher said he *did* hear a little girl shouting, but he only heard the word 'liar,' and he thought you were joining in with the boys. That's why he didn't turn round."

Amanda nodded. "Thank you," she said. "You've been very kind. You do believe us, don't you?"

"Of course, dear. It's just that some people might find the whole thing a little unusual."

"I can understand that," said Amanda, happily.

The Westerly weather bureau was a modest, unprepossessing building behind Town Centre, which gave little indication from its exterior design of the work that was carried on within.

The three satellites which straddled the earth on polar orbits at planes of 120 degrees transmitted their data to receiving stations which, in turn, passed on the information to analysis facilities in the world's major cities and from there on down in pyramid formation.

It was a mass—nay, a mess—of data, and the task of local computers was to extract the intelligence which was relevant to their regions and recommend from fed-in principles and precedents the best way to counteract conditions which could be counteracted—a function more prevalent in the neurotic co-ordinates near the equator (where, for instance, a shower of magnesium sulphate could halt a hurricane)—and forecast the likely duration and results of the conditions in more settled climes so that folk knew what to expect, at least, and could make their own arrangements to meet it.

Development of the satellite system had not yet reached the stage where each orbiting satellite could deliver an individual read-out for the region over which it was passing. Hence the need for localized computer units.

This, then, was the eye of the whirlwind, as Charlie had christened it in one of his less formidable moments.

Here he went to prepare his little parameters, feed them like biscuits to the great columns, and then hand on their reactions to the men of the forecast department.

To be truthful, Charlie knew enough about weather in general to know what questions to put to the machines and enough about computers to be able to punch out the necessary programmes, albeit at the close direction of the forecasting staff.

His frustration was at his own incapacity to do either function well enough to be hailed as a prize. He was not a failure, but neither was he a success. Everything he tried, he could do just so well but no better. And therein lay the greatest discontent. Failures can invent lies to cover themselves. Charlie was merely inadequate and no tissue of dreams could disguise that state; no sympathy was spared for the ninety-five percenter.

Every day, Charlie entered the building and scanned the systems for inspiration; some time-and-money saver that would revolutionise the process; some item for the suggestion box that would give him that extra five percent. And every day, Charlie tasted anew the bile of ineffectuality and slouched to his console unsmiling.

Today was different. For instance, Charlie was too preoccupied with his problems to seek out the opportunities. For instance, Charlie had a query that might well start the forecasters feeling inadequate. And that was better than nothing, he reckoned.

When he took his mid-morning coffee break, he saw that Amery was sitting alone in the restaurant. Of all the forecasters, Amery was the most blatantly brilliant. Charlie took his problem to Amery.

"I'm wondering how a windless zone can be created," he said as he settled into the seat opposite the forecaster. "I thought if anybody could tell me, you could."

Amery did not even bother to acknowledge the flattery. He just said, "It can't."

Charlie smiled. Was Amery giving up so easily? He wanted to come right out and say, "Of course it can. I've got one." But Amery's unhesitating reply disturbed him. Perhaps the mystery lay in his own description of the phenomenon.

"I mean, an area which seems to be without wind when everywhere else is bending before a Force 9 blast," he said.

Amery set down his cup with deliberation.

"Obviously," he said, "something is acting as a windbreak. Like hills . . ."

"No hills within miles," said Charlie.

". . . or a strong line of trees . . ."

"No trees that strong . . ."

". . . or eddy viscosity."

"That sounds interesting. Tell me about eddy viscosity."

"If I thought you were taking me for a ride," warned Amery.

"No, truly," said Charlie, dropping the vaguely facetious tone. "I've got a reason for asking."

"Well, think of it this way," said Amery. "Air moves over the surface of the earth like a car travelling on a bumpy road. It is subjected to various little disturbances as it goes, like hills and trees and upward currents of hot air, and these are typical of turbulence.

"In turbulent motion, large . . . like . . . lumps . . . of air called eddies move in all directions as they are carried along by the main current. Perhaps the eddies transfer momentum from one level to another—air in the lower layers may have been slowed by the roughness of the ground and gets mixed up with faster-moving air from above and vice versa.

"Anyway, the result is a braking effect on the air as a whole. This is eddy viscosity, and it produces frictional effects.

"Now when the term representing eddy friction is brought into the equation of motion, the balance is upset, and the resulting steady motion is no longer parallel to the isobars, but slightly across, inclined towards the centre of low pressure . . ."

Charlie let the forecaster talk on through the geostrophic and gradient wind equations. If this was how he remembered it, fine. He would get to the point eventually.

"So, if it is assumed that the flow of air is incompressible—that is, the motion does not change the density of the air—it follows that the pattern of the flow must be such that nowhere does the air pull up or thin out. It is impossible to have horizontal flow into a region from all sides—there must be an upwards motion to prevent accumulation."

"In other words . . ." Charlie was beginning to feel he was getting somewhere. "In other words, if two or more such flows met at a certain point, they would rear upwards like motorcars crashing head-on. And just at that point, in the area over which they are poised, a sort of vacuum forms."

"Exactly," said Amery, so excited over the prospect that he quite forgot Charlie had taken his punch line. "Do you know some place where this has happened?"

"Yes . . . no," said Charlie hurriedly. "I just like—to think about winds, you know, and the things they get up to. I'd like to forecast myself some day." He smiled. "Hey, look at the time. My computers will be dying of malnutrition. Thanks for your help."

He left the restaurant quickly. Amery watched the door for a long time after it had closed behind Charlie. Then he stood up and walked to the phone booth. He checked a number in his notebook and then dialed.

"Eccentricities," he said, when the connection was made.

"File your report."

"Is it all right if I . . . This is the first time I . . ."

"Take a deep breath," said Eccentricities. "Compose yourself. Compose your thoughts. There is plenty of time."

His hair against the telephone ear-piece was wet. Perspiration beaded Amery's brow. The plastoid receiver slipped and slithered in his hand.

He took out a handkerchief and dried his hands and his right ear.

"Now," he said.

"File your report."

"A man, Charles Parkwood, has just been inquiring about freak wind conditions—whether, in fact, an area might be left completely free of turbulence by any natural means. I made various suggestions, and he seemed satisfied. Nevertheless, I suspect that, deliberately or accidentally, he has been able to create an atmospheric situation. I thought I should tell you. His home is on Acacia Avenue in the Helm section of the city . . ."

"We know it," said Eccentricities. "Good of you to call."

"I felt it was my duty," said Amery. But the line was dead.

Old Hiram ate his lunch in a bewildered silence while Beth kept up a stream of inconsequentials in a vain attempt to get his attention.

Both had suffered the encroachment of doubt that morning, old Hiram more deeply but less tangibly than Beth.

She had directed the weekly wash and placed the garments on the garden rotary hoist to spin themselves dry in the wind, gone out an hour later and found them still hanging, limp and dripping, from the immobile arms.

Yet she heard wind somewhere, the rustle of it, the subtle conversation of it beyond . . . beyond the boundary fence?

No. It was a distant engine. It was the monorail.

The children had picked the overnight haul of autumn leaves off the lawn just before they left for school, but no more leaves had scattered since then across the grass.

Now they dropped vertically, spinning only in the draught of their own downfall and raising a natural funeral pyre around the base of the garden chestnut.

Beth stuck her head over the gate and looked along the street. The blast dusted her eyes, and she withdrew with tears brimming. Sure, the hedge sheltered the garden. And what about above the hedge? Wasn't there—what was the word?—"turbulence" at every level?

She raised a hand experimentally and tested for some pressure on her wrist, her palm, her fingertips. But it was impossible to tell whether the flutter in the digits was the passage of air or climbing circulation.

Hiram, leaving the house, had toured the front garden extensively, even climbing onto an ornamental wrought-iron seat so that he could see over the hedge.

He saw the weather vane on the distant church steeple twisting hither and thither in an orgy of activity. He saw the trees of the avenue with their branches bending before the wind. He saw leaves blown in whirling eddies down the road and people hurrying with collars turned up, eyes masked against dust and clothing wound tightly about their limbs.

He watched as a man might watch from a sealed room, through an unyielding window. He was remote from the elements. And they from him.

And now he played with his meal, locked in on his thoughts and doggedly determined that he would not be drawn into fruitless discussion with Beth.

Beth, the while, kept her doubts to herself for fear of exciting the old man and starting up his suspicions again.

"Can't understand it," said Hiram to himself and broke off his lunch to search for pencil and paper and then fill the paper with navigation-velocity equations. He left a great deal of his meal and ascended to his attic bedroom, still without speaking to Beth.

Beth noted the time and resolved to telephone Charlie at the bureau when he had returned from lunch.

Grandpa sat in his window, watching how the rest of the world moved in the face of the storm.

By and by, he had worked some sense into the situation. It was the work of the Black Baron. He was on his way here with a bomb, and he had dispensed with local wind resistance so that it could not affect the drop. The baron had never been much of a mathematician, Hiram recalled, even when they had clashed time and again over northern France. The times Hiram had outwitted him with a tight turn that brought him into an attacking position on the baron's tail, only to have his 18 mm's jam just as he had the Junkers in his hairline sights.

But this was the final insult, bombing a man's home. Hiram had to get off the ground to meet him and down him forever in a dog-fight well away from the house.

His mechanic had his Sopwith turning over on the runway.

Hiram, urgency trapping his fingers, buckled his helmet as he walked out along the narrow strip to the runway. He climbed into the cockpit, strapped himself securely, and gave the thumbs-up to his mechanic. "Chocks away," he shouted.

He taxied to the edge of the runway, moved the engine up to full throttle, and began his run. The wires sang above him, the wind tugged at his silk cravat. He adjusted his goggles, eased back the stick, and was off the ground, moving out over the town as the residents looked up, pointed, cheered him on.

> "I'm an airman, I'm an airman,
> And I fly, fly, fly, fly, fly
> High in the sky,
> See how I . . ."

Then he nose-dived abruptly into the Parkwood drive.

A police patrolman was bending over Grandpa when Beth reached him.

"He jumped off the roof," he said without emotion. "Several people saw him."

Beth looked down upon the broken body and felt sickened—not by the ugly sight but, for some reason, by the audience of ghouls which pressed ever closer up the path.

"He's dead, naturally," said the officer. "Relation?"

"My—husband's father."

"Is your husband 'Charlie'?"

"Charles Parkwood—yes. Why?"

"Something the old man said just as I got to him. The only thing he did say. Sounded like 'Charlie sent away the wind.'"

Beth felt her reserve go. She sobbed uncontrollably. She let the patrolman lead her back into the house.

He made her strong, sweet tea while the ambulance came and went— "No point in going with it. You can catch up later."

And then she talked—about old Hiram's World War I service in the Royal Flying Corps; about how the passage of years had brought a withdrawal into his remembered glories as though the approach of death had sent him scurrying desperately backwards across time in search of refuge; about his late preoccupation with the wind and his association of Charlie; a weather-bureau employee, with the disappointment he felt when the elements defied the demands of his imagination.

The patrolman took it all down in copious longhand.

"I'll have to make a report," he said. "If there are any matters arising from this, we'll be in touch."

Then he departed, leaving Beth to weep afresh before she contacted Charlie.

Station-sergeant Malloy of Helm Division read his patrolman's report on Hiram Parkwood's death fall and dismissed the man with a nod.

"A thing of beauty," he said. "I'll show it to the chief, no less."

He entered the chief's office hard behind his warning knock and handed the report without ceremony across the desk. The chief ran a quick eye over it, picked up his telephone, and dialed confidently.

"Eccentricities," he said, when the connection was made.

"File your report."

The chief went straight into it:

"Incident report on death fall at 79 Acacia Avenue, indicates victim carried conviction that he could fly. Dying words to officer were —quote—Charlie sent away the wind—unquote. Inquiries showed— quote—Charlie—unquote—to be son of deceased Hiram Parkwood. Patrolman satisfied with daughter-in-law's explanation of statement. Are you?"

"Leave it with us," said Eccentricities. "We already have information about this family and this address. Good of you to call."

"My pleasure," said the police chief. But the line was dead.

Charlie sensed before he picked up Beth's call that something of major importance had occurred. She did not make a habit of calling him at work because she knew his routine was irregular and any call might find him at an inopportune moment. Charlie, then, took the receiver with some trepidation. But not nearly enough.

"Charlie? Charlie, something terrible has happened."

Beth had considered asking Charlie simply to come home, but she knew he would press her to be more specific—even as his bureau chief would press him before letting him go.

"Grandpa jumped off the roof."

"*Jumped* off. But why? How?"

"He must have been having one of his—games. He's been inaccessible all day. He kept asking me this morning whether you'd send the wind away."

"Me! How the . . . how could I send it away?"

"I don't know, Charlie. He was afraid because he talked to you the way he did this morning."

"But that was forgotten."

"No."

" 'No' what?"

"Not forgotten. The last thing your father said before he died was, 'Charlie sent away the wind.' "

Charlie found a seat and pulled it towards him so that he could sit down. He felt sick and he was wringing with cold perspiration.

It was enough that the old man was dead. He could encompass that fact. Hiram had lived on the edge of extinction for years now, and Charlie had conditioned himself to the inevitable. But to find now that his father blamed him . . . He had to get Beth to say it again. There might be some misunderstanding.

"He said this to you, did he?"

"No. He said it to the police patrolman who found him. The policeman asked me who 'Charlie' was."

"And you told him?"

"Well, of course. He was bound to find out sooner or later. Look, don't worry about it. I explained about Hiram's . . . ramblings. He seemed to be satisfied."

"He might be, yes. But what about his superiors? Do you think he'll bother to put all that in his report?"

"Well, if he doesn't, we'll have to explain it again. At least he'll say if they ask him that I had told him already."

"I don't know."

"But, Charlie, what's the mystery?"

"No mystery. It's just been one hell of a day, and I don't think it's over yet."

"Come home, Charlie. Let's shut it out together."

"I'll come, Beth, as soon as I can. But I don't think it's going to be a simple matter of shutting the front door."

"Hang on, Charlie. Here are the children. What's the matter, Mark? It's no good, Charlie—I'll have to go. They don't seem to have had much of a day, either. Get home as quickly as you can."

Beth hung up. Charlie went to plead his case with the bureau chief.

The Department of Eccentricities was somewhat bizarre in itself, comprising as it did one phone-talk device programmed with every conversational gambit contained within the combined experience of the BIWI agents and one tape-recorder equipped to take messages.

The premises of BIWI—the Bureau for the Investigation of Weather Inconsistencies (a lump of a name, let's face it)—lay two stories below Charlie's computer room and around the side of the building, behind a door marked "Stores."

BIWI had been conceived in panic—the agencies were ever mindful of espionage and intrigue and anti-social behaviour, and there was no reason to believe that the weather might be any more trustworthy than the Chinese embassy.

But so far the bureau, blessed with an enviable network of agents in all walks (and not a few of the dead ends) of life, had been forced to confine their screening activities to the occasional water-diviner and the even more occasional rain-maker.

No volcano vomited fish upon its island populace, or even lava. Earth tremors were few and easily explained and damage was little—buildings in quake regions, constructed on podia, merely braced their legs and took the strain.

Nobody tried to dye snow blue; nobody tried to capture moon-beams in a jar; nobody tried to direct lightning into the local street-light system. Nobody, in fact, tried anything that might interest BIWI even remotely. Until today.

Today, one Charles Parkwood, whose name appeared in several dictapes drawn from an unusually busy phone, had been accused by his father of his murder. And accused of sending away the wind.

Of course, the old man could be crazy or vindictive or scared. But then there was an entirely independent report on the Parkwood children.

Operative Tyler lined up the reports on the table in front of him and studied them. Then he shuffled them and studied them again. Operative Tempest stood poised and alert at his elbow.

"Looks like the job we've been waiting for," said Tyler, eventually.

"Great," said Tempest. "What do we do now?"

The men came just as they were finishing dinner, unsmiling men who wore their raincoats like uniforms. They introduced themselves.

"I'm Tyler, Helm division chief, BIWI—that's the Bureau of Investigation of Weather Inconsistencies."

"Never heard of you," said Charlie. "I work with weather myself, and I've never heard of you."

"Still not surprising," said the second man. "We are not a publicised, glamourised service. I'm Tempest."

Charlie smothered a grin. "Is that a name or a department?"

"Take your laughs while you can," said Tyler.

A snowfall started in Charlie's stomach. He led the two men into the parlor and indicated chairs. The men ignored the gesture. They moved over to the old-fashioned fireplace and regarded the naked conflagration at first with suspicion and then, as it warmed them, with a momentary glow of well-being. They held their hands over the flames.

Charlie cleared his throat. The men returned their attention begrudgingly to him.

"What was it—you wanted?"

"We had word . . ." started Tempest. Tyler halted him with a glance.

"Certain information has come into our possession throughout today regarding incidents, seemingly unconnected in themselves, which have all been traced back to this address."

Charlie was puzzled. "Oh . . . you mean the old man. Look, my wife made a statement to the police. I have spoken to them myself. It's a family tragedy, but I don't see why it should interest you."

"We've come about the wind," said Tempest. Tyler regarded him with ice-cold disapproval.

"That's right," he said eventually. "There's no wind blowing round this house. Why?"

"How the hell should I know?"

"You work for the weather bureau."

"I'm a technician, not an expert. A guy in the office said something about eddy viscosity, and he could be right for all I know."

Tyler produced a thin sheaf of reports from his raincoat pocket with a flourish. "Do you want me to read them to you?"

Charlie sat down heavily. Dear heaven, what a day!

"Go ahead," he said. At least he might get some inkling of what the man wanted.

"Eight-thirty," said Tyler. "Public operative one-seven-three-oblique-M reported mania of aged male resident at this address for quote flying and wings unquote and quote standing on the roof looking for the wind unquote.

"Ten-thirty: Public operative eight-five-seven-oblique-T reported two children—your children—claiming they had quote killed the wind unquote or quote scared off the wind unquote.

"Eleven-fifteen: WB operative seven-oblique-Met reported you questioning natural likelihood of windless zone."

"Maybe you were working on an alibi," cut in Tempest.

"But . . ." countered Charlie.

"*Thirteen*-thirty: Police operative two-three-nine-oblique-Pat reported fatal fall-type mishap at this address and quoted dying words of victim as quote somebody stole the wind unquote."

He folded the papers methodically and stuffed them back into his pocket.

"It sounds like a murder conspiracy," he said. "A convenient way to get rid of the old man."

"But why would I want to kill him? I *loved* him." Charlie rested his aching head in his hands.

"You would say that, sure."

"What motive?" said Charlie, weakly.

"Maybe he was a nuisance," said Tyler. "And maybe he was an experiment. Once you could harness the wind, think what you could do. This gets to look like a conspiracy against the State, damnit."

"But I *can't*," screamed Charlie.

Beth Parkwood was in the room suddenly, closing the door carefully behind her. At one glance, she took in the men standing stiffly near the fireplace and Charlie sitting with his shoulders heaving in an armchair.

She moved over to the chair, sat down on the arm, and gently but firmly pried Charlie's right hand away from his face. He dropped the other hand and lay back in the chair, eyes shut. Soon he grew calm.

Tempest looked to Tyler for inspiration. Tyler shifted his weight from one foot to the other.

"You might as well know straightaway," he said, "that your husband has been accused of some very serious charges."

"Like what?" Beth was undeterred.

"Conspiring with meteorological forces to overthrow the State," said Tyler. "Causing the death of Hiram Parkwood."

Beth stared at him disbelievingly. "I won't even pretend to understand," she said. "Who are you, anyway?"

"Bureau of Investigation of Weather Inconsistencies."

"An unlikely-sounding title if ever I heard one. Now who are you really? Some kind of maverick market researchers?"

"Madam, I assure you . . ."

"Never heard of you," said Beth, with an air of finality.

"Not surprising," recited Tempest. "We are not a publicised glamourised service."

"And what is your real reason for coming here? I mean, you can't honestly believe any more than you can expect me to believe that my husband's got the weather at his beck and call. As for the other thing, well . . ."

There were still tears left unshed for old Hiram, but when Beth viewed the tragedy against Charlie's present predicament, she emerged dry-eyed.

"My husband loved his father," she said. "As for causing his death, he wasn't even here."

"He didn't have to be," said Tyler.

"Then how . . . ?"

"He just took away the wind."

Beth's mind fled to the clothes that would not dry, the leaves that fell like stones. In the tense silence that surrounded her, she listened for some sound of a passing current, a solitary rattle, a whistle through unlicked lips. She laughed, a laugh pitched slightly higher than her usual rich chuckle. "That's ridiculous."

"Not on the weight of evidence."

"What evidence?"

"We have independent reports here," said Tyler, dragging the papers from his pocket.

"It seems we have been spied upon," said Charlie from a great distance. "By the tradesmen, the kids' teacher, the men in my office. It is hard to believe."

"We have to safeguard ourselves," said Tyler defensively. "This isn't autocracy. It is just a matter of internal security. Our authority over the weather, though it may appear complete to all intents and purposes, is still subjected to occasional boobs and jiggers. We have to keep a watch on every detail."

"If we can control it, anybody else can," contributed Tempest.

"Including your husband," said Tyler. "Particularly your husband, because he works at the bureau."

"As a programmer," echoed Charlie. "I told you, I don't have the know-how to pull off these things you claim."

"Well, *somebody* does. And we have to make a complete investigation. You'd better get the rest of your family in here."

"No!"

"Do it, Beth," said Charlie. "For the sake of my sanity."

Beth went to the door and called, "Mark . . . Amanda."

The children came promptly, glad to be free of the stunned silence that had followed on their father's cry and away from Grandpa's empty chair and the place Beth had laid for him unthinkingly.

Charlie called the children over to his chair and sat them one on either knee.

"These nice men are going to ask you some questions," he said. "It's like a game. Only you must tell the truth. There's a forfeit if you don't."

"What forfeit, what forfeit?" clamoured the children.

"A *big* forfeit. I might have to go away."

"That would be a terrible forfeit," said Amanda.

"Now just tell us," said Tyler, endeavouring to affect an air of benevolence, "what happened that was unusual today."

"You mean about Grandpa?" asked Mark.

"No—before that."

"Right from this morning?"

"Right from the time you got up."

"That was when Daddy dropped the mirror," said Mark.

"I didn't drop it," hastened Charlie. "The wind . . ."

"I *told* you," said Amanda to Mark. "I *told* you it was the wind. 'Seven years' bad luck for the wind,' I said."

"Ohmigosh," breathed Charlie. "Seven years . . ."

At 21.35, nocturnal inversion began to absorb the solid little aura of warm air from the Parkwood chimneys that had enhanced the westerly thermal wind as it moved in to meet the surface easterly fronting a cold depression. The two forces, locked in a convergence that turned them up and over, fell apart; and as the warm air rose, so the cold rushed in to replace it.

The temperature dropped close to the night minimum. The weathercock on the distant steeple caught itself by the comb and did an abrupt spin-turn.

One leaf and then another moved on the Parkwood lawn. The grass stirred as though an invisible hand strayed over it. The front door opened.

"It's colder," said Tyler, chucking up his collar. Tempest felt a draught at his ears. "Wind's sprung up," he said.

They stepped down onto the path to allow their prisoner foot room. Then it hit them.

"Wind's sprung up," repeated Tempest, half in disbelief. "All right, clever fellow. What have you done?"

"What could I have done?" Charlie turned his face to the breeze. "You were with me the whole time. Did you see me flip any switches? Did you hear me mouthing any incantations?"

"All right, all right. We've still got you for murder."

"But how? How did I do it? You admit I haven't been fooling round with the wind—so how could I have taken it away so that Grandpa could fall?"

Tempest chewed his lower lip. Tyler shoved his hands deeper into his raincoat pocket. When he encountered the report sheets, he withdrew them. He shredded them carefully and deliberately. Then he threw them into the air in a gesture of defiance . . . a lost gesture because the new wind caught them and dusted them against his coat.

"Don't bother to pick them up." Charlie was in pursuit already, chasing the elusive fragments across the moonlit garden.

Tyler and Tempest went down the path and out through the gate without looking back. In the middle of the lawn, Charlie discarded his overcoat and then removed his jacket. He shivered luxuriously as the mounting wind plastered his shirt to his body, head back, eyes on the sky, lungs filling with the very essence of the wonderful, moving air.

He saw the moon overwhelmed by great cotton mountains of cumulus and was frozen out of his nuance by the attendant chill. By the time he had regained the porch, rain was beginning to fall.

Diagonally, fitfully, encroachingly.

He opened the front door and called, "Beth."

"On leaving the residence of the accused Parkwood, we observed that there was no longer a marked absence of wind in the region.

"Since there had been no opportunity for Parkwood to restore natural conditions by any manufactured means, we ascertained that the phenomenon complained of (do you think that sounds okay, Tempest?—never mind) the phenomenon which was the subject of the investigation had been caused by some inexplicable inconsistency in the elemental flow.

"Parkwood was therefore attended all proper courtesy and released."

Tyler dragged his first case history from the dictype and carried it to a file close to the office central-heating unit. He singled out the P section and slipped the report away.

Tempest had followed him to the file, almost as though he could not bear to miss the final act of the pantomime. He leaned now on the unit, warming his hands absently before the convector.

"That coal fire was something, wasn't it?" he recalled. "Perhaps one day they'll bring back coal for everybody." He felt benevolent towards subject Parkwood. "I think a man should be allowed one idiosyncrasy," he said. "I don't see much harm in an open fire."

Tyler was only benevolent towards Tempest and himself. "I think we handled it pretty well. Our first case, at that. We couldn't have done better if we'd got a conviction."

"Says something for the bureau that they can find a person innocent," said Tempest. "Well . . . occasionally."

Beth woke in the early hours, sensing that Charlie stirred beside her. Rain spattered the bedroom windows; the wind moved hollowly about the pipes.

"Charlie?" He took her hand and squeezed it three times in their secret pressure code for "I love you."

"I'm sorry—did I disturb you?"

"No. What's the matter? Can't you sleep?"

"I could, I suppose," said Charlie. "I'd just rather listen awhile."

They listened. They heard a rumble and then, a long second afterwards, a splintering crash. "Another beautiful slate gone," said Charlie. "It's nice to have things back to normal."

"Not quite normal. It cost us a life."

"Then it's . . . nice . . . to be able . . . to mourn in peace." Charlie discovered a sudden difficulty with his voice. "It's a pity Dad . . ."

They wept together as the Force 9 northeasterly hammered about the house.

SAME AUTUMN
IN A DIFFERENT PARK

Introduction

Some people have said this is allegory; others have contended that
the business of molecular rejig units and the theoretically sound
juggling with genetic codes places it squarely on the side of the
groundlings.

For myself, I have seen many more meanings in it since it was
written than I ever knew in the construction. Joe Ross, when he was
editor at *Amazing/Fantastic,* and Judy Merril, when she was collecting for her *England Swings SF* (published in Britain, in part, as *The
Space-Time Journal*) pointed out some of them to me.

Others I saw for myself and not all are relevant—too many hangers
and not enough coats, you might say. Anyway, certain of the ac-
coutrements have now been removed and I should be honoured indeed, dear reader, to learn what you make of it.

MM/DD REF SHELTERCHILD SNAP FOUR

DARLING DASH DAMN THESE TELETYPES COMMA THEY TAKE ALL THE
WARMTH OUT OF A CONVERSATION STOP DARLING DASH I DON'T CARE HOW
STUPID IT LOOKS IN PRINT COMMA I'M STILL GOING TO SAY IT STOP DO YOU
THINK OUR CHILDREN ARE REALLY RIGHT FOR THIS SELF-SUPPORT BUSINESS
QUERY I MEAN COMMA WE'RE NICE PEOPLE STOP WHAT HARMFUL IN-
FLUENCES ARE WE GOING TO EXERT ON THEM QUERY ENDS

DD/MM REF SHELTERCHILD ANSA FOUR

HONEY COMMA TRY TO ACCEPT VERNACULAR DASH ALSO FINDINGS OF
COMMISSION ON UPBRINGING RE EVILS OF PARENT OBLIQUE CHILD INTER-
COURSE STOP I QUOTE PAR ONE EIGHT (18) SUB HYPHEN SECTION L (L)
COLON

QUOTE IT HAS BEEN NOTED FROM DEPOSITIONS OF JUNIOR JUDICIARY
PANEL MEMBERS THAT INSTANCES OF CHILD MISDEMEANOUR ARE SEVEN
TIMES BRACKET OUT OF REPRESENTATIVE TEN BRACKET DIRECTLY RE-
SULTANT FROM PARENTAL FAILURE COMMA ID EST COMMA PREVIOUS
AND PROVEN CRIMINAL TENDENCIES OF HEREDITARY NATURE COMMA
DISCERNIBLE MORAL INADEQUACIES COMMA RELUCTANCE TO ADMINISTER
VITAL CHASTISEMENT SEMI HYPHEN COLON AND TWO POINT NINE SEVEN
RECURRING (2.97%) TIMES TO ENVIRONMENTAL FACTORS COMMA EXEM-
PLI GRATIA COMMA RICH HOME COMMA POOR HOME COMMA SPOILED
CHILD COMMA CROWDED OUT CHILD STOP BRACKET SEE FOOTNOTE

FOOTNOTE STATES COLON

APPARENT EXISTENCE OF TWO EXTREMES COMMON TO SAME CON-
DITION SHOULD NOT BE TAKEN AS CONTRADICTION STOP CONDITION ONLY
SERVES ALL MORE TO ILLUSTRATE INADVISABILITY OF SUBJECTION OF
MINOR TO ADULT INFLUENCE OF ANY FORM ENDS UNQUOTE HONEY
COMMA NOW YOU KNOW STOP ENDS

MM/DD REF SHELTERCHILD SNAP FIVE

BUT WHY DO WE REPEAT WE HAVE TO BE APART QUERY WHY DO WE HAVE
TO SPEND OUR LIVES IN THESE LITTLE CUBICLES MANOEUVRING DREAMS
QUERY ENDS

DD/MM REF SHELTERCHILD ANSA FIVE

BECAUSE INEVITABLE DISCUSSION OF METHODS WOULD YIELD ONLY CON-
FUSION STOP EACH OF US MUST GIVE OF HIS BRACKET AND HER BRACKET

BEST STOP MASCULINE AND FEMININE UTILITIES ARE CLEARLY DEFINED
STOP SEEK COMFORT FROM FACT THAT ALL OVER SHELTERCHILD SITE HUS-
BANDS AND WIVES ARE SO PARTED STOP RE DREAMS QUERY COMMA IS IT
NOT BETTER TO BE IN POSITION TO MAGIC UP CHILD DREAMS AND DESIRES
THAN TO HAVE THEM BENT BY TOO MUCH TELEVIDEO AND TOO MUCH
JOHNNY ACTION TOYSHIP QUERY ENDS

MM/DD REF SHELTERCHILD SNAP SIX
WHAT ABOUT LOVE REPEAT LOVE QUERY

DD/MM REF SHELTERCHILD ANSA SIX
LOVE OF US QUERY LOVE OF CHILDREN QUERY BE EXPLICIT COMMA
HONEY STOP ENDS

MM/DD REF SHELTERCHILD SNAP SEVEN
LOVE OF CHILDREN COMMA OF COURSE STOP CHILDREN MUST HAVE LOVE
STOP ENDS

DD/MM REF SHELTERCHILD ANSA SEVEN
THOUGHT YOU MEANT US STOP SO YOU ARE GETTING EMOTIONAL AGAIN
STOP REMEMBER SENTIMENTALITY ONLY LEADS TO EXAGGERATED VALUES
COMMA IS THEREFORE HARMFUL DASH AND UNNECESSARY STOP ENDS

MM/DD REF SHELTERCHILD SNAP EIGHT
IF I HAD MEANT US COMMA IT WOULD NOT HAVE BEEN UNNECESSARY
COMMA I SUPPOSE STOP LOVE IS PREROGATIVE OF ADULTS STOP COSY STOP
I DONT LIKE YOU STOP

DD/MM REF SHELTERCHILD ANSA EIGHT
YOUR ATTITUDE MERELY PROVES ACCURACY OF COMMISSION FINDINGS
STOP TYPICAL OF DOMESTIC SQUABBLE LIKELY TO UNBALANCE RESIDENT
CHILDREN STOP NO MORE TO BE SAID STOP ENDS

MM/DD REF SHELTERCHILD SNAP NINE
I STILL SAY CHILD NEEDS LOVE DASH AND SUCKS TO COMMISSION STOP
ENDS

Tina mounted the bird of yellowing privet and rode at the speed of
a gentle breeze along the top of the hedge.

The fine high wall of shrub followed the whole meandering pe-
rimeter of the garden, shifting at will to encompass its unchartable
moods.

Borne upon a product of its leaves, Tina crossed hump-back

bridges over unopening gates and skirted great green spinning-top creations.

It had been a magnificent idea. Tina thrilled even now to its ingenuity as she jogged on, invisible and ever watchful of the bowers and half-hidden spinnies for some sign of Addison.

Once she thought she saw him standing near an MR booth, but she could have been mistaken. The molecular recomposition units had an inherent hallucinatory property. Nothing in their region was ever quite what it appeared. Or it *need* not be.

So it was with Tina. Skipping as usual, having again evaded Addison in the maze, she had come upon the garden boundary with its topping of foliate heraldry.

How much better to ride, she thought. On a bush bird.

She entered an adjacent cubicle and dialled.

Behind the rejig controls, the unit searched for a common codon, translating the DNA code of the Tina gene into the messenger-RNA template required for the new triplet base, forming the attendant spiral.

Then it fed in simulant functions—respiration-photosynthesis, sepalody-glandulation. It stored a little of this, paid out a little of that, until the body was the bird and the mind was a pure psychomotor, balanced astride in the conscious guise of a rider.

An off-shoot of the hedge ran inwards, following a path Tina did not recognise and she determined to veer right and follow it.

But she did not anticipate any effort and she was past the turn, bewildered, before she realised the difficulty.

She was a motile, vivacious and thinking and dreaming in terms of action. It took a little time for her to work out her predicament.

Her muscular distribution and her tensile qualities had been deposited at the MR unit. Which meant that her only mode of movement now was the wind, presently whitening the leaves spasmodically, and any telekinetic surge she could will from her doubly impulsive mind.

She felt annoyance and stamped an imaginary foot. Her idea had suffered a setback. It was no longer brilliant. It was no longer even bearable.

The bird jerked fitfully along the hedge-top until it came to another MR unit and promptly disintegrated. It took all Tina's meagre strength to dial her genetic home-code, "G . . . I . . . R . . . L."

In a remote corner of the garden, Addison wandered. Just today, he was Addison.

It was a new game and they were still on the As. Correction—he was still on the As. The girl cared for no such discipline. She fancied a name, picked it, and pinned it to her. Today, this day, this now, she was Tina. Probably.

Already, he was beginning to feel a discomfort low down in his virus-resistant stomach. If he had known the word, he would have called it "foreboding."

The setting was idyllic. They did what they pleased, which was little enough in any event. Sometimes, they walked together along the avenues, naming the trees; but more often, pursuing each other throughout the shifting co-ordinates of the garden.

And there was this early uneasiness. If he had known the word, he would have called it "apprehension."

The pursuit was a matter of Ideas and Tina—if she were still Tina—was the one with the Ideas. This was not as it should be, Addison thought. He preferred the walks, she the chases.

Whenever they were together, her eyes darted hither and thither like humming-birds. Then, when they came to a rejig unit, she would enter quickly, dial a code, and be gone, crawling like a caterpillar, drifting like a leaf.

The unit, a miraculous device programmed against impossibility, nevertheless set a restriction on its activities. The dialling had to register originality. A second-hand idea produced no response.

Addison (before he was Addison) had spent a number of day-times moving about the MR regions, seeking some tangible link with a power source. There was none—he was sure of that. The machines had to operate by a wave pattern or an encephalographic principle.

If he were to stay with the girl, he must think as she thought. And even then, the very fact that two of them shared an impulse made it redundant.

He had to think ahead of the girl—or else chase butterflies hopefully or ignore the challenge altogether, wandering as he wandered now.

Despite the pain of her presence, the garden was no fun without the girl. Somehow, he had to out-manoeuvre her.

DD9/SHCHLD HQ REF MM9 SNAP NINE

APOLOGIES FOR REMARKS RE COMMISSION STOP WIVES ARE COMMA AS YOU SO RIGHTLY POINT OUT COMMA RATHER MORE EMOTIONAL THAN IS GOOD FOR THEM STOP I SHALL COUNSEL HER STOP REMARKS GUIDE RE-QUESTED STOP ENDS

SHELTERCHILD HQ/DD9

SUGGEST YOU SAY NO MORE RE SUCKS REMARK STOP HQ IS ABOVE FEEL-
ING OFFENCE FROM MM9 OUTBURST STOP DIRECT MM9 THOUGHTS TO
VALUE OF TEACHING CHILDREN HORROR OF COMMA FOR INSTANCE
COMMA NUCLEAR WAR AND FASHION GARDEN ACCORDINGLY STOP ENDS

DD9/SHCHLD HQ

THANKS FOR GUIDE STOP POST HYPHEN WAR PHASE ACTIVATED STOP
ENDS

DD/MM REF SHELTERCHILD SNAP TEN

CO HYPHEN OPERATION REQUIRED FOR N WAR SYMBOLISM PHASE STOP
TRUST THAT THIS IS ACCEPTABLE TO YOU STOP ENDS

MM/DD REF SHELTERCHILD ANSA NINE

ANTI HYPHEN WAR CONCEPT ACCEPTABLE SINCE IT REQUIRES LACK OF
HATE STOP IS THIS THE BEST YOU CAN OFFER QUERY ONLY DOUBT DASH
IS FRIGHT RIGHT WAY TO BANISH AGGRESSIVE INSTINCTS QUERY STILL SAY
LOVE STOP ENDS

DD/MM REF SHELTERCHILD SNAP ELEVEN

NO TIME FOR HALF HYPHEN BAKED FEMALE PHILOSOPHY STOP FOR NOW
COMMA JUST DO AS YOU ARE DAMNED WELL TOLD STOP ENDS

It all began with the strontium doll. Tina found the pitiful bundle
lying in the middle of the path. She picked it up and then thrust it
from her hastily, repelled by the charred clothing and palsied limbs.

Some sleep-fed reflex told her dolls should be pink, rounded,
well-frilled.

"It is a victim toy."

She nodded to acknowledge the intelligence, unsurprised at its
prompt emergence since she had never known any inadequate
pause, any barrenness of expression.

After that first time, she and Addison found many such playthings,
placed rather than scattered about the garden.

Addison stumbled on a curious construction of cold black slimy
steel, running his hand along the tube, moving the butt almost unconsciously to his shoulder while an itch started up in the first crook
of his right index finger.

"It is a laser gun."

Always the voice that sounded so much like his own, yet spoke of
things he could not possibly know.

Then there were the mutants—terrible creatures of withered limb and disarranged features, explosive body chemistry and hormonic disharmony.

Addison and Tina came upon them together and found a new but short-lived closeness in shared nausea.

"These are the overkill people."

Two voices like their own, explaining, explaining.

When they opened their eyes again, the mutants had gone and their purpose had been served.

DD/MM REF SHELTERCHILD SNAP TWELVE

I HAVE WITHDRAWN POST HYPHEN BOMB PHASE AND CHILDREN ARE RESTING STOP TIME FOR SLEEP FEED STOP PLEASE ACKNOWLEDGE AND ADVISE OF SLEEP FEED PROGRAMME STOP ENDS

MM/DD REF SHELTERCHILD ANSA TWELVE

SO WE ARE SPEAKING AGAIN COMMA ARE WE QUERY ACKNOWLEDGE SLEEP FEED STOP PROGRAMME EXCESSIVE VIVID PROMPT OF RIGHT HY-PHEN WRONG STOP SUBJECT BOY STOP AND I STILL THINK LOVE MATTERS STOP ENDS

Addison stirred on his bed of leaves and heard an attendant rustle a few feet distant. Tina—still Tina?—was back. He listened for some sign of wakefulness but heard only the even rise and fall of her breath.

He rose silently and tiptoed to where she lay, squatting and look-ing down on her sleeping face.

When peace had smoothed some of the lines of youthful deter-mination from her brow, she looked more like her ten years.

When he was fortunate enough to find her in genuine slumber and not just feigning sleep until he turned away and she slapped his calves, he often sat just so, trying to piece together some kind of beginning for himself.

She had not always been with him—at least, he did not think so. Certainly, the whole time they had been in the garden, they had been together. But when he hovered protectively—in the face of what?—over her sleeping form, he could pick out recollections as insubstantial as thistledown of locations and places which might have been memories but might just as easily have been dreams.

Tonight, for instance, his mind moved along streets in a city of prisms, where some eternal sun at horizon height cast a million paths for him to follow, and as many broad patches of shadow where he could find an illicit coolness and a refuge from the spectral rays which coloured this strange rainbow city, dappling his hands and his moving back.

For miles, it seemed, he had been following a violet train, stepping from one pin-width of light to another to find some constant path that would take him wherever about the city that he wanted to go. But then the violet way petered out into darkness.

He stepped onto a nearby green way and kept to it as best he could, weaving among the great glass edifices. More miles before a broad, unnavigable belt of shadow separated him, at one extreme of the green band, from its continuation.

He saw no other person in all his journeyings hither and thither across the city; but something moved within the shadow. Something which had a loud voice and many feet but used them all silently.

He stepped onto a sweet blue walkway and went weaving again among the prism dwellings which carried only a yellow light at their apex and washed the wide, trafficless, formless, directionless streets with a showerfall of primary hues.

The blue trail ended. As did the red. Addison found himself, face pressed against one prism, trying to see beyond it, to perceive the yellow light that hung like a sun at its core.

Like a sun.

He must get to the sunward side of the city, but how?

He tried, knowing full well that he would not succeed, to scale the prism, but his hands and feet slipped and were done on the smooth sides.

Then he must go round the prism. And there was a shadow away from the focal points, where the colours radiated across the patchwork spaces.

He began to edge his way cautiously along the wall, his eyes fixed on the yellow core. He felt the increasing weight of the darkness on his back.

The something that inhabited the darkness raised its voice to a whisper, to a million million whispers that set his skin crawling and his ear-drums fluttering as though a breeze played through his head.

He was round the side of the prism now but the weight was not lifting. He moved fast but not too fast in case he should trip and take his eyes from the glowing core, which was changing to a horizontal shaft.

"Fall . . . fall . . . it is not bad to fall. . . ."

His fingers traced the line as though it were some Braille umbilicus and by and by he was at the back of the prism and a clear golden road stretched across the darkness to guide his feet. He embarked upon it, strolling purposefully into the eye of the sun.

MM/DD REF SHELTERCHILD SNAP THIRTEEN
RETURNING CHILDREN TO YOUR DIRECTION STOP SCHEDULE SAYS FREE EXPRESSION STOP OF COURSE COMMA I DON'T KNOW WHAT YOU HAVE IN MIND STOP ENDS

DD/MM REF SHELTERCHILD ANSA THIRTEEN
SCHEDULE GOOD ENOUGH FOR ME STOP HOW LONG DO YOU INTEND TO KEEP THIS UP QUERY ANIMOSITY GETS THROUGH ON MOTIVATION PARAMETERS STOP DON'T THINK ME COMMA THINK MOTHER STOP ENDS

MM/DD REF SHELTERCHILD SNAP FOURTEEN
THINKING MOTHER STOP ENDS

Tina stirred uneasily, summoning Addison to his outer world. Shortly, she sat up and gazed at him curiously with wide eyes.

"Where were you this afternoon?" she asked. "I looked for you. I had the most marvellous Idea."

"You wouldn't have been able to tell me," said Addison and looked down upon his crossed legs. "Ideas don't speak. At least, not your sort of Ideas. They may buzz a little at times, or develop a scent of bougainvillea . . ."

"Well, I'll tell you now. I was a bush bird."

The full meaning was not immediately apparent to Addison.

"But you've been a bird before . . ."

"*Not* made of privet," countered Tina with a gesture of pride. "I went right round the garden on top of the hedge."

"Did you . . ." Addison checked himself; a vague guilt had been born a minisec behind the question.

Now Tina was watching him, almost defying him to complete it, as though the broken sentence, the hesitation, was an indication of inferiority.

He shrugged the doubt away. "Did you see any of the outside?" he asked quickly.

Only when she reflected on it did Tina realise that she had not once turned her eyes away from the garden.

"There was some kind of sight-shield," she lied and then, just in case he should clamber up the hedge and look, she qualified her answer. "It is nothing visible. It is some kind of strong undesire to turn the eyes to unfamiliarity."

"You didn't look." This time, at least, Addison could see through the deception.

"I *couldn't* look. Try yourself."

She knew he wouldn't take up the challenge now that he could believe she had lied; he would not care to be seen taking that much notice of her pronouncements.

Back on his bed of leaves, he wondered why the unknown bothered him so. Surely he had everything he wanted.

But then, how did he know what he wanted until he knew what there was to have? And did the unknown bother him because it *was* unknown and for no other reason?

He cried quietly. A six-year-old knows no other way out of frustration.

Tina, hearing his distress, found her hand straying again to the scar on her left side. It was a habit, she supposed, like the way she enjoyed the feel of a leaf's sharp edge between her fingers or folded into the palm of her hand; like the way Addison still sucked his thumb occasionally.

There was some connection between Addison and that scar. She stroked it to comfort him, incapable of any other consolation.

Gradually, his sobbing receded. She thought he had fallen asleep, until he said:

"Why don't we know anything about the Outside? I mean—if we know it's there, why aren't we told anything about it?"

"It's a matter of obedience," said a voice like Tina's. "A matter of doing what we are told."

"But what are we told?"

"We are told not to concern ourselves with the Outside."

"But why?"

"Because," said Tina.

"Because what?"

"Because, because."

"That's stupid."

Addison leapt to his feet and moved across to Tina. For a moment, she thought he was going to strike her, and indeed he was until his programmed serenity won control and he stood above her awkwardly, swaying from side to side.

"That's stupid," he repeated limply.

"There are good reasons—you must be content with that."

"But what are those reasons?"

Tina pulled him down beside her and put a sisterly arm round his shoulder.

"I don't know," she said, and felt him go tense with returning annoyance. "I know only that they are good reasons and that that should be enough for us. Perhaps further knowledge is . . . harmful."

"Perhaps it's something to do with the strontium doll . . ." Addison entered into the speculation and felt better. "And the overkill people and the . . . the"—again a curious guilt made him hesitate— "the laser gun."

"Something it is better for us not to know," said Tina conclusively. Addison nestled against her. "All right," he said.

A little later, he asked another question, drowsily—"Why were you here first?"

Tina found her hand moving back to the scar below her ribs.

"Sometimes, disobedience springs out of lack of responsibility. That was what happened before . . . This time I have the responsibility."

But Addison's head lolled suddenly and Tina knew he had heard no word of her explanation. She heard it alone.

MM/DD REF SHELTERCHILD SNAP FOURTEEN
I NOTED A HOSTILITY READING FROM THE BOY LAST NIGHT STOP I THINK HE NEEDS TO BE SHOWN LOVE STOP I AM NOT TRYING TO PROLONG THE ARGUMENT COMMA DARLING COMMA BUT I AM AFRAID THAT HIS NEED MAY FIND ANOTHER OUTLET STOP ENDS

MM/DD REF SHELTERCHILD ANSA FOURTEEN
CONFIRM HOSTILITY READING STOP WHAT BOY NEEDED WAS ANSWERS STOP REPORT EXISTENCE OF INHERENT IMPATIENCE STOP GIRL COULD SHOW RECONCILIATION STOP CAN I LEAVE TO YOU QUERY ENDS

MM/DD REF SHELTERCHILD SNAP FIFTEEN
I AM SURE YOU ARE WRONG STOP LOVE IS ALL ANSWER HE WANTS STOP ENDS

MM/DD REF SHELTERCHILD ANSA FIFTEEN
REPORT IMPATIENCE DASH OR I WILL STOP ENDS

MM/DD REF SHELTERCHILD SNAP SIXTEEN
BLIND BULLY STOP ENDS

The children breakfasted on the usual nuts and fruit, complemented with a filling cereal they found in a seeming never-ending store in the dwelling shelter.

"Who are you today?" the boy asked the girl. He allowed her first choice habitually because he liked to know where he stood—for the first few moments of the day, at least. After that, she would probably add further to his frustrations. She would not keep to the disciplines they had shared at the outset—spasmodically he remembered a better time and this was what he understood by the outset —and he felt a new indignation at each fresh infringement.

"No. You must be first," answered the girl. She waited, forming an A silently with her lips.

"Why?"

"For a change."

"So you can try some other trick on me."

"For a *change*," said the girl emphatically. "I'm *always* first. I want you to be first so that we'll know where we are and we can play together all day."

The boy pondered the new arrangement.

"'Able,'" he said finally. "'Able' because I can do anything. Now you."

"I think I'll take a little time to think about it. I'll let you know."

"That's not fair. I told you my name. Now you must tell me yours. How can we get in touch with each other?"

"I'll get in touch with you."

"It's not fair. You don't even stick to the As . . ."

He sat hunched in his rustic chair, sulking. "You don't make it much fun for me. You should, you know. You have a duty."

The regretful words, dropped unsubtly into the conversation, caused the girl a twinge of conscience.

What he had said was true, perhaps more true than he knew. She did have a duty to him. As yet it was still obscure; but she knew with certainty that she must deter him from any whim that might endanger their existence in the garden.

While she exulted in her own Ideas, made her own enjoyment out of her superior capacity to use the garden's strange gifts, he was left alone.

He was younger and less likely to reconcile himself to the life, building his own satisfaction within the meandering hedges; more likely to look for diversions and not always the wise ones.

She recollected how his finger had begun to curl round the trigger of the laser gun.

The younger you were, the more difficult it was to be strong—because you had no reason to try and could understand no cause.

She watched him now with a certain warmth. The soft curve of his cheek, the slight snubness of nose, the pursed perfection of his presently petulant mouth—it all filled her with a weak-kneed quality she could not comprehend.

"All right," she said. "I'll promise. I shall be an A all day. See if you can find me."

She rose quickly from the table and paused as she passed his chair to run her fingers through his curls. He turned his head away angrily.

"You don't want me," he said.

The words hurt her. "How can you say that? You know——"

"I'm a burden to you. You can't have the things the way you want them because you have to think of me. So you try to deceive me all the time. You try to be cleverer. I know, well, I'm sorry. I'd go away, but you won't tell me how."

"I don't know how." The girl bit back the words. She had reacted only to his last comment when sense told her she should have considered the whole of his outcry. But if she stopped to think, it would be too late.

"Oh, so you'd let me go." It was too late already. "You're all I've got and you want me to go. Fair enough. I hate you."

"Boy," she said gently. "Able . . . I didn't mean it like that . . ."

But Able (just today, he was Able) was gone down the path, hiding his reddening eyes.

The girl gathered up the platters and vessels and carried them back into the shelter. The exchange had shaken her. She was not at all sure what she could do.

As she stacked the crockery in the washbox, she went over the dialogue again, concentrating on what she had said to Able.

She had promised to be an A all day. She had invited him to find her. Perhaps, if she made it a little simple for him . . .

MM/DD REF SHELTERCHILD SNAP SEVENTEEN

AM RECEIVING ANXIETY PATTERN FROM GIRL STOP BOY MUST BE SHOWN SHE DOES NOT MEAN WHAT HE THINKS SHE MEANS STOP ADVISE YOU USE MINDSWEEP SO HE CAN FORGET STOP ENDS

DD/MM REF SHELTERCHILD ANSA SEVENTEEN

NO STOP MINDSWEEP WOULD ONLY FACILITATE MATTERS FOR GIRL
STOP CONTEND UP TO GIRL TO MAKE MOVE STOP BOY TOO YOUNG TO AC-
CEPT CONCEPT THAT TAKING BLAME IS LINE OF LEAST RESISTANCE STOP
ENDS

MM/DD REF SHELTERCHILD SNAP EIGHTEEN

QUIT BEING SMART STOP BOY MAY HAVE NOW PASSED BEYOND STAGE
WHERE APOLOGY WOULD SUFFICE STOP SUBMIT IT IS NOT FAIR TO GIRL
TO EXPECT HER TO KNOW WHAT TO DO NOW STOP ENDS

DD/MM REF SHELTERCHILD ANSA EIGHTEEN

TELL HER THEN STOP ENDS

The path down which Able disappeared in such haste led indi-
rectly to the school zone. There was an MR unit in the classroom
to facilitate their physics studies. She could place herself there—for
a while at any rate.

Once inside the booth, she dialled A . . . L . . . P . . . H.

The unit slotted her request into the calcium programme and
she felt the chemistry beginning its chain.

Alphabet peered down from the blackboard with her twenty-six
eyes, but there was no sign of Able within the school precinct or
moving in the parkland visible through the window.

She waited for an hour and then willed the chalk characters from
the board and drifted the dust into the booth for recomposition.

She tried the recreation runs next, waiting while the local unit
shunted her formula into the resin-bank and then lying, blunt head
down, in a quiver for another hour before allowing the breeze to
direct her feather flights back to the booth.

Then she turned her steps to the playroom, but again, Able was
not to be seen. She digitised A . . . B . . . A . . . C and waited
while body ferrum and sulphur drew a match which made her a
wooden frame with parallel wires which carried brightly coloured
counting beads.

But Able did not come. Even though she finally forsook any pre-
tence of sport and called his name until her throat was sore, Able
did not come.

MM/DD REF SHELTERCHILD RUSH ONE

GIRL HAS GONE TO EXTREMES TO CONTACT BOY STOP NO SUCCESS STOP
FATHER MUST REPEAT MUST ACT STOP ENDS

DD/MM REF SHELTERCHILD SPEC ONE
PRODUCING NON HYPHEN VIOLENCE MOTIF DISCIPLINE STOP DON'T PANIC
STOP ALL UNDER CONTROL STOP ENDS

Able did not come because he knew she was looking for him. He heard her shouting, but instead of responding, he found a molecular rejig unit in a distant corner of the park and tried his own words on the dial.

First, he fingered out H . . . A . . . T . . . E.

The machine went dead. The silence which followed seemed to take on a definite personality.

"You shall not kill," he heard himself say. "You shall not kill."

An unseen hand propelled him forth across the garden. He stumbled on the strontium doll.

"She was a victim toy."

He found the laser gun suddenly in his right hand.

"This is a killer."

The mutants barred his path and he fell upon his knees before them, dislodged by the sudden withdrawal of the force.

"These were killed without dying. These were dead though they still drew breath."

Then the force picked him up again and carried him on.

"You shall not kill. You shall *not* kill."

Unexpectedly, he was back in the booth, breathless and frightened. It was as though some person watched how his fingers moved on the dial.

"I shall be an A all day," the girl had said.

He dialled A and his imagination failed him. He tried to dial A . . . B . . . C . . . D as proof of his desire to obey, but his nervous fingers slipped on the digits.

Instead, he dialled A . . . B . . . A . . . D. And all restraint and hesitation withdrew with a terrible sigh, like an agonised breeze through bare, wounding branches. But the machine clicked and hummed its inevitable way.

A . . . B . . . A . . . D . . . D . . . O . . . N

The boy felt his mind bulked with horrific knowledge; his heart extinguished with cold water; his fearful tears dried before they could surface. Of an instant, he knew the easy beauty of the darkness and the tainted deviations of the prisms.

DD/MM REF SHELTERCHILD RUSH TWO
BOY HAS JAMMED MY OUTPUT STOP DON'T ASK HOW STOP AM NO
LONGER IN EMPATHY WITH HIM STOP GIRL MUST REPEAT MUST CONTAIN
HIM UNTIL I CAN RENEW CONTACT STOP ENDS

MM/DD REF SHELTERCHILD SPEC TWO
AM PUTTING GIRL TO FLIGHT STOP IF BOY IS ANGRY SHE IS NOT GOING
TO BEAR BRUNT STOP I TOLD YOU HOW TO CONTROL HIM STOP MAKE YOUR
OWN CONTACT STOP ENDS

Abaddon laughed. He considered the garden. He revelled in the
limitlessness of his own devilment. He strode purposefully through
the vegetation, trampling it before him.

The girl had found her way to the MR booth in the shadow of
the hedge where she had ridden the day before. Now, she could
hear the thrashing progress of some thing, a sound that came ever
nearer.

Able was taking his spite out on the garden. It must be he.

She must avoid him. But how? And should she still play, in fairness to him, in a last bid to appease him?

She would change. He would pass her by. But at least she would
have retained her good intention. Her thoughts fled to the classroom, to the wall-chart there.

"A is for Apple. A is for Apple."

MM/DD REF SHELTERCHILD RUSH THREE
I FEAR FOR GIRL STOP I WARNED YOU STOP

DD/MM REF SHELTERCHILD SPEC THREE
DON'T WASTE MY BLOODY TIME WITH THREATS STOP IT WILL WORK
OUT STOP ENDS

The rolling apple touched Abaddon's foot as he walked. He
picked it up and polished it while he looked for the tree from which
it had fallen.

Then he sank his teeth into it, deliberately ignoring the small scar
that marked its glistening surface and amusing himself with the
scream that seemed to cleave to the roof of his mouth and filter
through the crowded chambers of his brain.

He threw the core down carelessly on the grass verge. After that
the gates out of the garden opened easily.

MM/DD UNSPECIFIED
CHILD KILLER STOP I WILL GET YOU STOP ENDS

SHELTERCHILD HQ/DD9 CLASSIFIED
WE HAVE RECEIVED GRAVE COMPLAINT FROM MM9 STATING YOU DE-
LIBERATELY ENGINEERED DEATH OF GIRL AND BOY WE HAVE BEEN
FORCED TO DESTROY STOP STUDY OF YOUR TAPES REVEALS MM9 PERSIST-
ENTLY WARNED YOU OF NEED FOR SUBTLER METHODS BRACKET LOVE
STIMULUS BRACKET STOP WHY DID YOU NOT CONTACT US FOR ADVICE
QUERY REFUSE TO BELIEVE THIS WAS MERE BAD JUDGMENT ON YOUR PART
STOP SHELTERCHILD PROJECT NOW BECOMES RIDICULOUS STOP COMMIS-
SION ON UPBRINGING DEMANDS YOUR SCALP COMMA MY RESIGNATION
STOP WHAT IS YOUR EXPLANATION DASH AND IT HAD BETTER BE MEM-
ORABLE QUERY ENDS

DADDY9/SHCHLD HQ RE MUMMY 9 CLAIM
BOYS WILL BE BOYS STOP ENDS

DEAR WITCH HAZEL,
MY BIRDS WON'T FLY

Introduction

When a writer tells you he starts off without any idea, suspect him. The idea which sparked this work was a half-baked thing indeed. Supposing birds didn't fly south for the winter because . . . Because the metals they had taken in from the air and with their foods had made them too heavy—discarded. Because the magnetic pull of the earth was providing too great an attraction for them to get off the ground—discarded. Because said metals were affecting the magnetic elements of their uncanny orientation—*can't* be discarded.

A small aside: I thought I was safe (even clever) likening the darting movement of swifts to that of a sewing needle. The story was produced for the British Milford II at Barton-on-Sea and it was during that Milford week that I went to Lyndhurst and discovered three books of nature essays by Richard Jefferies . . . discovered Richard Jefferies, in fact. In one of the essays, sure enough, there were swallows darting like needles. But that painful coincidence happily led on to some wonderful moments with the essays of Jefferies, to whom I would refer you all.

Still with Milford II—one of the workshoppers, Peter Nicholls, said this tale was one of two he would have nebulated for a Nomina (I've been *dying* to do that!) . . . given publication, that is. Well, time may tell.

But it wasn't written for a Nebula. It was written because I have started looking to the birds with some concern at certain times of the year and wondering how it is they have the extent of forgiveness that keeps them singing for us. Richard Jefferies (1848–1887) might have had the answer. Witch Hazel, I fear, would not.

Melanie Michaels lived in the Northern Hemisphere, let us be as vague as that. From the north, migrating birds fly south and that is the point at issue.

Melanie's house was as green as you could get with the grey and oxidous closing in, a renovated cottage that nestled two miles beyond one building line and three miles from the next. The cottage had eaves and a garden. The eaves and garden sheltered and gave succour to birds.

Melanie loved them as only a nine-year-old can—not as a buff with their fine Latin titles at her tongue-tip but as an observer unspoiled by disciplines, who saw one breed as cheeky, another as romantic, yet another as sly, and yet a fourth as constantly put upon.

In her bedroom while little claws scratch-scuttled across the overside of her ceiling, she wrote:

Dear Witch Hazel,

This is about the birds in my garden. You said for me to write about what interested me and my birds interest me.

I know a lot about them, not the sort of things the tutor boxes tell you but what you learn from watching them. I love the blackbird because he is always the first to wake up in the morning and he has the sweetest song. Sometimes I see him in the half-light on the top of our line-post and he is there again in the dusk seeing all the other little birds off to bed. Perhaps it's his job to switch the day on and off.

I love the sparrows because they are cheeky and talkative and most like little children of all the birds. I see crowds of them on the trellis work and it is just as though they are holding a conference or a parliament or something.

And I like the thrushes not because of the way they whistle but because I have noticed something about them by myself and with nobody telling me. Some of them *hop* and some of them *run* and every time I see a thrush standing still and listening for a worm, I think, Which do you do? And sometimes he does it just to show me but whenever I try to guess I am wrong.

I feel sorry for the starlings because they have such sore throats and they don't seem to get on with anybody except other starlings. And the young ones, when they have to look for food first of all in

May, seem to be such big babies. I know children who do not like starlings. I would not go that far.

But I do dislike pigeons. They are messy and greedy and they chase off all the smaller birds when I put down bread and bacon rind. I suppose they are bigger and they have to eat more but they annoy me because when I chase them away the other birds won't come back either. Except the sparrows.

I don't see much of crows and rooks because they live in the park down the road and I expect they think my garden is a bit cramped. But I do have a robin and he is my friend in winter when I see him down on the muddy part of the lawn or under the chestnut tree looking for grubs. Once I thought he was three birds because he has three songs, a whistle, a peep, and a real little talking melody for different times of the year.

But my favourite of all are the swallows and swifts because they are mysterious. They live under our roof during the summer and you see them darting like my gone mother's sewing needle first thing in the morning and at twilight. They squeak and I used to think until I saw pictures that they didn't have faces. You watch them flying, Witch Hazel, and you'll never see their eyes or mouths or anything and you'll wonder where the squeaks are coming from, so that's one mystery, and you'll never see them on the ground and that's another one.

I did see one once. There was a bang on the window and when I looked out, there was a little bird lying on the flower-bed. I felt sick because I thought he was dead but then he shook his head and got up dragging his wings as if they were too big for him.

I wanted to pick him up but I was sure he was too delicate and I would break him. My daddy said when he came home that if you find a swift you should pick it up gently and throw it in the air because the air currents on the ground are not strong enough for it to take off but when we went to look for this swift he had gone. I hope no cats had him.

And here's a third mystery about my swifts. They are still here and it is October. Why is that, Witch Hazel?

Love,
Melanie

—and fed it to her tutor box.

APUS APUS/DELAYED MIGRATION
DOA DOSSIER 178/79-Oct.
Genesis: Woodbine Research Centre
State: Incomplete pending PM findings

Backgrounder:

Swallow (*hirundo rustica*) migration occurs between August and October on a fairly leisurely basis. Swift (*apus apus*) departures are unvarying and in direct relation to depletion of aerial insects with the onset of lower temps in the northern latitudes. Adherence to these behavioural patterns is essential, since many factors hinge upon them, food-finding and sunsearch being only the most superficial. All known motivations for south-journeying are being examined against existing irregularity.

Pathological prognosis: None.

Random projections: Without path. prog., these lie too far on the wilder side of possibility. Some medical or psychotic parameter is essential and needs firm path. basis.

Conclusions: None.

Melanie called her tutor box after the real Witch Hazel, who had provided a regular Country Corner in Primrose Times, one of the finest comic papers ever to come from a wall-chute.

Melanie was beyond the Primrose Times stage now but she had been encouraged to endow her new teaching machine with an old familiar identity and here it was—a link to the thinkpile with a name out of a fairy-tale.

It was handy not having to wait two months for an answer to a country question, anyway. She had inundated the original with a welter of woodland lore and a barrage of pastoral imponderables, unmindful of the six-issues-in-hand mechanics of printing, and had agitated for answers. It was her attention that had led largely to the good lady's retirement to some hollow, faraway tree, if only the truth were known.

Her questions, nonetheless, relinquished no part of their intensity. The quicker one was settled, the hastier came the next. Ned Michaels had liked the tutor idea but he wasn't so crazy about the machine-time bills.

He called her down from her perch underneath the bird ballroom when he got the October (1) account, intending to instruct her on controlling her interrogations. He had been an hour struggling with the printout proofs that came with the invoice and now he thought he had a place to begin.

"Melanie."

"Daddy?"

"I have had a bill for the teaching machine and it is rather large," he said—and then added, "The bill," because his daughter would have come back like lightning with, "The teaching machine? It's only as big as a doll's house, Daddy."

"You always told me," said Melanie, "that a good education was more precious than gold."

"Cumulatively," he countered.

"What's 'cumulatively'?"

"Gathered up over a period. I didn't mean it was worth a king's ransom three times a month."

"I'm sorry, Daddy. I'll try to—to only be as curious as we can afford."

"I don't want to sound like a pinch-penny, honey. Perhaps . . . perhaps we could save questions which don't require immediate consideration for more affluent times or you could invest a little of your birthday allowance or something like that. For my part, I'd like you to be learning the value of money and—well—brevity."

"I keep my questions as short as I can, Daddy."

"True, flower, but the effect is only to give you more time for more asking. No, I think we might try a little test here. If you like, you can pretend we are trying to outsmart the machine. Let's see if we can get the same amount of information from—say—half the number of questions. Some of the queries you put to the tutor last week were less than vital."

He sifted tearsheets for the example he had marked. "You wrote an essay on the birds in our garden—and I enjoyed it, Melanie, I have to say I like the way you work with the tutor—but then you ended it by asking, 'Why are the swifts still here in October?'"

"That doesn't count." Melanie came round the breakfast table and leaned on his shoulder to read the printout.

"Why not?"

"Well, it shouldn't. Because I didn't have a proper answer. They shouldn't make you pay for information I never had."

"Not a proper answer?"

"No. Look, you've got the response here. 'This file is suspended pending revision.'"

Ned Michaels tried to remember if he had ever seen the term before. Of course, he must have done. There were bound to be files out of circulation all the time while the data were amended.

"That may be so, Melanie," he said, "but it doesn't alter the point I'm trying to make. This was not a vital question."

"It was to me."

"What we have to ask ourselves, lovely, is whether our studies suffer by the absence of the requested information. Had you been given a project on migration?"

"No, Daddy."

"Then it could have waited."

"Please don't think I'm arguing with you, Daddy, but I thought it was important for general knowledge. You see, I can still hear the swifts squeaking now in the roof and it is mid-October, and . . . and if the file has been withdrawn so they can put some more information in it, there must be something we don't know."

Michaels took his coffee into the garden. Melanie went with him. He ran his eyes along the roof-rim of the house. There was a fair amount of feathered coming and going, but was it uncommon? To be truthful, he would not have known in any event.

He gave his attention to the temperature of the day.

"It's not cold," he suggested.

"That's just by the way," said Melanie. "It's cold for birds."

"It hasn't started being cold yet," her father defended his observation.

Melanie, up to his elbow, seized his hand and pulled him down the path to the chestnut. She caught a low branch and showed him yellow nibbling inwards from the edge of a leaf. "The trees know," she said. "And birds know. It may be warm now but there could be a frost tonight. It's time for the birds to *go!*"

"You're sure?" asked Michaels uneasily.

"Daddy—"

"Of course you're sure," he said with sudden decision. "Will the lady let me come to her bedroom?"

"Yes—but why?"

"I'm going to spend some money with Witch Hazel myself."

He let Melanie lead the way upstairs, waited with a wry smile while she cleared her consol for him to sit down.

Then he typed: WHAT WAS THE DATE OF SWIFT AND SWALLOW MIGRATION LAST YEAR QUERY ENDS

Witch Hazel's reaction was prompt: SWALLOW SOUTH FLIGHTS WERE STAGGERED BETWEEN AUGUST 27 AND OCTOBER 2 STOP SWIFT MIGRATION WAS IN ONE FLIGHT ON SEPTEMBER 29 ENDS

Michaels typed: WHY HAVE THEY NOT LEFT THIS YEAR QUERY ENDS

The tutor growled and muttered like a dog with a biscuit and put up: THIS FILE IS SUSPENDED PENDING REVISION ENDS

Melanie shrugged. "What now?"

"I have words with Uncle Max," said her father, "and he won't charge me."

Then they listened to the sounds on the ceiling. If I were more of a romantic, thought Michaels, I'd picture them pacing up and down on that plasterboard wondering what the hell to do.

But he didn't tell his daughter. She was still and already a romantic.

Melanie Michaels was naughty but with love. When her father had departed for his business in town she lost no time in renewing her acquaintance with Witch Hazel.

Her father had said to watch her questions and never ask two where one would do. She asked Witch Hazel, WHAT DO YOU HAVE ON RECORD ABOUT BIRD MIGRATION QUERY ENDS

The outcome was such a blizzard of material that she had to press the override button and cry, "Enough!"

For a long time she picked over the pile like a hobo after rags. She read what she could and found a lot she could not.

The phrase "Earth's magnetic field" kept coming up and even though the nuances were lost on her, she knew magnetism had something to do with the North Pole.

When Mummy had been alive it had been a leg-pull with them, the way Daddy turned up sometimes with presents that were better suited for a boy. Mummy said Daddy had bought them because he secretly wanted them himself. Daddy said not so, there were things that would benefit a girl.

Like a compass? asked Mummy.

Like a compass, thought Melanie, and started searching through the chest of drawers.

She found it, balanced it on the palm of her hand, and pirouetted. The needle kept going north.

There had been a man called Gustav Kramer who carried out experiments she couldn't quite understand with mirrors and magnetic fields and noted how they affected bird behaviour.

And if birds were supposed to go north, perhaps it was a real struggle for them to go south every autumn. Perhaps they had decided this year not to bother.

She telephoned her father and said, "Daddy, ask Uncle Max if my swifts are magnetic."

And Ned Michaels, having little enough else to put to the expert, agreed.

Max Norstadt, brother to the late Sara Michaels, was a bird himself, like those early mobiles that always seemed to be attracted to a glass of water until the weights in their nether regions snapped them back to the upright to begin their swing again.

He pecked now and came up with a piece of paper. Ned was surprised to see it in his hand and not his beak.

"If you had a dead swift for me—"

"I don't," said Ned. "They're not moribund, they're just . . . pacing up and down."

"Where?"

"In the roof recess. What's that paper?"

Norstadt seemed to have forgotten what he was holding. "This is a dissection record from a guillemot," he said. "The latest thing I can find."

"We don't have any guillemots."

"You don't have any dead swifts, either. This isn't a complete waste of time. You came here with nothing and I'm giving you something. This bird apparently died of starvation in the Irish Sea. There is no shortage of food."

"Then—"

"Then it's a contradiction but unfortunately it isn't new to us. It's trace-metal poisoning."

"Metal." Ned made a note of the word.

"Right. We used to put it down to PCB's—that's poly-chlorinated biphenyls, industrial solvents. Oil tankers are washed out with them and when there's an oil spill, PCB's are in the detergent that clots the oil and sinks it."

"But I always thought the oil was the real threat to sea-birds."

"They're *both* real threats. The steps taken against pollution are no better than the pollution. The oil affects the birds externally—messes them up, burns them, clogs their pores. The detergents are a bit more subtle by being once removed."

"Eh?"

"—Given a gift wrapping, Ned. My word, you're anxious, but you'll have to hear me out. If I don't explain it all, you won't understand any of it. . . . There's very little in oil to harm fish. It's mostly nutrient and all comes from the bottom of the sea, anyway. . . . No, I won't go into that. By the time that the fish get to the Double Devon clotted oil, it's impregnated with PCB's. The fish eat those, the birds eat the fish, and the poison's on its way up the food chain. Are you following?"

"Closely." Ned was tapping his fingers, out of patience. The man was Sara's brother but the two were—had been; grief, he still had to keep correcting himself—as different as chalk and cheese. Sara had been so much of everything he needed; this brother rattled on like a pair of bone dice. And now she was— It was uncharitable to wish the two were juxtaposed; but that was just what he did wish as Max mumbled on now, testing his tolerance. Enough! He couldn't change it, so he must make the best of it. At least, he was able to secure private audience on demand with the Department of Agriculture's big man on birds, this little man, Max Norstadt. "So far you've said nothing I haven't read in the *Readers' Digest*."

"I don't know why I like you, Ned."

"I'm sorry, Max, but I'm in a hurry. This dilemma is now. You said something about 'used to.'"

"Yes. So we come back to this guillemot. Undoubtedly. PCB's entered into its demise but there was a whole lot else, too. This is a list of what we took out of its liver—40 parts per million of lead, 38 ppm arsenic, 15 ppm mercury, 82 ppm selenium, 950 ppm zinc and 12.8 ppm cadmium. That's a multi-lethal combination—in other words, any one of those is close to the limit and could have been the killer."

"But you said the bird starved to death."

"That's the trace-metal spiral—loss of appetite, reduced food intake, resultant loss of flesh, mobilisation of more accumulated metallic and other poisons, increased inability to hunt and survive, self-perpetuating and self-intensifying."

"Poor guillemot."

"That's just one, Ned. It's happening all over. Particularly this time of the year when they're having to look a bit harder for their food."

Ned sat up and took notice. "This time of the year is what concerns me particularly. Migration, you know? These—metals—that are finding their way into birds' bodies—are they magnetic?"

"What difference would that make?" The tangential thought had left Max Norstadt in the dark.

"Well, they might draw the birds north instead of south."

"I—I don't know."

"Is it so ridiculous?"

"Not at all, Ned. It's an extremely fine original thought in a field where we're a bit too close to the problem to get fine original thoughts. But it doesn't seem evident in the case of the guillemot."

"Oh?"

"Because the bird is non-migratory."

"Then what—?"

"Lead is not magnetic, some of the others only slightly so. That means we'd have to be talking about arsenic, mercury, selenium, zinc, cadmium—plus anything an inland bird might pick up which a guillemot might not and that's quite an alphabet. Antimony, beryllium, copper, manganese, nickel, pica, strontium, thallium, uranium . . . coupled probably with greater intensities of mercury or cadmium. . . . We still can't explain migration, except to say that we have considered genetics, hormones, biological clock, even good old common sense, and they all fit. But the idea that a magnetic pull from the opposite direction can divert them or even just make them stay where they are—well, that's an innovation. It isn't ridiculous, by any means, but . . ."

"Unlikely. It was Melanie's idea. I promised I'd put it to you. So we're no nearer finding out why her birds are still here."

"And I wouldn't say that. She could well be right but these are early days. Until I find dead swifts in Iceland, I can't start building up a case."

Ned Michaels stood up. "What can I tell Melanie?"

"Tell her I'm thinking about it. That's no lie, Ned. You see, one effect of metallic poisoning is disorientation. If these swifts' navigational equipment has been impaired, it could well explain why they're not moving. On the other hand, it could just be that new central-heating equipment of yours, keeping them cosy under the tiles. Southern Africa is a long drag when you're comfortable where you are."

Michaels turned at the door. "You don't really believe that, do you, Max? I mean, should I say we've been worrying for nothing?"

Not for nothing, Norstadt was sure. It had to be something and it had to be crucial. But so far he was a long way from an explanation and alarm was hardly likely to speed the process. On the contrary . . .

He said: "Just tell Melanie to keep an eye on them. They may need a friend."

DEPARTMENT OF AGRICULTURE
WestM: Teletype Rapid and Scramble

Woodbine:
Am in receipt of your apus apus data but find myself no wiser.
Why such absence of detail or even conjecture? When is post-
mortem finding likely to be available?
Norstadt.

DEPARTMENT OF AGRICULTURE
Woodbine Research Centre
Attent. Norstadt and Scramble

Cannot help you on imminence of post-mortem finding because
we do not have corpus apus apus. This lack also explains our igno-
rance in other areas you mention.
David Dundee (Director)

Norstadt/Dundee (scble)

Your answer is less than adequate. WHY do you not have a dead
swift when your contention is that the birds are still readily
available?

Dundee/Norstadt (scble)

LIVE ones are available. We are debating wisdom of taking bird
for tests. There may be no PM explanation while conduct of live
bird may be enlightening.

Norstadt/Dundee (scble)

You excuse the gaps in your dossier by citing "pending PM information." You explain your inability to answer me by saying a
laboratory PM may not reveal the necessary indications. One or the
other, Dundee, but you can't have both. I am going elsewhere.

Norstadt at the Department of Agriculture had a link with the
Department of Defence through the Westminster data exchange.
He digitised his geophysical concern and the DOD connected him
verbally with Grant Wheeler. Norstadt was not sure whether tele-

phone was going to be a true conveyor of his need. Since the DOD offices were only a matter of a walk across the square, he made his introductions and asked if Wheeler would favour him with an interview. Wheeler was free directly.

By the time Norstadt had found his way into the DOD building and down to the geophysical section, where time would not wither nor earthquake destroy, he was even less convinced of the wisdom of his inquiry than when he had set out. It was a child's idea, anyway.

But Wheeler was affable and gave him the run of the drinks keyboard and very soon the words were beginning to form.

For opening, he tried: "What would you do if the birds stopped flying south for the winter?"

"You win," said Wheeler. "I never heard anything like. I'm illogicised."

"It's not a game." Norstadt couldn't help the edge of irritability that crept in. "It's a serious, sincere, genuine question."

"You mean they have? I didn't notice . . . Hey, wait a minute. Our satellites monitor cranes. They've said no such thing."

Norstadt sighed. "Imagine the birds have stopped flying south."

"Then they haven't?"

"*Assuming* some have . . ."

"My first move would be to inspect myself and my department for culpability."

"And if you found yourself and your outfit blame-free?"

"I'd ask myself why I was asking myself. . . . Look, what's behind all this? Are you levelling a complaint? Have you got facts to back up what you're accusing me of?"

"I'm not accusing you or your section of anything. The problem was raised—"

"Then the problem is *real.*"

"The *projected* problem was suggested to me. Why are you defence people so defensive?"

"By whom?"

"By my brother-in-law. Well, by my niece."

"So we're theorising."

Norstadt was moist and short of breath and wondering more than ever whether this subterranean interview was worthwhile. He decided submission was the best form of attack.

"Presently," he said, "but with a serious purpose. In fact, you were the only person qualified to weigh up the projection for me. My niece seems to have plucked the word right out of the air."

Now Wheeler was looking bemused. Norstadt was almost pleased he had started giving as good as he got.

"What word?" asked Wheeler.

"Magnetism."

"She thinks magnetism is preventing the birds from migrating? In what way?"

"That's the point. With her, it was just a word that came to hand. Her father tried to give it some semblance of credibility when we were talking about trace metals. And I, when I was going over what had been said—well, I tried to rationalise it further with my own professional knowledge."

"And what's the result?"

"Not impressive. We don't know so much about the chemistry of animal migration that we could dismiss it altogether, but I would say if there were any effect at all it would be minimal. The suggestion was that the birds were being attracted north instead of south, or that the pull from the north was sufficient to stop them flying south. When my brother-in-law and I were talking, the theory was developed to the point where trace metals lodged in the birds—and that's no speculation; lodged they are and lots of them—were the cause of the attraction."

"It's not practical."

"I wouldn't say—"

"It's not practical. Look, Doctor, you're missing out on the fundamental fact. Any such attraction is not from the magnetic north, it's from the centre of the earth. That's what gravity is all about. If these birds were suffering in the way you describe, they'd never get off the ground. Like your theory. Are they flying?"

"According to my information."

"Then they *are* real."

"Yes . . . Look, I'm not trying to be abstruse with you. It's just that the thing is so—premature—at the moment that it could be any one of a million phenomena. I have to deal with it in the abstract."

"All right—if that's an apology, I'll accept it. Fill up your glass and let's see how abstract we can get. What is there in your particular science that would support such a theory? I can't honestly believe you overlooked gravity."

Norstadt coloured slightly and hoped the flush wouldn't show with the dogged pallor of the lighting. He *had* forgotten and now he had to come up with something to justify his dalliance with the idea. It arrived with surprisingly little trouble.

"I must confess it threw me for a minute," he said. "I was carried along with the man's enthusiasm. Then when he had gone, I started exercising my mind on points like the one you've raised. And it still came back to me that quite a large number of the winter havens favoured by northern birds are in the South Africa/South America regions where the field strengths are pretty high and hurricane genesis is just one of the manifestations. Then again, when the birds make their flights south, they allow for such things as the Coriolis Force, which would seem to indicate they know a lot more about earthpull than we understand . . ."

He tailed off because Wheeler was fiddling with his nails.

"It's all pretty desperate," the DOD man said.

Norstadt found he couldn't take issue with that. Wheeler was right and the word *was* "desperate."

"Forgive me," he said. "I suppose I favoured the concept because then, at least, we might have been able to do something about it."

Wheeler crooked an eyebrow. "And what would that be?"

"We could have stepped up the attraction of their usual haunts."

"How, for crying out loud?"

"By nuclear means, perhaps. Controlled explosions like Project Plowshare or space adjustments that could irradiate the areas—making temporary holes in the ozone layer so that more gamma rays would get through the earth's atmosphere—"

"Hell's teeth, I think you're serious."

"What's the matter with it?"

"People, that's what's the matter with it. The poor people who live right under where you want to throw your gamma rays or right over where you want to blow your megatons."

"It's mostly ocean."

"All right, a few more hurricanes generated and several tsunamis for good measure. At the end of their runs . . . people. Are people worth less than birds? Do you honestly believe you could get the support you would need for a programme like that?"

Norstadt swallowed and thought about it. "Then the theory really had nothing to commend it. It was just as insoluble as the one I'm coming round to believing."

"Which is?"

"That the build-up of trace metals has reached the point where the birds can't find their way anymore. That they've lost their site tenacity and that this human race you're pleading for is responsible."

Wheeler opened a box on his desk, extracted a cigar and pared it. "That sounds much more like the situation. I'm glad to have been of service."

It was a signal, but Norstadt was reluctant to be away. The exchange had gone as far as was possible, he knew. Still he was unresolved. With all the dead alternatives dispatched and the one concrete fact staring him squarely in the face, he was diminished.

Wheeler came and stood over him, careful with the cigar smoke and ash. "Was there anything else?"

"No." Norstadt regained his feet so fast that his head swam and small lights blinked. "Nothing anybody can do, I suppose."

Wheeler walked him to the door. "I think you're wrong," he said. "Of course, it's not for me . . ."

"You mean my theory?"

"I mean the way you've given up hope. Listen, this little girl of yours—does she love her birds?"

"Of course. That's the reason I—"

"Then I suppose she wouldn't mind keeping them warm and fed through the winter, domesticating them, if you like. Teaching them new habits for their new circumstances. She might even enjoy it. . . ."

By the time Norstadt had digested the full import of Wheeler's parting comment, the man was gone behind his door.

"Thank you very much," he said. He kept saying it all the way back to the surface.

The telephone rang when they were at dinner.

Ned Michaels had been silent with his own thoughts. Melanie had been chewing over a prospect more tasty than her food and waiting for the right time to tell it.

Her father took the call and she could hear only the usual imprisoned bumble-bee hum from the other end of the line.

"You mean us?" said Ned.

Then, "Well, I suppose . . ."

Then, "What would it involve?"

And, "Now you're sure, because I don't want her to—"

And, "Right, I'll tell her."

He came back to the table. "Melanie—"

"Daddy!" His daughter beat him to the punch. "As long as my birds are going to stay here, couldn't *we* look after them?"

Ned Michaels laughed. "I suppose it's common sense if you're a child. It's taken your Uncle Max and me all this time to come up with it. Now here's what we do. . . ."

That was the end of the silence at the dinner table.

November came and Melanie sat down and asked Witch Hazel a question out of pity, since the old dame had been second-placed for so long.

WHAT DO SWIFTS LIKE TO EAT IN WINTER QUERY ENDS

THIS FILE IS SUSPENDED PENDING REVISIONS, responded the machine.

"Now you're sulking," said Melanie and went for the umpteenth time to check the level of mercury in the attic thermometer.

But it wasn't that. Dear Witch Hazel, it wasn't that.

What Max Norstadt put into the thinkpile, Melanie Michaels would take out. It was an arrangement he had not seen fit to mention to her father, since it rendered him a buck terminus and Norstadt never liked people to believe him infallible.

He was only human (like, to err is only . . .) but humans had to script the data banks, a point which the masses seemed quite content to overlook.

The machine claims it is infallible, so heap blame on the machine.

And when the task was beyond the programmer, what then of the machine? It was Max Norstadt who had suspended the swift file for "revisions." Max Norstadt prodded and delved and went to see people and listened to little girls' feather fantasies. The relief he had felt with Wheeler's short-term solution had lasted just a little beyond his evening phone call to the home of Melanie Michaels. Then a whole new batch of questions started forming. And he still had to keep the swift bank out of action.

December came and the scarlet part of December when the holly hung in clumps from mirrors and pictures and Ned Michaels pinned a painting of a log fire to the hardboard panel beneath the mantel.

Melanie, meanwhile, continued her regular ascents to the roof-space. The swifts slept more now and seemed to eat less, the one perhaps complementing the other. The old theory had been that they hibernated and it was scotched when birds were marked and traced.

But perhaps hibernation had predated migration when more of

the world was ice-unrelieved and the new habit was an old habit reawakening.

In any event, Melanie stood atop the attic ladder and listened to the soft bird breathing, a weird and wonderful sound which turned the recess into an organ loft. It was a comfort to the house and a comfort to her. Two dozen heads tucked under wings. She had given them a home and they thanked her by trusting her enough to sleep in that home, by not waking in panic at her coming.

She didn't know which she preferred, this whisper of utter contentment or the scratch-scatter steps of the brighter days when her charges exercised their limbs, spread their wings and pecked at the pure-protein titbits she had brought for the attic wildlife.

She never stayed too long in their presence because she was still afraid they would flee. Yet there were no spots of daylight in the roof or along the eaves to indicate access.

And when she ran her light along the beam-ends, she found tidy little fillings of cotton waste and feathers cemented with saliva and the warmth persisted at summer level.

Coming down the ladder now, she found her father waiting.

"Well?"

"They're fine, Daddy."

"Food?"

"They don't seem to have left any. They are sleeping now. I suppose if they sleep and eat, they must be all right."

"That's a fairly safe criterion," said Ned.

"Criterion, Daddy?"

"Hard-and-fast rule. A sign you can rely on."

"And that's what eating and sleeping means—they're healthy."

"Right."

"I love you, Daddy." Melanie got her arms round Ned's hips and squeezed. "You've made this winter so—interesting."

"The only thing is—" said her father.

"Yes?"

"Nobody knows how interesting it is."

"What do you mean?"

"You're not telling anybody. I don't think you've addressed a single remark to Witch Hazel for a week. I know I've told you about asking it—her—questions, but I've put no brake on observations. You're privileged, Melanie. Not everybody's got this chance."

Melanie freed herself. "You mean there are only a few of us looking after our birds?"

"I know of only one."

"But that's terrible, Daddy." Melanie was dealing with a lump that had risen suddenly in her throat. "You mean people don't care?"

Ned demurred. He had not realised the ill-chosen words would go so surely to the heart. "No . . . Lots of people don't have swifts for neighbours anyway."

"And I thought—" It had all been very simple to Melanie. Everybody who had birds was keeping them as she was. Surely, nobody would want to miss out on that hushed and gentle respiration or the tickle of tiny feet. "I thought this was a new habit for all the people as well as for all the birds. If we don't do it together, how will either one of us get into the habit?"

"All the same . . ." Ned was edging her gradually towards her bedroom. "I think you should put your experience on record. Who knows, you might be adding to the thinkpile. And that's not bad for a little girl of nine."

"You're just saying that to make me work."

"And don't you think you should?"

"I—I'm sorry, Daddy, of course I should. Forgive me."

Ned Michaels ruffled the short hairs behind her ears as he might fondle a favourite dog's head. She almost laughed because she recognised the gesture and he did not. It made her happy, anyway, to think that even as the swifts were her pets, so she was her father's fond possession.

For Ned, meanwhile, the gesture meant thoughts elsewhere. He had tried to make her feel conscientious about recording her task on the pretext that the information might have a common benefit. In fact, it was just for her.

In childhood, it was easy to believe the pleasant things could last forever. In maturity, when you knew they were going to be reduced to memory all too soon, the game was to make them as thoroughly documented as possible.

On the unresolved matter of the birds, he saw it having extra urgency because the hope of a new and lasting relationship was only a hope.

He watched Melanie go to her keyboard—and prayed that Witch Hazel was briefed well enough to know the game.

This was December in the office of Max Norstadt—a close study of Gustav Kramer's experiments in bird orientation, a sifting work with the papers of S. T. Emlen and Jean Dorst, a session of talks with the personnel of Slimbridge Wildfowl Trust on the Severn Estuary, and a coffee break with Kenneth Mellanby.

If swifts had been fish, he would have had the answer.

Snow lay six inches thick on the tiles in January and drifted in the valleys between the gables. Melanie's journeys to the thermometer became more anxious and more regular until she could see for herself that the presence of the crystal layer was not bringing down the temperature.

"Why is that, Witch Hazel?" she asked the machine.

WHY IS WHAT? countered the machine.

Melanie could not be bothered to rethink the question. She went downstairs instead.

"Why is that, Daddy?" she asked, and Ned Michaels, who knew where she had been and what she had wondered, said, "Eskimo principle."

His daughter looked askance.

"Igloos out of ice-blocks are some of the cosiest homes round," he said. "The ice traps the warmth inside. Snow on the roof does the same."

She considered it. "How did you know what I meant?" she asked eventually.

"Empathy," said Ned. "That's what gives me the edge over the computer every day. I pick up your vibrations."

"I'm glad," said Melanie.

"What? Are you falling out of love with Witch Hazel?"

"Well, she has let me down over the swifts, but I didn't mean that. I'm glad I've got vibrations. They sound nice."

"They're beautiful," said Ned. "And I'll tell you something else. You know how you go and listen to your little birds breathing and the hum fills the attic?"

"Yes, yes?"

"Vibrations."

Melanie fidgetted at her book for nine minutes and twenty-seven seconds (she counted till her patience ran out) and then started up the stairs again.

"More eyes on the temperature?" asked her father absently.

"Vibration check," she assured him.

Max Norstadt blinked away the lesson of Minamata, read and noted the cadmium findings in Celtic Sea shellfish, tried to relate

Swedish neutron-activation-analysis records to the situation as he knew (or rather did not know) it, suffered with the Huckleby family, mad as hatters in New Mexico, and wrote nothing upon his master pad.

His theme had been thresholds, his success less than negligible. That was January for the man who scripted Witch Hazel.

You had to take February with a pinch of salt. Frost one day and first daffodils the next. The birds above the ceiling didn't know how to take it at all.

Their responses to the undulating glass were fitful, usually a day late and short-lived, as though the message was getting through too late for them to act.

Melanie began to speculate that they were jaded or even heading for a nervous breakdown.

She took her anxieties to Witch Hazel. "Can birds have nervous breakdowns?" she asked.

IN THE SENSE OF NEURAL DETERIORATION PERFORMANCE HAS BEEN SEEN TO BE AFFECTED BY SUCH STIMULI AS ARTIFICIAL LIGHT OR PRO-LONGED ABSENCE OF LIGHT, OVERCROWDING, AND CHEMICAL ABSORP-TION, volunteered the tutor in quite the longest speech since autumn.

IN THE SENSE OF EMOTIONAL CRISIS, IT HAS NOT BEEN POSSIBLE TO ISOLATE CAUSE AND EFFECT.

Melanie was quite taken aback by the garrulous computer though, in fairness, there had been no let-up in the software forthcoming on other subjects.

"What about my swifts in the attic?" she tried.

Fuss and scrabble and spit and here came the blocker: THIS FILE . . .

Melanie wrenched out the paper without reading the rest. Father's homecoming was hours away. Instead, she went to the window and listened to the garden regulars.

Shouting sparrow, laryngitic starling, whistling blackbird all sounded suitably robust.

"But then, you're no cri-criterion really," she told them.

February upon the face of Max Norstadt. Deepening lines and dip-down mouth, brain-cells weighed down with trace-metal knowledge subliminally if not actually from the London air that kept coming through his window.

He quit his office and sought the company of birds on Hampstead Heath. No crow dropped dead at his feet, no robin ploughed skywards in lemming gesture and then fell spent in the corner of his eye. Not a word or a whisper from any member of the feathered family as to why the swifts had decided to sit out the winter.

At home, cleaning off his shoes, he found a crocus imbedded in the heath mud on his heel. It was little to show for five months of being more anxious than Melanie Michaels.

On March 10, the sun shone all day and the overcoats came off like nobody's business. By evening, a forty-eight-degree F isotherm was lying near the land and dewpoint was late and insignificant. On the morning of March 11, the sun was hot from its arising and the unseasonal belt of high pressure persisted.

Melanie Michaels woke late for two reasons. The muffled scratchings and machinations in the bird ballroom above her head on the previous evening had kept her eyes open long after her brain had elected slow delta rhythm. This morning, the roof-space alarm had not sounded.

She came awake with a start, listening. Though sunlight rested squarely on everything she could see from her bedroom window, there was silence overhead. A terrible, sick-making silence that was all wrong.

She was halfway up the attic ladder with the rungs cutting into her bare soles before her thoughts caught up with her movements. She was pushing open the trap door with a haste that would have scattered her charges screaming . . .

. . . if there had been any left.

Fingers of new day poked at her from a dozen holes in the eaves. They confounded her vision so that she could not tell whether the attic had any occupants. All the same, she knew.

Dear Witch Hazel, my birds have gone. . . .

She dropped from the ladder, landed on her knees, and was away downstairs to the garden with her father emerging from his bedroom. "Melanie? What's the matter?"

She did not hear him and would not have answered anyway. In the garden, shivering upon the cold grass, she identified and counted out the bird songs one by one and watched in vain for her sheaf of arrows moving among the trees, banking and turning for home, washing their backs with sunbeams.

Ned Michaels wrapped his dressing-gown around his daughter

and lifted her feet clear of the dew. But he didn't take her indoors.

Instead, they toured the garden, her eyes on the sky, his eyes on her face.

"Where are they, Daddy?" she asked eventually, so quietly that he had to bend his head to pick up the murmur.

Ned had tried to read up on migration and fallen down on the new factors, the intangibles that had come about here in this one happy winter. He said, "I don't know," with authority, but it still sounded like "I don't know."

"Perhaps they're just exercising," said Melanie.

"Perhaps," agreed her father. "But you mustn't . . ."

"Mustn't what?"

Mustn't build up your hopes, he thought. "You mustn't mind," he said, "if they live their own lives. They're grateful to you for keeping them alive all through the winter, but they can't say thank you."

"They said it." Melanie was almost arrogant with the information but it was only to mask her upset. "They said it each day they stayed."

He kissed her gently on the forehead and felt it fever-moist. He turned his steps towards the house. "If they thanked you for each day you gave them, there's no debt."

"No." Melanie was biting her lip. "They don't owe me a thing."

Then she wept.

Ned's gaze lingered on the sticky buds of the chestnut and knew there was a message now as surely as there had been in autumn. But he could not pinpoint it and Melanie was in no condition to translate.

In the kitchen, he kept her on his lap until the kettle boiled and filled her with cocoa until the tears stopped.

"I could ask Witch Hazel, I suppose," she said quite calmly.

"Why don't you?"

She was back in ninety seconds. "There's still a block on the subject."

"Well . . ." Ned stood up. "No news is good news. And now I'll talk to Uncle Max. Why don't you go and dress?"

He telephoned Max Norstadt. "I can't come round and see you," he said, "because I have a crisis on my hands. Even so, I'd be glad of some answers."

"Then ask the questions," said Norstadt.

"Statement of fact: the birds have flown."

"Oh, no. Sweet heaven, no."

"Well, what's the matter?"

"That is a crisis."

"How can you know that? We can't even say where they've gone."

Norstadt sounded suddenly old and tired. "There's only one way —north."

"But why?"

"Because they're *supposed* to fly north from their winter quarters at this time of the year."

"I thought the trace metals had put paid to all that. I thought they could only stay where they are."

Norstadt was silent. Ned prompted him further. "You mean— magnetic north? Melanie was right?"

"No, Melanie was wrong. We were all wrong."

Michaels waited for an explanation. What he got was a hollow laugh from the other end of the line. "What—?"

"All except Sigmund Freud," said Norstadt.

"How does he fit in, for crying out loud?"

"He was the one who said the sex drive predominates."

"But . . ." Ned was at a loss. "But is that such a terrible thing?"

"As terrible as this—I'll have my dead swifts in Iceland, more evidence than I need—"

"Good grief." Ned Michaels's stomach turned on the size of the tragedy. He saw Melanie at her desk, begging Witch Hazel for answers. He saw the familiar holding key: THIS FILE IS SUSPENDED FOR REVISIONS. But the damn computer would soon start broadcasting now; no chance of telling a pretty lie.

"Max," he said weakly. "Look . . . I'm sorry to tax you further but I'm completely out of my depth. What do I tell Melanie?"

"I suppose you'd better tell her about the birds and the bees." Then Norstadt put down the phone and went away somewhere.

Ned Michaels found Melanie lying on her bed. Looking at the ceiling.

CRUMBLING HOLLYWOOD
MANSION,
CRUMBLING HOLLYWOOD MAN

Introduction

Admit it—you did not think to find the song-writing virtues of Tom Paxton and Jim Webb discussed in this context.

The exercise has three validities and the first is a declaration of intent. Words are music and a statement can be meaningful in lyric or literature—in my understanding, we all travel the same minstrel road.

If I have tried to do anything with this story (and with several others) it is to marry up the two media without necessarily writing in verse or strict metre.

Second, Ejler Jakobsson asked, when he took this tale for Galaxy, whether I had ever had any songs published—and thereby digitised a secret dream.

I am a failed song-writer. For instance—

> Country love and poison rain,
> They're two different kinds of pain.
> One a stranger, one a brother,
> Each one deadlier than the other—
> Country love and poison rain . . .

—which didn't even find a place in my novel of that title because I couldn't think of a second verse.

But music defeats me. Like Glyn Roderick, of that work, all my melodies sound the same—and those, like somebody else's.

Third is that I like to credit the artist whose work gives me pleasure in that field—and to feel that while we are both offering commodities, it could be more of an exchange than a small payment off a mounting debt.

Even so, there must be recognition of excess. One suspects that having David Bowie, inventor of the hunting knife, render a screen version of Robert Heinlein's *Stranger in a Strange Land* is a little over the top for both those spectacular gentlemen. One would gladly be proved wrong.

The most worthwhile match is between us and contemporary folk, despite and in anticipation of symphonic arguments from Jims Ballard and Blish.

Jim No. 3—Jim Webb—has swung rather late into my line of vision. Anybody who knows Tom Paxton's "Crazy John" will see an affinity with this following tale, though in fairness to myself, the idea was in my mind long before I found it in his; likewise, "Whose Garden Was This?" with its "pictures of flowers" and "records of breezes" must have taken the words out of many mouths as well as mine (and *not* off many pages). Nevertheless, the observations are more topical than technical and do not make the best example for that reason.

Webb's "Wichita Lineman" comes very close to the model incorporation of open-road tradition, scientific credential (his singer inspects high-tension cables), and gut eloquence of (musical) phrase.

This story appears under the original title, which intended a kind of melodic presence. Unfortunately—as well as Jake's objection to the celluloid capital—I can imagine it was a space-hungry extravagance in his small-format Galaxy.

Paxton or Webb—which one of them, I wish and wonder, could best set to music and finalise this heartsong? It begins with the couplet . . .

CRUMBLING HOLLYWOOD MANSION,
CRUMBLING HOLLYWOOD MAN . . .

The overgrown and choking garden was shaped like a guitar with a hedge of pure Gibson box, the jaded magnificent dying room was furnished in Spanish cherrywood, he slept last night in a Fender cut-away and, sweet Pete Seeger, even his home telephone exchange had twelve strings.

Jacob Grass. Gone today, maybe here tomorrow. The world stopped listening and advancing years impaled the minstrel. He calls himself a victim of bad taste but in actuality it was just the taste, any taste, new taste, that polished him off.

Jacob Grass with a bowl of hot wax upon his knee and golden hands working in it, salvaging the joints, dispelling the cramps for a small while.

Then the digits came up like candles and he towelled them clean and reached for his peeling Gallacher. Jacob was going to sing his song before finger warmth and all daylight went. Daylight was vital though he played with his eyes shut. In darkness he could not see to mix the wax.

How do you equate an active telephone exchange with a lifeless electric system? Jacob Grass had no lights, which he needed, and a dozen primed lines which he did not. Why?

Hope.

Hope doesn't need light but it does need contact. Jacob had heaved himself clear of the Nashville debris and headed for Hollywood with some idea about him and the old dear dying together. Finding a place was easy enough—their doors were open and begging along upper Hollywood Boulevard when he had been expecting to hike deep into the Cheviot Hills.

The Haunted House, some seer of the sixties had called Hollywood, and that was just how it was now only more so, with the rest of the midway packed up and gone and the squat hulks hardly holding up under the weight of the winter.

And to find a dwelling so given over to the motif of his heart, so sympathetic in vibrations, that was more than good fortune. That was the beginning of hope.

So the phones stayed, though the power company came and looked at the ghost town and then sent an in-spectre to scare Jacob into paying his bill. One look at Jacob, though, and they knew it wasn't worth the legal trouble because you can't get blood from a rocking horse.

Maybe they were even plotting with the phone company but something kept Grass safe and whenever he picked up his handpiece, the buzz invitation was there, sure and penetrative: "Make your call, sir."

Likely there was an engineer somewhere along the lines who remembered Jacob Grass with affection for the songs that had said all that the engineer had always wanted to say about war, women, work, or whimsy.

No doubt about it, Jacob had spoken with the tongue of tongues once upon a merry time. Now he composed to himself and swore because the rhymes were ragged or the metre didn't run true.

Jacob Grass and Hollywood. A strong affinity and the only affinity you would find here anymore, eccentric and accidental.

The people walked out on Jacob. The people walked out on their celluloid dreams. Time had been when Fox, Warner, Universal could dictate the direction for mass escapism with only a limited number of other choices. But at the thin end of the millennium now, there were so many brands of reality and so many eyes with which to view them that dreams were redundant.

For instance, in a typical day:

The Northlands satellite was beaming the survival struggle of a crashed plane crew in the Arctic Circle by daily episodes. Any time —maybe tomorrow, folks—the pilot, dragging his broken leg, was going to start hacking chunks off his dead Eskimo passenger or the copilot or the beautiful mortified stewardess for fresh meat and strength.

Spangles McGraw was plugging his/her latest crunch every time you turned up your transvestite radio.

There was "Show Your Cards," an extravaganza from Central Africa where the Malawi Young Pioneers would have lined up another round dozen unpolitical animals and were proceeding to burn their homes, pillage their limbs, and wreck their wives just to see how much it took to make the dissidents join the Party.

Seoul Brothers, the recruiting splurge from the Indo-China theatre, was always good for a laugh.

You could watch people dying on a dozen different channels, near and far, traffic control or Skylab mortality quotient.

With all that, who needed fantasy? The cameramen had gone to the top of the pile. There was even "If It Kills Me . . ." a kind of television consequence game that got through its production staff like crazy because that was the sum total of the scenario. The producers and directors? When facts speak for themselves? They were back in the splicing rooms or wielding a hand-held or dead.

And Hollywood continued deserted, left to wraiths like Jacob Grass who came to stay forever while ancient stardusts drifted in doorways.

The same manifestation. Jacob had sung protest songs and the enlightened had listened. But the mass had gloried in the very things he decried and he bothered them. When he waded in the water, as Tom Paxton had put it, they couldn't see the old reflections. Crazy Jacob. Chase him away. And kill off his listeners. All flesh was not Grass.

> I'm the man who taught the people
> How to think before they sing,
> How to look for little hitches
> And examine everything.

And somebody moved upon the thickening grime of the boulevard. A young man tensed to the sound, the faint jangling like a music box in a high and distant room.

He put his weight against the fluted magnificence of the gate. Its rustings came away on his glinting hands and his fibrous suit but it gave inwards and before he was three paces up the path the oxide had been shaken off like sand.

Following the music to its source, he skirted spent azalea bushes, trod carefully upon fissured mosaic, and came at last past a fall of bougainvillaea to a patio and an open French door.

By which time the guitar had stopped.

Jacob Grass had heard no footsteps save his own for a very long time. Suppliers of sustenance stopped their vehicles to unload cartons at his gate. Mailmen opened his box and collected the small checques for the butcher, the baker, and the candle-wax maker. The other envelopes—the offers of work and the fan letters he had written to himself—they authorised with a hand-stamp and replaced. All out of his ear-shot.

But now there were footsteps. And stepping from light into gloom, a young man of slightly soiled elegance with a miracle looped to his wrist. Jacob Grass knows a camera when he sees one.

"Well, for crying out loud," said the young man. "A living soul. Dr. Living Soul, I presume."

Words crawled in Jacob's throat but were reluctant for utterance. A second voice, suddenly. Let it speak its fill and let me listen.

The youngster chuckled and panned the room with his eyes, cutting from pool of shadow to splash of light, sunfall to gyrating column of dust.

"Are you at one with this place, dad? Is it yours or do you squat?"

Jacob found expression at last. "It's mine."

"How long? Mercy, I never thought to find anybody actually still here. Then I heard a guitar. You got records?"

"I've got fingers," said Jacob. The Gallacher lay across his legs, last resonances still murmured in mansion corners, and only now the intruder's vision was coming round to him.

"You mean you play?"

"I play." Jacob didn't like the way the kid said it as though there were some dishonour involved.

"Here?"

"Nowhere else."

"But why?"

"Because I want to."

"What are you doing here?"

"What is anybody doing anywhere except waiting to die."

"Wait a minute—do you mean to say you're—like—in sight of death?"

Jacob couldn't see the point of the questions and the boy was supercilious anyway. "What if I am?"

"Well, maybe I can help you."

"To die? No thanks. That's one job I keep for myself. . . ."

"No, pop. Don't misread me. What I mean is—somebody at a low ebb like that. Sometimes it helps to have a friend. Like, pushes the tide back."

"You mixed your metaphors. I noticed that. I keep it out of my lyrics."

"Lyrics?"

"Songs. I have written songs that are loved the world over."

"Great. Are you David or Bacharach, Killjoy or Vespucci?"

"Jacob Grass."

"Jacob Grass?"

"Do you know the name?"

"Sure I know it. Er—folk songs." He could tell by the acoustic guitar.

"Protest."

"Protest I meant."

"There's a difference."

"I appreciate that. Dylan made the point—"

"Listen, I had more to say than Dylan and I said it better."

"Of course you did, Jacob. But just the same, now you're—"

"Dying?"

"Living. Living, Jacob, here in this—string mausoleum. People should know . . ."

"They'll know soon enough. I get offers all the time. It's just a matter of picking the right one."

The young man was aiming his Minolta, swinging it hither and thither, watching how the black-box attachment set him right for film-speed and aperture as he dry-shot darkness, light, and Jacob Grass.

"I know I can help you," he said. "I have some friends who would be transported by this old house and you and—and the whole scene. Do you mind if I bring them?"

"Do you have a name?"

"What? Sure—forgive me, Jacob. Clements, my name is, Asa Clements. It's kind of funny . . . like, you get 'ASA' on films? Or maybe you don't know that. . . ."

"Asa Clements," Jacob was echoing.

"Do you know the name?"

"Of course. You take pictures." He could tell by the camera.

"You're playing a game, Jacob."

"Your game, Asa. You don't know me from a bag of grit."

"That's not true, Mr. Grass. And let me tell you—before long people will be falling over themselves to get to know you."

"With your pictures."

"Maybe a little of the glitter will rub off on me, yes."

"So tell your friends. There'll be enough glitter for all."

Past the bougainvillaea, across the cracked tiles, through the barren bushes to the gate, Asa Clements was counting his friends. Not the ones he had, because he had none. But the ones he was going to make as a lone-wolf cameraman with some off-beat footage.

The networks beckoned. Asa went to sell his project and beg some film.

> I'm the man who told the people
> Life is not what it appears.
> Media lie and they've been
> Doing it for years.

Control room subdued of illumination and numbers crawling like flies upon one wall while above them Amazon natives fried a missionary in high colour. Mr. Gianni Intermezzo was post-synching birds with their songs, cicadas with their rattles, screams with their sources.

"And you say this man is dying?" He did not hesitate in his work. Cut, thrust, splice, run, and all the time the jungle sounds learning to be punctual.

"He says he's dying," said Asa Clements, "and that makes it more authoritative. Just a thousand feet, taken at the proper time, would do it, Mr. Intermezzo."

"Why come to me?"

"Because you're the best."

"The best what? The best push-over?"

And here a little self-respect crept in. "I'm not asking for a hand-out, Mr. Intermezzo. I'm seeking the wherewithal for a project that will do you far more good than it will ever do me. Slap your name all over it but just give me camera credit."

"How certain are you this—Grass—won't welsh on us?"

"Welsh on us?"

"Carry on living. Waste our endeavours."

"Because he volunteered the information without knowing who I was."

"Does he know now?"

"Of *course* not. What do you think I am, Mr. Intermezzo?"

"Would you believe a vulture?"

"I'm a buzzard in a buzzard world, Mr. Intermezzo, and anybody who tries to pass himself off as anything else is just airs and graces."

Clements watched the airs and graces on the flickering wall. The woodland fire was burning low and some of the natives were risking their soles to prod the crackling body at the stake. His stomach turned. As a defence against nausea, his mind put up one of the maxims beloved of his profession: If you don't like the heat, stay out of the kitchen. But suppose, Harry S. Truman, that the kitchen covered the world.

Intermezzo watched on unmoved.

"What—" Clements swallowed. "What do they do next?"

"Nothing."

"Nothing? Don't they eat him or—some kind of ritual?"

"What for?"

"Well, it's . . . I thought it was practise."

"They don't need practise. They did it very well—"

"No, I mean . . . custom. What's expected of them."

"Where's the thrill in the expected?"

"I'm not sure we're talking the same language, Mr. Intermezzo. Where's the thrill in doing nothing?"

The film was backtracking now, over the treetops, higher and higher until the river was a ribbon and the jungle was unbroken. The incident and the lost life were gone, as simple as that, like a pebble beneath the surface of the sea. Intermezzo let the question hang until fadeout.

"All right," he said. "Because we may do business, I'll honour you with a context. How to make sense of this scenario. The missionary was burning at the stake. Why?"

"I—" Clements stumbled. "I—guess they didn't like what he said."

"What did he say?"

"I don't know. Maybe he made vague promises."

Intermezzo lit up his workroom and grinned. "You're getting the picture. Would you say that was enough reason to kill a man?"

"I've heard of slighter reasons."

"In the context."

"No."

"Then what are they doing?"

"Putting him to the test?"

"Splendid. And what were the alternatives?"

"They could kill him or let him live."

"You're going away from it. They've mounted the test. What then?"

"When the fire's lit, he can only die."

"Perhaps he claimed differently."

"Then he's a fool. There's only one likelihood. The rest are impossible."

"Even with faith?"

"Faith doesn't make the steamroller jump over you. It just helps you to know whether what you're dying for is worth it."

"That's more profound than I had expected, Mr. Clements. I am beginning to like you."

"I'm gratified, Mr. Intermezzo, but I'm not sure I grasp your meaning."

"Think about it. You see, that film finished where it did because the natives had made their point. No melodrama, no special effects, no impossibilities. That's what I call integrity. And when I give you five hundred feet of film, it's what I want."

"*Five hundred.* But that's barely enough to . . ."

"Keep a record? It's all you need. There'll be no second take. Pick your moment and economise, Mr. Clements. Economy is such a virtue. And listen—when I talk about integrity, I mean integrity from Jacob Grass and integrity from you."

"You'll get it," said Clements weakly.

Intermezzo stabbed his thumb at the blank screen wall. "Make your point in five hundred feet. Make sure Grass knows what he's dying for. Otherwise . . ."

Otherwise, thought Asa Clements, it's me for the torture stake and somebody else's five hundred feet. If you don't like the heat . . .

> But the world goes on burning just the same
> And there's no volunteer to take the blame.

Asa Clements answered to Gianni Intermezzo. Intermezzo stepped to a different drummer. He locked up the control room, donned a Polaroid visor against the intensity of the downtown Los Angeles light, and headed for the nearest hologram terminal.

There he dialled up his sponsor, no less than Frank Baker, the protein millionaire. No chance of getting to Baker, of course, but today was a good day. He came within three doors of the top. The man whose foreshortened features shaped up on the hologram link was Charles Natchez, a well-advanced chief of staff he had met before. Natchez remembered the movies with affection and kept a soft spot for flotsam like Intermezzo.

"Gianni," he said. "Always a pleasure."

"Pleasure's all mine," conceded Intermezzo. "Charles, I have set an item in motion."

"Well, you know we respect your judgment, Gianni."

"My judgment's all right. I'm calling to apprise you, is all. I can't give you a completion date, although the feeling I have is that this is a quickie."

"How many reels, Gianni?" Natchez loved the chance to get into the vernacular.

"I advanced the boy five hundred feet of film. It should be more than enough for the project he has in mind."

"Are you going to tell me about it?"

"This old folk-singer. Name of Jacob Grass."

"Jacob Grass . . ."

"You know him?"

"I can't be sure. I'm just making a note."

"Well, I know him and I remember he used to be good. There could be some beautiful things said—"

"Not too many, Gianni. Not to match five hundred feet."

"Forgive me, Charles, but I know my limitations. Twist it any way you like, but it doesn't take long to say 'I'm dead.'"

"And you believe he'll do this."

"Naturally."

"And *mean* it. We have to have the action, Gianni."

"I am assured he has no stamina to change his mind even if he had the intention."

"Just the same, he'll have to be checked in the usual way—checked that his insurance is paid up, that he has no friends who might dissuade him, that his medical degeneration is rapid, that he actually *wants* to go."

"My contact claims all these requirements are fulfilled. Grass is tired of living."

The head of Natchez, projected there at the mouth of the tube like a genie, blinked and nodded. Intermezzo had an insane desire to reach out for the image, tear the head from its moorings, smash it to the floor just to see what happened. But he kept his hands out of sight, knowing it was an impossible murder. There would be no more effect than a flickering of colours on his swinging fists and, more, Natchez would see the movement and recognise the intention. It's hard to go on talking business to a man when you've just proved you'd like to kill him. Intermezzo kept his hands and his thoughts out of sight.

Natchez was still nodding. "You know it only takes a good idea to change a person's mind in these circumstances."

"That's a gamble I'll take. Believe me, if there was a good idea to be had, Jacob Grass would have had it. I'll organise the usual safe-guards."

"Otherwise—" Charles Natchez laughed and brought his hands up over the edge of his desk. Intermezzo could see them there in miniature like moth wings. Then the little hands were sweeping across the expanse of the image. Muscles tightened in his neck as he realised what Natchez was doing. What he could not afford to do. "Otherwise," chuckled the genie, "heads will roll."

> I'm the man who thought the people
> Would be glad to know the score,
> With a great big smile of welcome
> When they opened up the door

The telephone rang. It shuddered the ancient chandeliers until they shed dust like rain upon the startled house. It jerked Jacob Grass's hands so that he spilled molten wax upon the dull tile floor and put his feet in it and toppled before he knew what he should do about the phone.

And it kept ringing.

Asa Clements, at the other end, reasoned that Jacob was finishing a solo or mesmerised in some other form and waited while motes fell and Jacob cursed and scrabbled. Waited and thought how kind he was.

Eventually—

"The Jacob Grass residence. Who wishes to consult with him, please?" Grass doing his wrinkled retainer bit.

"I wanted to speak with Mr. Grass if he is not too busy," said Clements, grinning at his own sophistication. "My name is Clements. He may remember me."

He had to remember; it was only yesterday.

"The man with the camera." The voice was the same. Grass had wearied of the game. "Of course I remember you, Mr. Clements. I wasn't expecting you to phone."

Jacob was not expecting anybody to phone. For some reason, he had the cameraman earmarked as someone who would come through the French door again next time. All the same, he was curious. He hastened to amend and explain. "What I meant was, I didn't realise you had my number. Is it—?"

Clements read him. "Yes, it's listed, Mr. Grass. Large black capitals. JACOB GRASS, PROTEST SINGER, HOLLYWOOD BOULEVARD. It looks just fine." He had taken the number off the hand-unit at the house the previous day. There were no capital letters, no book of names.

"You lie too easily, Asa," said Grass. "You lie for almost no reason at all."

"I—" Clements dried up.

"You what? Were you going to deny it? Were you going to compound your felony?"

Five hundred feet of film and Asa Clements had been wondering whether it would be enough. The danger now was that he would not get to use any of it.

"I'm sorry," he said. "I—I try to be kind. If an old man has a dream, I try not to spoil it or trample on it. In this ghost town, the directory is full of dead numbers, Jacob, that's common sense. I thought you knew that and I was echoing your charade. Don't think too badly of me because I have some good news."

"Is it the truth?"

"It is as good as that. I have been invited to make a film about you."

"What do they want me to do—jump off the roof? I'm afraid I couldn't climb up there."

"No, Jacob. A film about the way you live. Your songs. It could do you a lot of good, bring you a lot more work. . . ."

"Are you still trying to humour me, Asa? I see films. They all have one ending these days."

"Truly, Jacob." Well, he could put it in a way that wasn't too much of a hypocrisy. "I have five hundred feet of film to use on you. You can do what you like, say what you like—play what you like. And if my contact likes the result, there could be more footage. Don't say you wouldn't enjoy being a star again. . . ."

Jacob Grass looked down at the cute little receiver in his hand and wondered if he could be brave enough to replace it on its cute little stand. The cameraman's offer was seductive, allowing for any and all consequences.

But there were other entirely professional considerations. He needed time to think on those.

"You can't come here," he said. "I don't want to see you. The hell with your five hundred feet of film—and I still have enough strength to break a camera."

For courage, read cunning, he thought as he cradled the receiver. Clements would be across the ferrous-oxide threshold and lurking in the shrubbery with very little delay because he was already committed to Grass. Keeping his distance but waiting his chance.

Jacob, meanwhile, had all the time he wanted to work on his act.

> I'm the man who begged the people
> It was truth I had to say,
> But they just turned up their 3V sets
> Until I went away.

On his last day in the crumbling mansion, Jacob Grass awoke laughing. Hammering life back into his stunted hands, laying them to thaw in the sunlight upon the window-sill, he perceived what he could do.

This very window-frame. The others around the house. All could be utilised. He drew his fingers back into the shadows and set them searching for screws and driver.

Twelve screws to the top of each window-frame, grouped in twos, twelve screws to the bottom and paired. See how far they went.

And when he had used up his own supply of loose screws, he toured the house dismantling doors, discarding mirrors and pictures and handles. He vandalised fine furniture for the small spirals that kept it together. He plundered comforts for the joints that made them so.

And in the end, ten window-frames were studded top and bottom, couple by couple.

So much for the mechanics. Now for the art.

He used half his remaining supply of wax to resupple his hands and kept the rest for a more vital purpose. As hunched as Quasimodo, he scaled the stairs to the attic and burst open a box which bore its age in cobwebs.

Strings. Curled, looped, plaited, laid flat. Catgut, steel, nylon. Knotted together, they could reach the moon but Jacob Grass needed them as individuals. All bore small labels identifying their key. He shoved and pommelled the box to the top of the stairway and dragged it to the first floor.

Then he started on the first window.

Working from left to right, a bass string and then a treble wound at either end round a screw—E,A,D,G,B,E.

He left them slack and moved on to the next window—bass E, treble E, bass A, treble A, bass D, treble D, and on into G and B and E again.

Moving on. Take a pair of laughing E's, a brace of A's, a deuce of D's . . .

He made a song out of it. Not up to his usual standard, maybe, but then the lyrics were not important because this time there would be no lyrics.

Five windows strung and Jacob Grass humming. Seven windows and Jacob gritting teeth against the pain in his paws. Ten windows done and now came the tough part, the part that cried out for craftsmanship.

His fingers needed wax but so did he. And if his fingers didn't get it, the strings never would. He split the small block in two again, made it liquid before the fire, laid his digits to rest.

It was mid-afternoon and he hadn't eaten, his stomach told him. He committed his hands to the towel hurriedly and scrambled for bread and cheese, not heeding the extra taste from the remnants of wax.

Leaving the morsels unfinished, he returned to the windows with the screw-driver and began tuning—one twist to top, one twist to bottom and pluck and listen. Little by little, bass E. Up a tone, little by little and treble E. To A, to D, a tone apart; G to B, an octave span, B to top E the same. He was less than satisfied over-all because even the give of the wood in the frames robbed the chords of accuracy. Perhaps he sought too much, perhaps his ears were only accustomed to perfection.

He ran his hand across the width of the window. The effect was mellifluous and melodic. His throat knotted and his eyes stung.

The second window. As good and easy as the first.

The third needed more time and he knew chill fear as the sun began its downward arc. The fourth came right as simply as the first two. The fifth had woodwork in the frame and try as he might, Jacob could only achieve a bass sound from his treble strings and a dry, dead, rope twang from the bass.

He moved on in hazard, aware that he had wasted too much time. Sixth, seventh, and eighth windows performed admirably. On the ninth, three feverish screws had been forced in against the thread and refused to budge. The whole was a mess because they broke up the chord.

Tenth and, sweet Woody Guthrie, Jacob was doubled over with the pain in his wrists. He cursed arthritis, cursed the waning wax, screamed at his own madness—and came up with a bridge as clear and true as the best he had ever fingered. Hearing it thus, he whispered, "I love you," to the faithful catgut and blessed the numbness that had been an anaesthetic to his tattered fingers.

His blood on the guitar-strings at every window. His stain on every note they played, ever.

There had been no hint or whisper of Asa Clements all day but he knew the boy was out there biding his time and conserving his footage.

"Tonight," he shouted at the darkening garden. "Bring your friends tonight."

Then he sat down to wait for a breeze.

> And the world goes on burning just the same,
> So I guess I'm going to have to take the blame.
> No, there's no other hand out for a share.
> I'm the man who bored the world too stiff to care.

The night jagged with noise and the ear-phone men screaming with the pain and the vibe counters running up off the dial and Gianni Intermezzo taking Asa Clements by the scruff of the neck and hurling him into the presence of Jacob Grass.

The old man was sitting in his upright chair with the Gallacher across his knees and his shoulders hunched against the open window cold.

In the darkness, Clements could not see the tears along the lines of Jacob's cheeks and Grass wasn't about to tell of his grief when the wind had sprung up and rendered his Aeolian strings shrill and unmelodic, tortured and meaningless.

Besides, the camera fiend was still smarting from Intermezzo's invective. Boiled down to the functional, what he had said was: "Get in there and save this production."

Clements knew exactly what he meant by that and had come with Minolta at the ready. Now here was Grass sitting in his chair, not moving, not even going crazy or threshing about.

"What do you want me to do?" The old man said as loudly as he could against the keening wire hum.

"What?"

"How do you want me to end it? Am I all right here? I can't move very far or very fast now."

"Don't. Not yet." Desperation had removed any subtlety from the Clements approach.

"I mean, that is what you want, isn't it?"

"No."

The chandelier burst apart in a crystal blizzard, showering the pair of them. Clements, unhurt as he stood, brushed splinters from his hair and opened a cut in his left palm. He sucked at it because this gave him something to do but no words came with the salt taste.

"Why don't you admit it?" prodded Grass. "Come on, now it's inevitable let me hear you say it. Let me go with you being honest."

"Please, Jacob—" And the words were gone again. A dilemma without articulation. How do you say "You're not dying the way I want you to"?

"Then guide me." Grass could read the pause.

"Jacob, this noise. It's tearing me apart—"

Something fell in an upper room. Something slid on the Camelot slopes of the roof.

"Say it, Asa. Say you wanted me dead."

"What does it matter?"

"It matters to me what the last man I'll ever speak to is thinking."

"You're neurotic, Jacob. I came to promote your music, to give you a new chance."

"And how do you like my hand-made synthesiser?"

"Fantastic. It's only ruined everything."

"Why?"

"Good grief, man, we can't record the event in this—this bedlam. All our sound instruments are going haywire. . . ."

Clements could not be sure, but he fancied that Jacob Grass chuckled. There was too much volume. The feel of it was coming right up through the floor, climbing his legs, jetting up his backbone, socking at his brain. "Why yourself?" he screamed. "Why go to all this trouble?"

On the upper landing, a mirror which had been left against a wall when robbed of its screws reeled or was shaken clear, staggered like a drunken man on its curlicued edge and disintegrated.

Pinpricks sabotaged Clements's eardrums so that he had to struggle to get Jacob's reply.

"I thought you were used to dealing with professionals."

"I am, but what has that—?"

"Then you should know."

Wire-cutters. The simple answer. Short work at the windows. The peacemaker. Relief swathed Asa Clements like cotton wool.

"I don't know," he said. "Tell me."

"A true artist never goes on stage without an encore ready."

Pete and Paxton, Cisco and Joni, it was sweet to say those words again. The goodness warmed Jacob against the blast.

And Clements missed them, running for the door.

Jacob set his fingers like a caress on the neck of his Gallacher, closed his eyes, and finished his lifesong without fuss or film coverage.

Clements, back with the tools and racing from window to window, didn't even look at the crumbled Hollywood man.

Gianni Intermezzo's back-up cameraman got some fine telescopic shots of panic and wire-cutters before the Hollywood mansion crumbled upon Asa Clements.

"That's integrity," said Mr. Intermezzo to the silent night.